FAR FROM NEVERLAND

RIVER HALE

Written by River Hale
Previously published under Rylee Hale
Cover artwork by Martino Paulis

ISBN 979-8-9867508-0-4 (paperback)
ISBN 979-8-9867508-1-1 (ebook)
ISBN 979-8-9911454-6-6 (illustrated cover)

PUBLISHED BY VICIOUS CITY PRESS

NOTE FROM THE AUTHOR

FAR FROM NEVERLAND is a dark romance, a darker kind of fairy tale for the adults who dream of returning to Neverland, the ones who always secretly wished to see the heroes and the villains turn from enemies to lovers.

Everyone's definition of *dark* varies, especially when it comes to romance. This book may be too dark for some and not dark enough for others. Please stay safe and check the trigger warnings if needed.

For specific content warnings, playlists, and to sign up for my newsletter, please visit my website: www.riverhale.com

*To those who always dreamed of Neverland,
of flying, and of falling in love with the villain.*

Though my soul may set in darkness, it will rise in perfect light;
I have loved the stars too fondly to be fearful of the night.

—SARAH WILLIAMS

1

HOOK

Neverland hasn't been the same since Peter Pan left. It's been so much *better*. Fourteen years of peace, and I've been basking in it.

Sure, not everything is perfect, but it's a hell of a lot more preferable than the alternative. The obnoxious presence of that vile and despicable child ensured I had headaches every single moment of every goddamn day. He flew around here like he owned the whole bloody island, but all he was was an infuriating pest that I couldn't squash, a rash with an itch that I couldn't scratch.

Despite the state of the map on the desk in front of me, it was worth it.

Standing from my wingback chair, I turn my back on the blasted map. I absentmindedly run my hook over the many silver and gold rings adorning the fingers of my right hand as I peer out of one of the large windows that look out of the stern of the Jolly Roger.

It's the middle of the day, but it sure doesn't look that way. The sky is a dark gray, heavy with thick clouds. Honestly, it's just the way I like it.

Everything is dark now.

I don't miss the sun—Neverland's star. It left when Pan left, like it simply died out. Good riddance. I like the dark. The island is lit now only by whichever star is nearest, which is clearly too far away to keep the island warm, sunny, and dry.

Snow drifts down over the dark water, landing on the thin blanket of ice over the sea. Thanks to the small fire in my captain's quarters, it's warm in here.

But it turns out I don't mind the cold so much either.

Running my one hand through my hair, I return to my seat at the desk. I lean back and put my boots up, resting them beside the map that I really don't want to look at right now.

Several gold doubloons litter the desk, and I pick one up to roll it across my knuckles. The map is surrounded by a bunch of the coins along with a compass, a pistol, a couple of my best daggers, and a few other trinkets. The glow from the small fire keeps most of the cabin in shadow, including the bed tucked in the corner, the miniature bar, the numerous shelves of treasures I've collected in my many, many years.

When I start to get a bit too warm, I drop the coin, pluck a leather string off my desk, and tie my hair back at the nape of my neck.

When everything changed fourteen years ago, I embraced that change and sliced off a good chunk of my dark, wavy hair. It barely brushes my shoulders now, and since time doesn't really move in Neverland, it's never grown back. But I'm okay with it.

Picking up my tricorn hat next, I place it on my head,

tipping it down a little past my eyes as I settle back in my chair. The only thing I have to do right now is wait on news, so I may as well sleep in the meantime.

I barely manage to drift off before a knock comes at the door. I groan.

"Enter," I say as I drop my boots to the ground.

The door opens, and Mr. Smee, my boatswain, enters the cabin. He appears nervous. Though, that in and of itself is nothing new. His red stocking cap is in his hands, and he's twirling it over and over. I'm surprised the threads haven't unraveled by now with how much he worries it, leaving his white, wiry hair to branch out in every direction.

"What is it, Smee?" I'm already miffed by his mere presence. "Have they returned?"

The portly little man nods and blunders forward. He approaches my desk and stops on the other side. His eyes are down on the cap that he continues kneading in his hands. When he finally looks up at me, his spine snaps up straight.

I can only imagine what it is he sees there.

I'm not known for my patience. I *am* known for my temper.

Everything has been so much better since Peter Pan skipped Neverland, including me. However, that doesn't mean his exodus made me a completely different person. Happier for the most part, sure. Doesn't make me any more capable of dealing with bumbling idiots.

Id est, the one standing before me.

My eyes narrow, and I can see the fear grow in Smee's own eyes.

"Sorry, Captain." He scrambles over both his words and his cap as the scrap of red fabric falls from his hands onto the floor at his feet. Smartly, he leaves it and instead reaches for what he came to show me.

He pulls it from his belt—a piece of rolled up vellum. Cautiously, he moves a candlestick on my desk out of his way, his fingers shaking.

I always knew I was capable of striking fear in the hearts of men, but something else is clearly affecting him. My stomach dips at the thought, dread settling there, heavy as lead.

Smee lays out the vellum. It's a map, identical to the much larger one that's spread out over the majority of my desk. Both maps are of Neverland, though mine is a lot more detailed and a little more accurate.

However, they do share one striking similarity that's impossible to miss.

A sizable portion of the island had been painted over in midnight black ink, obscuring any familiar landmarks.

As I study both maps, that dread from earlier grows and grows. When I look up at Smee again, I see his gaze isn't on the maps. It's on me.

I stand so fast my chair nearly falls backward.

"It grew twice as much as last year!" I snarl as though he can't see that for himself.

"Aye, C-Captain. And we l-lost two of our crew this time to the shadows."

I swear to the gods that a fire alights somewhere inside me and that I very nearly expel flames from my eyes when I glare at my boatswain.

"Excuse me?!" I take off my hat and throw it clear across the cabin. "*Fuck!*"

Smee shrinks back as though he can make himself smaller. It doesn't help my rage.

Raising my hook in the air, I bring it down with so much force that nearly an inch of the pointed tip becomes embedded in the desk. I let all my frustrations out in a roar.

As soon as the deafening noise that comes from somewhere deep within me fades into nothingness, I take an even deeper, shuddering breath. I yank my hook out of the wood, splinters flying, then slump over, both my hand and my hook resting on the surface of the desk as I hang my head.

I don't want to look at either map anymore, but I force myself to. I have to see the extent of the damage.

The scouters I sent out had mapped the current line of the shadow that had fallen over the island and grown like a cancer ever since Peter Pan left. It had started slowly, a darkness at the outer western edge of the island, growing little by little every year. A tiny acorn that's now an imposing oak.

If only I could cut it down.

It's not like the darkness that exists outside of this ship, like the overcast, dreary sky. No, it's utter darkness. Suffocating. A cold, Cimmerian void.

Anyone who's crossed the line into that shadow has never been seen or heard from again.

Last year, the shadow covered only a little over a third of the island. It had forced the American Indians from their lands and their villages. The fairies must have thought their natural light could help, but they were apparently dying off one by one. As the shadow began to creep into the lagoon, even the mermaid population seemed to be thinning.

The new map on my desk shows that the shadow has now encroached on Marooners' Rock. Which means that by this time next year, it could reach the Never tree where Pan and his Lost Boys once lived.

The thought nearly causes a smile to creep onto my face.

I haven't been back there since they all left, but the idea of it blinking out of existence brings me some sort of sick satisfaction. Like even the memory of them would be erased.

Too bad I can't let it get that far.

I know what I have to do to fix this. I just don't *want* to do it. At all. Letting the shadow take over the whole goddamn island almost sounds better than what I have to do to get rid of it.

Smee's grating voice finally breaks through the tense silence. "Does that mean it's time, Captain?"

Resigned, I sink back into my chair, shoulders slumped. Dark thoughts swirl in my mind. I've tried so fucking hard to come up with ideas on how to make the shadow retreat—or at the very least to stop growing—but I've only come up empty handed.

Only one person can make that happen, and it's the last person I ever wanted to see again.

"Send Starkey in here," I demand, dismissing Smee with a wave of my hook.

The boatswain nods, picks up his cap, and shuffles out the door.

It's only a few minutes later before there's another knock.

"Enter," I say again.

The door opens, and my first mate walks inside, closes the door behind him, then approaches the desk. He stops exactly where Smee had stood moments before, and that simple fact makes my blood boil.

"You requested my presence, Captain?"

My left eye twitches. My voice comes out harsh, restrained. "You led the expedition to track the shadow over the last few days, did you not?"

"Aye."

"You know its extent and what this means?"

"Aye," he answers again, though slower as though he's proceeding with caution.

I raise a brow, my gaze raking down, down. Over his pecs and to the valleys and ridges of his abs peeking through the dark blue tunic that's unbuttoned nearly to his navel. "Can you imagine what kind of mood I'm in, Starkey?"

He doesn't answer this time.

Taking his silence for acknowledgment, I flick my eyes back to his. "Then you should know what side of the bloody desk you should be on."

No argument or hint of objection leaves his lips. In fact, they turn up at the corners, though I can see him attempt to suppress the smile. As soon as he rounds the desk and is on his knees in front of me, I reach out, placing my hook under his chin and tilting his head back.

"Did you miss me while you were away, Starkey?"

His lids hang low over hazel eyes that spark with desire. His rough voice comes out breathy, needy. "Aye, Captain."

"Then open your mouth," I say as my hand goes to my belt.

I have it undone quickly, freeing my thick, hard cock from my black trousers, ready to fucking explode.

My first mate is used to my moods. I'm sure he could tell the difference between my *I'm so angry I could gut someone* and my *I'm so angry I could fuck someone* moods. Sometimes the two do tend to overlap a bit, but considering I already lost two men today, I suppose I should resist shedding any blood.

Or at least a considerable amount of it.

My hand goes to Starkey's hair. It isn't quite as long as mine, but it's still long, the perfect length for me to grab a good fistful.

Not gentle by any means, I force his open mouth toward me. I need a release of all this tension, all this fury at what I have to do. I need to forget it completely.

He takes my entire length, and I feel my cock hit the back of his throat as I thrust up. I groan, letting my head fall back.

Being a pirate has its perks—one of them being that no one

gives a fuck about what you do to get your rocks off and with whom. I lost track a long time ago of how long I've been in Neverland, and I barely remember what it was like to be with a woman. I remember enjoying it once upon a time, and I'm sure I could again. But even in that mortal place, it was common for us men of the sea to seek pleasure in whatever ways we could.

I didn't mind it. Not one bit. I've always been attracted to men as well, and some of my crew were young, fit, appealing. Especially my first mate.

Even if I wanted a woman, there were none in Neverland other than those of the American Indian tribe who resided on the island, and they would sooner shoot an arrow in my eye than lay with the likes of me.

Of course, I could have one if I wanted. I may be ruthless and barbaric and would gut a man without blinking, but there are some lines not even I would cross.

Besides, Starkey's mouth is warm and welcoming. I love what he's doing with his tongue, rolling it around the head of my cock every time his head bobs up.

Then his hand comes up and massages my balls, and I can feel them tightening.

With a strained grunt that fills the entire cabin, I grip his hair tighter, forcing him to stay in place as I roughly thrust a few more times before coming down his throat, letting some of my tension be swallowed up as he sucks me dry.

I'm not sure it's enough.

Releasing him, I sink into my chair, panting. Eyes closed. Head back. A few moments later, I hear footsteps fading and the door to my cabin open and close.

Starkey knows the drill.

The inside of my eyelids continue to flicker with stars for several minutes, and I feel at least a little lighter than I have in days.

Unfortunately, it doesn't last long.

Those dark thoughts creep back in—the shadow. It ruins everything.

I don't want to leave Neverland. I like it here. There's no growing old and dying. I can sail, pillage and plunder, ravage and be depraved for all of eternity.

Except the shadow's threatening that way of eternal life now. The darkness will eventually take over the whole island. Neverland would be no more.

I can't allow that to happen.

The decent mood that Starkey's mouth put me in barely lasted five fucking minutes.

I have to find Peter Pan and bring him back to Neverland.

2

PAN

Instruments clatter on the white linoleum floor of the community college band hall as soon as I open the door of the soundproof practice room. I step out with Cora, the sophomore I had been tutoring. She carries her clarinet case close to her chest and peers awkwardly between me and Simon, one of the other music department staff members. He's scrambling around to pick up the fallen drums, snares, and cymbals.

"Go ahead," I say to Cora with a smile. "Good luck at the concert this weekend. You'll do great."

She nods, then scurries away and out of the band hall.

Walking through rows of chairs and instruments, I head over to where Simon is still righting parts of the drum set that he knocked over and begin helping him. His blond hair falls in front of his chocolate brown eyes, and he keeps having to push it back to see what he's doing.

It's no wonder he knocked the damn drums over. *Again.*

"You really don't have to do that, Peter," he says.

"I know." I flash him a grin as I pick up the cymbals. "It's no problem."

"I'm such a clutz."

"I know," I repeat. When he looks at me, I laugh. "I'm honestly not sure why they let your arse around all of these expensive instruments."

Simon groans and holds the snare drum up for me to see. There's a hole ripped right through the head. "They probably shouldn't."

I laugh again, shaking my head. "Get out of here. I'll take care of it."

He frowns. "Are you sure?"

"Yes," I answer forcefully as I take the snare from him. "You have that meeting at USC first thing in the morning, don't you?"

He nods.

"Then go. You need your beauty sleep."

"Thanks, Peter." Simon gives me a one armed hug, then practically skips out of the room.

Heading over to one of the storage closets against the white walls of the hall, I carry the snare drum with me under my arm, humming quietly now that I'm alone. I find a replacement head, take a seat on the nearest stool, and get to work switching it out with the broken one.

Anyone else may have bitched and moaned at having to fix something else that Simon had accidentally broken—it happened more often than it should—but I don't mind so much. I love working with instruments. I have for as long as I can remember. Besides, Simon is a brilliant musician, even if he is equally as clumsy. The school's lucky to have him.

Simon will be off to better things soon, I'm sure of it. We both work at the community college in our small coastal town a couple hours north of Los Angeles, but he's been talking about making the move south for so long.

As for me, I'm still not sure what I want. I love my job. I love this town. It's quiet, peaceful. I don't think I could ever live in a city as big and bustling as LA. I know that's where all the opportunity is, all the fame and the fortune, but I'm pretty content with everything I have here.

Sometimes I miss London. And the Darlings. But here, I get to see the sun so much more often. I love the sun, the light, the warmth.

I moved here right after secondary school. I don't think I ever felt at home in London. The Darlings were the best family I could've ever asked for, of course. They found me, along with several other lads, fourteen years ago. None of us had any family, no home. I don't have many memories from that time, but one theory everyone had was that we were from some illegal workhouse that had been shut down before the police could crack down on it. I don't know if that's true. I suppose I'll never know. I don't remember my life before that, but it is what it is. I never really tried hard to remember.

They weren't even sure of my age at the time, but they estimated I was around twelve. Which would put me at about twenty-six now. Still young but old enough that it's time I start thinking if this is what I want to do for the rest of my life.

Still humming as I work, I remove the ripped drum head and chuck it in the trash. I place the new one on and begin tightening the bolts into place.

I still have a little time, so I'm not in a big hurry. But I am looking forward to dinner with Wendy.

Oh, yeah. Wendy followed me here from London. She had said because she's my best friend she couldn't let me go alone. I had appreciated that more than I ever expressed. I didn't want to be alone. We shared an apartment for the first year, but then her high school sweetheart—well, that's what he would come to be known as over here in the states—ended up following her a year after she followed me. So she moved out to live with him instead.

I'm not upset about it. Really, I'm not.

Glancing up at the clock on the opposite wall, I see that it's almost six. I get so excited that I stand up fast, nearly sending the snare drum crashing back to the floor, which probably would've broken it worse than the last time.

Okay, maybe I'm just a little lonely.

And the tiniest bit disappointed that I'm not meeting Wendy at our usual place.

We found the Coastline Cafe during our first month here on our first trip to the beach. We've gone there almost once a week for the last eight years—minus the two visits to London and the vacation Wendy and Jeremiah took to New York a couple years ago.

For today, Jeremiah apparently made reservations at some fancy restaurant downtown.

Don't get me wrong. I have absolutely nothing against Wendy's boyfriend. Jeremiah Nibs was one of the boys found with me fourteen years ago, and we had stayed in touch. He had been adopted by the Darling's next-door neighbors.

Don't get me started on Slightly though. He had been taken in by Wendy's aunt, and I still feel sorry for that old woman.

After I shut off the lights and lock the door to the band hall, I head out of the small, white-brick building and toward my moped parked in the lot.

I smile when I see the sun shining off the forest green paint.

Wendy still thinks I should've bought myself a car instead, but she doesn't get it. How can you feel like you're flying when you're driving a car, without having the wind whip through your hair like it's caressing you?

Exactly. You can't.

My moped is my most prized possession. Her name is Lily. I don't care what Wendy thinks of Lily. I'm sure she's just jealous.

I remove the D lock from Lily's back wheel, then climb on, smiling again as she purrs to life.

Heading off campus, I make the turn for my apartment. It's nothing special—a standard one bedroom that I traded the two bedroom Wendy and I had shared for. It's a small complex of four yellow buildings with a neglected garden, trees, and a walking path in the center.

Despite the fact I'm only going to be five minutes, I lock Lily's wheel, not wanting to take any chances.

I climb the stairs to the second floor of the back building and enter my apartment. The living room is on the left, a floor lamp right beside the door. There's a small television in the corner, but the room is mostly filled with instruments—guitars on stands, a drumset, and wind and wood instruments hanging on the cloud-white walls. Passing the small dining room on the right that connects into the kitchen, I continue down the hallway to my bedroom.

There's one window beside the queen-size bed. The dying daylight seeps in through the thin blinds, casting a glow over the wrinkled dark green sheets on the mattress. There's a nightstand on either side and a small dresser across the room. The space is kind of a mess, but it's mostly clothes that are strewn about. Okay, and maybe a couple of empty glasses.

Wendy was the neat freak, not me.

After scouring my closet for something decent to wear, I pull on a pair of black slacks, black dress shoes, and a hunter green dress shirt. Before leaving, I attempt to tame my slightly wild auburn hair in the mirror. I manage to get a few pieces to lie flat but give up on the rest of them.

I'm pleasantly surprised to see that the color of my shirt almost matches my eyes perfectly.

Of course, if we were going to the cafe instead, I wouldn't have to dress up at all.

Forcing down my grumbling, I leave the apartment, hop back on Lily, and head to dinner. I find the restaurant easily enough after driving through the narrow streets of downtown for about five minutes.

Wendy and Jeremiah are both standing outside. The smile on Wendy's face is so big, brilliant, and bright that it's nearly blinding. Her long brunette hair is loose, cascading down her back in waves. She's wearing a baby blue babydoll dress, staring up at her boyfriend with the biggest brown doe eyes I've ever seen.

I hop off my moped, lock up the back wheel, then approach my friends.

"I hope you're paying, Nibs," I joke, staring up at the restaurant's sign as I skip up onto the sidewalk. It's a French name that I couldn't pronounce even if I tried.

"Actually," he starts, glancing at Wendy with a matching smile, "yeah, tonight's on me."

Regarding the both of them, my eyes bounce back and forth, and my brows knit in suspicion. "Okay," I drawl. "What did I miss?"

Wendy looks between me and Jeremiah now. His dark brown skin is practically glowing as he straightens one of his signature brightly-colored ties—today, it's a canary yellow. I don't think Wendy's smile could grow any bigger.

But as she raises her left hand in the air, it does.

The diamond on her ring finger catches the setting sun, glinting in the light. It's even more blinding than her smile.

"We're engaged!" she squeals.

I blink. Then blink a few more times. She stares at me expectantly while I stare back silently, incredulously.

Finally, I tilt my head. "Weren't you already?"

"Peter!" She swings her brown handbag around, and it makes solid contact with my shoulder.

Howling with laughter, I block her second attack. "I'm sorry, I'm sorry!" I'm still laughing by the time she finally stops hitting me with her bag. She crosses her arms and glares at me, but I don't stop. "I'm just saying. It's about time."

"We wanted to be in a good place," says Wendy, still pouting at my joke.

"I know, Wen." I take a step toward her but stop and hold up my hands. "You're not going to attack me again, are you?"

She raises her chin. "I haven't decided."

Deciding it's worth the risk, I close the distance between us and wrap my arms around her. "I'm happy for you, Wendy," I whisper in her ear.

She's stiff for a moment, then sighs—that familiar noise she makes when she can't stay mad at me no matter how badly she wants to. She finally hugs me back with a grin that she had clearly been trying hard to repress. "Thank you."

After our hug, I turn to Jeremiah and embrace him next. "Congratulations, Jer."

"Thanks, Peter," he says, patting my back.

When we pull apart, I look over at Wendy again to see her still glowing.

"Shall we?" Jeremiah asks, opening the door to the restaurant for us.

I let Wendy enter first, then motion for Jeremiah to follow while I grab the door. I enter behind them, and the scent of freshly baked bread and French wine reaches my nose. My mouth immediately starts to water.

Staying a few steps behind, I watch as he walks with one arm around Wendy's waist. He gives the maître d' his name, who then leads us to the table.

The walls of the restaurant are covered in yellow wallpaper with intricate patterns and fleur-de-lis. The tables are all square and draped with white tablecloths. It's quite busy for a Monday night, but it's not all that surprising with the delicious aroma wafting through the place.

I let Wendy and Jeremiah sit at our table first before taking a seat beside Wendy. Jer orders a bottle of their best wine.

I'm happy for Wendy. Really, I am. For them both. They're two of my favorite people in this world, and they deserve each other.

But there's always been a quiet, nagging voice in the back of my mind for the last seven years ever since Wendy moved out that's been telling me I'm going to be alone forever.

What if it's right?

As I sit at the table with them, that voice seems to be screaming now. I silently tell it to shut the hell up. I'm here to celebrate with my friends, so that's what I'm going to do.

What the fuck does that voice know anyway?

3

HOOK

Many of Neverland's fairies have perished in their attempts to hold back the shadow, but there's still a few left.

I just hope there's *enough* left.

Fairies and their fairy dust are just a couple of the things that keep Neverland alive, so naturally I know where their nests are.

I know everything about this island.

Except for how to save it.

Pushing those dark thoughts away the best I can, I trek through the snow-covered forest with my first mate and two of our crew. The white powder crunches beneath our boots and trickles down in a steady drizzle from the overcast skies between breaks in the canopy above. Everything is dark skies, white snow. Hardly any green from the trees. It smells like frost and ozone, sweet and pungent.

Other than our breaths and the crunch of snow, it's quiet. *Too* quiet.

The fairies used to make a lot of noise around the island, their singing like birdsongs, their wings like bells and gentle chimes.

Even so, they've always avoided us pirates, so they didn't make it easy to track them. We've already gone to one of their nests to find it empty. Either they were hiding from us more than usual, or their numbers are dwindling more than we've estimated.

Fortunately, the next nest we come across has a few. Not as many as it should have, but I'm not too worried.

If—no, *when*—I get Pan back here and he saves Neverland, the fairy population will bounce back. They've been keeping their numbers down on purpose, not wanting to overpopulate the only habitable portion of the island that's shrinking day by day.

Normally, they fuck like rabbits.

So, yeah, they'll come back.

With that in mind, I approach the tree from behind. It's hollowed out, and there's a hole carved into the trunk on the other side, a pinkish glow emanating from within. Peering around the body of the tree, I hear quiet chimes and bells and whistles drifting out.

Once upon a time, that music filled Neverland.

I hated it.

With a wicked smirk, I whisper into the entrance of the nest, "There's no such thing as fairies."

The music ceases. Abruptly. My smirk grows.

Rounding the tree, I study the dark hole that still radiates with pinks and blues and purples. Fairy dust floats in the air, mixing with the snow. I swat at it and dust it off my black frock coat with the back of my hand.

I reach into the tree. My face screws up in a grimace when I feel a tiny body. Pulling it out, I glare down at the fairy corpse. It fits in the palm of my hand, its skin already a cadaverous gray and cool to the touch.

As though it's a bug, I flick it away, and it lands in a pile of snow.

Reaching back in, I feel what it is I'm looking for. I pull my hand out and look down at the scoop of dust. It sparkles, glimmering like tiny pastel stars. Turning my nose up at it, I motion for Starkey. He approaches with a small glass vial in his hand, uncorks it, and holds it out for me. I deposit the dust inside. It swirls and drifts within the glass before settling. After he closes it up and hands it to me, I store it in the inner pocket of my coat.

"Okay, mateys." I turn to my crew. "Starkey, you're in charge while I'm gone."

"Are you sure you don't want me to come with you?" he asks.

I shake my head, knowing exactly what he's thinking—that I'll need him the moment I first lay eyes on Pan. And he most likely isn't wrong. My blood boils just thinking about it. It's not quite the fuck someone kind of angry, but it probably wouldn't take much to get there if I had the chance.

Still...the other world has changed. I know that from my visit in the 1930s. Peter Pan had no idea I left. He didn't think I had any happy memories, so he didn't think I *could* leave. Let alone that I would leave and ever come back. But I did. Just once. It was shortly after Pan took my hand, and I thought going back was what I wanted. I thought I wanted—

It doesn't matter. I left and came back. That's all there is to it.

And now I really don't want to leave again.

"I need to do this alone. Besides, two eighteenth century pirates will draw a lot more attention than one alone. Time may not move here in Neverland, but it does elsewhere. And we don't know what that world has become."

"All the more reason if you need backup, Captain," says Starkey.

I do consider it for a moment, but the truth is that I *want* to do this alone. Peter Pan is mine, always has been.

Mine to capture.

Mine to bend.

Mine to break.

"You're staying here, Starkey. End of discussion."

Turning back to the tree, I once again reach into the hole in the trunk. I scoop up as much of the fairy dust as I possibly can, but there's not a lot left. I'm usually not one to hunt for a bright side, but at least I'm doing this now. If I were to wait much longer, there may not be enough fairy dust left for me to leave the island at all.

With the last of the dust in my hand, I take a step back and nod at my men. "Keep the crew away from the shadow. I'll be back as soon as I can."

The three of them mirror me, taking even more steps back to give me space.

I don't hesitate. I can't. Not in front of my crew.

Tossing the dust into the air above my head, I let it trickle down over me. It's pink and lilac and powder blue. It tickles my nose and smells like sugar and vanilla. I want to swat it away again, stomp it into the snow, blow it into the wind.

But I don't.

With the dust a part of me now, soaked into the fibers of my clothes, permeated into the pores of my skin, I close my eyes.

And think.

I think of happy thoughts.

It's a surprise I have any, I know. But Peter Pan has been gone for fourteen years. I've been happier in those fourteen years than I have in the last two hundred.

So that's what I think about. I think about the farthest reaches of the sea I've sailed to, at least until the ice became too thick, when there were open waters for leagues and leagues. I think about the peace of not having a nasty little child ruin every moment of every day. I think about the occasional fight with the other inhabitants of the island with no Lost Boys ambushing us and winning the battle for the other side. I think about the dwindling fairy and mermaid population and all the treasure they've left behind.

It's all enough. It gets me in the air.

When I open my eyes again, I'm hovering above the canopy of the forest, my men lost below the trees.

I don't look back.

I take off, away from the forest, away from the island, away from Neverland.

It doesn't take long until I'm far enough away that the air begins to thin and thicken all at once. The atmosphere feels a little heavy, a little heavier than air. Like gossamer.

It's the veil. The veil that separates our world from all the others.

I don't stop. I keep going.

And then I pass right through it.

For the briefest of moments, everything goes dark. I lose the ability to breathe. All the air is sucked out of my lungs, stolen by some mystical force. I panic for only a second, inhaling a whole lot of nothing. But then my breath returns, and I gulp down air, gasping as though I had been held under water.

Then the light returns too.

At first, it's flickering, like I'm barreling through a tunnel and the wall is made of billions of stars. But then it steadies, a burst of yellow that gradually shrinks to one circle—the sun. The blue backdrop all around is clear, but it's not quite as flawless, not quite that perfect cerulean, as Neverland's sky used to be.

Letting the wind guide me, I aim for land.

It doesn't matter where I end up. I already know I'm going to have to spend time hunting for Pan. After fourteen years, he could be anywhere.

I'm careful not to let anyone see me flying. The last thing I want to do is attract more attention than my clothes surely will. So I land somewhere secluded—a countryside with lots of trees and open fields—and make my way to the closest city. It's a long trek, scorching hot with the sun barreling down on me. My coat gets left behind somewhere along the way, and I transfer the vial of fairy dust into my pants pocket.

When I make it into the heart of the nearest city, that's when I realize the clothes I'm wearing are literally nothing like those that the people on the street have on—tight fitting and brightly colored.

That's my first priority. New clothes.

After finding a pocket to pick, I take the stranger's wallet to the nearest clothing store.

It's a small shop with racks of clothes and accessories. I try not to focus on how different everything is from the last time I was in this world. Instead, I focus on the thin carpet beneath my feet, the subtle smell of citrus and lemongrass, the path I take around the store to avoid as many people as I can.

There's so many of them. I'm not used to this many people.

The looks I receive aren't surprising. I was expecting them, of course. I had already lost the frock coat, but even without it, everyone still stares at me as though I stepped through time.

I suppose in a way I have.

Being in a different time, around this many people, has me

a little on edge. Or a *lot* on edge. So I do my shopping quickly, familiar with some of the styles and fabrics thanks to my time here almost a hundred years ago. I choose black jeans, a gray T-shirt, and a black leather jacket that seems to call out to me.

The vial of fairy dust is carefully tucked into the pocket of my new jacket.

The brunette woman scanning the tags I tore from the clothes so I could wear them out keeps staring at my hands. Or, more accurately, my hook. She's probably never seen anything like it. Her cheeks turn pink at whatever thoughts are running through her head. I maybe should consider an alternative, but the hook is a part of me as much as my left hand had once been. I'm not getting rid of it.

When the woman tells me my total, I open the wallet and am baffled by the fact there's no cash inside. *Fuck.*

"Um," I start as I rifle through the various compartments. "I thought I had..."

"Will one of those cards work?" the woman asks.

Cards?

With the wallet held to the counter by my hook, I remove a *card* from one of the pockets. It's hard plastic and dark blue with numbers on it. I hand it to her, unsure.

She takes it, unfazed, and scans it. There's a beep, and she hands it back.

"That's it?"

"That's it," she confirms, a friendly smile on her face. "Have a great day!"

After the clothing store, I wander around a bit and learn that I'm in America, Florida to be exact. It's too bright here, too hot. I imagine it's the kind of place Pan would like to live.

I find a small restaurant where I can sit outside and order food, something safe—broiled chicken and fried tomatoes. The food turns out to be delicious, but it's mostly an excuse to talk to the waitress. I ask her how I might go about finding an old friend.

Friend.

That one word leaves a bitter taste in my mouth, but I don't let it show.

The waitress prattles off a list of possible solutions to my problem. Google. Social media. Or if I was more old school, a phone book or directory assistance.

Of course, I hadn't heard of any of that.

What the fuck is a Google?

I thank her and finish my meal, paying again with the card from the stolen wallet.

Last time I was in this place, everyone's noses were in newspapers or books. Now, they all seem to be consumed by their little boxes. Only after seeing several people talking into them, I realize that they're phones. I know about phones from the last time I was here, but they were nothing like this. They didn't light up and have screens similar to televisions.

Which, by the way, those have changed quite a lot as well. Several televisions in the window of an electronics store are nearly as wide as I am tall, their images crisp, clear, colorful, no longer tiny boxes of black-and-white static. I may have let myself become a bit too entranced by their hypnotizing effects before I finally force my gaze away and enter the store.

I buy one of those *phones.* A cell phone, I find out it's called. I opt for a cheap one, thinking it will be easier to learn how to use.

The last thing I do for the day is check into a motel. The first one I went to wouldn't accept the card without identification. It's a good thing pirates make excellent thieves. I simply swipe a couple more wallets until I have enough cash. Even then, it takes awhile to find a motel that still doesn't require ID. When I do find one, it's a seedy, rundown building with one shabby couch in the lobby, threadbare carpets, and stained curtains.

Once I'm in the room—that's in even worse shape than the lobby—I'm done for the day.

I don't open the phone. I don't watch the television. I certainly don't read the Gideon Bible that's in the drawer in the nightstand.

The day was overwhelming to say the least. I'm in a completely different world from the one I'm used to, both literally and figuratively. I'm already missing the Jolly Roger. The lack of sunlight. The cold.

I don't like it here.

But I know I have no choice.

However, I decide the reason can wait until tomorrow.

Lying on the bed on top of the questionable covers, I stare at the ceiling and try to think about nothing. Nothing but the rocking of the sea and the snow drifting onto the deck of my ship.

I close my eyes and fall asleep and dream of Neverland.

THE NEXT DAY, I open the phone and power it on, and I'm instantly as overwhelmed as I was the day before.

After reading through the small instruction book the phone came with, I try my hand at navigating the tiny screen with my large finger, using the prepaid card it came with to set it up. It's not as difficult to use as I thought it would be.

Finding the information I need is a different story.

I manage to figure out what Google is—something used

to search for various things. I enter *Peter Pan* into the search field. Nothing useful pops up.

I nearly throw the fucking phone across the room.

Just the fact that I'm *searching* for a person I hate has me on a short fuse. Even more so because I'm not searching for him with the intent to kill him—which is what I would much rather be doing.

For the next several days, I try to pretend that's exactly why I'm here. If I let myself believe I finally get to end him once and for all, perhaps that determination will manifest in the luck I need. I search for him many more times and come across a few listings for the name, but none of them spark anything. I know in my bones that none of them are the Peter Pan I'm looking for. I've known him for hundreds of years. As much as it physically pains me to say, we're connected, connected by Neverland, by our everlasting feud.

When I find him, I'll *know*.

The days in the motel begin to blur together. I have to steal a few more wallets and a couple of purses to be able to pay for the room and food and more clothes, but I don't mind. I'm not worried about getting caught. I'm a pirate for crying out loud. I'm good at what I do. No one ever turns around. No one ever suspects.

I also break down and buy cigarettes. Since I left my pipe back in Neverland, I was craving a smoke.

One day, over a week later, I'm sitting on the tumble down bed, smoking and sipping on a bottle of rum that I probably shouldn't have spent money on, flipping through the channels on the television. I have nothing better to do. I've never felt so fucking pathetic.

But then the next channel I land on features a commercial that makes me suddenly sit forward.

It's a commercial for a cleaning service—Darling Cleaners.

Darling.

I pick up the phone from the bed. I've gotten better at using it, occasionally using apps to order food and Google to learn more about the world. Pulling up the internet browser, I type in *Wendy Darling.* I don't have to scroll far before...

There she is.

Wendy Darling, the children's book author.

My heart is racing. Everything that comes next happens in a fog. I figure out she lives in California and find a related contact—Peter Darling. I'm not quite sure what that's about. They don't appear to be in a relationship. I might have thought they would've ended up together, but it seems more like they're related. Of course, I know they're technically not. Perhaps the Darling family took him in after he left Neverland.

It doesn't matter. The only thing that matters is that *I fucking found him.*

Unfortunately, the fairy dust has worn off, so I can't fly. I try to buy a plane ticket—the idea of riding on a flying ship is pretty exhilarating—but they want identification for that, and I still don't have any. At least not one for myself. I've ended up with quite the collection of those I've stolen from. However, there is a bus company that will sell a ticket without it.

The trip to California takes a few days considering the bus doesn't make a straight shot there. By the time I arrive, I'm miserable. And in desperate need of a shower.

But I'm also hopeful.

During the trip, I researched more about Peter Darling. I know exactly where to find him.

The first thing I do when I get into town, though, is get a motel room. After taking a shower, I barely resist the urge to relax and recuperate from the long bus ride. But I can't. I'm too keyed up.

I have to go find Pan.

I take what they call an Uber to the college where Pan works in the music department. There was no picture of him on the website, so I'm not quite sure what to expect.

It's evening, and the campus is somewhat empty. Waiting in the car, I assure the driver that I'll pay extra. The door to the main building opens, and I hold my breath. I release it, disappointed, when I see a blond exit, knowing right away that's not Pan. I remember his reddish-brown hair, and this man doesn't match what I imagine he would look like now.

I wait a little longer. After another twenty minutes or so, the door opens again.

Then I see red. And it's not just from Pan's hair. It's from all the memories that flash before me.

Pan cutting off my hand.

Pan feeding it to a crocodile.

Pan being the most insufferable, vicious child I have ever known in my life.

Always playing, like everything is a fucking game.

Never growing up.

Well, he's definitely grown up now.

He still has the same hair, the color of burnished copper that's slightly disheveled and gleaming in the descending sun, the same tall and slender frame. Although, much taller, and I can see the muscle definitions of his back through his T-shirt even from a distance away.

So…not *quite* the same.

Peter Pan has grown up, and that fact momentarily shatters my reality. Because I can't believe the boy who swore to never grow up is now an adult.

Despite the fact that he's clearly older, he still has a boyish appearance thanks to his clean-shaven face and constant smile, though he's lost some of the soft lines in favor of sharper ones, particularly his jaw.

I probably shouldn't be spending so much time noticing those things, but it's hard not to.

He's the same Peter Pan, but he's so damn different.

When he climbs onto a small vehicle and leaves, I instruct my driver to follow him. We end up at an apartment complex. Paying the driver, I tell him he can take off. I get out of the car and watch Pan climb the stairs to the second floor, entering what I assume is his apartment.

Standing downstairs, I smoke a cigarette, considering confronting him now. But I take too long hesitating, and Pan exits only a few minutes later, dressed up for something, and leaves again.

I don't follow him this time.

I have a better plan.

4

PAN

Dinner with Wendy and Jeremiah goes about how I expected it would. We all drink way too much French wine, toasting several different times to their engagement. Wendy gushes over the wedding details—the flowers she wants, the style of her dress, the venue. There's never not a smile on her soft, heart-shaped face.

She goes on to say she's already called her parents and that they're going to start checking out venues around London. I'm not surprised Wendy wants to return to her home to get married, even though I'm sure her parents and her brothers, John and Michael, would travel for the wedding if they needed to.

I offer to invite our old friend Slightly.

"Don't you dare," Wendy says, cutting her eyes at me.

We all laugh.

"How about Simon?" asks Wendy, her glassy eyes gleaming mischievously. She tips her wine glass at me, totally tipsy. "Why don't you ask him to be your plus one?"

I sigh. "I already told you Simon isn't my type."

"Cute? Sweet? That's not your type?" She raises a brow.

Shrugging, I say, "I don't want to get involved with someone I work with."

That's true, but honestly, Simon really isn't my type.

Then again, I'm not quite sure what my type is, or if I even have one. I've been with several Simon-type men before—mostly soft, mostly sweet—and felt like something was, I don't know...missing. It's probably why I've been single for the past year and why I've never had a long-term relationship, which is strange considering my fear of ending up alone. I guess I just never imagined myself spending the rest of my life with any of the men I've dated. I always seemed to put my friends first. If I wasn't gay, I probably would've ended up with Wendy. She's my favorite person in the whole world, and I love her more than I could ever tell her. But I never saw her in that way.

She's known about that part of me since we were younger. Neither of us ever came right out and said it. She simply seemed to know. She always sort of just...got me.

Except about this Simon thing apparently.

"Well, you have time to think about it." Wendy tosses back the last of the wine in her glass. "You just better bring a plus one. It'll be sad if you don't."

I chuckle and lean back in my seat. "Gee, thanks, Wen."

"Okay, I think you've had enough to drink, fiancée." Jeremiah snatches the half full bottle of wine off the table before Wendy can grab it and places it out of her reach.

Wendy pouts, and we all laugh again.

True to his word, Jeremiah covers the bill. He then practically has to carry Wendy out of the restaurant. After he helps her into his silver sedan, he turns to me, shakes my hand, and gives me a pat on the back.

"I really am happy for the both of you," I say.

"Thanks, Peter."

He smiles at me and gets in the driver seat. I swear Wendy is already passed out in the passenger side.

Watching them leave, I try not to think past the haze of alcohol in my bloodstream. It's the only barrier between my happy thoughts and my lonely ones.

Once they're gone, I climb onto my moped, and Lily roars to life. I may have drank more than Jeremiah, a little more than I intended to drink, but at least I'm not three sheets to the wind like Wendy. As I head in the direction of home, the wind brushes against my face and whips through my hair, somewhat sobering me.

I park, lock the back wheel, and climb the stairs up to my apartment.

For some reason, it feels like there are more steps than usual.

Okay, maybe I'm still a *little* drunk.

That theory proves to be fact when I fumble with my keys, having a hard time getting the right one in the lock.

Strange. I'm usually better at getting things in a hole.

I laugh out loud at my stupid, silent joke.

The key finally goes in, and I unlock the door. I'm still chuckling to myself as I enter the apartment. It's dark inside, but I don't dare turn on one of the ceiling lights, not about to burn my sensitive, inebriated retinas. Instead, I pull the chain of the floor lamp in the living room after I shut the door, and a dim light floods the space.

My whole body goes rigid.

I sense it before I see it.

A presence.

My eyes flick to the corner of the room, and there it is. A shrouded figure—like it *is* the shadow, not that it's simply sitting in shadow—lounges in the corner of my sectional sofa, just out of reach of the dim light of the lamp.

The keys fall from my hand and clatter on the floor. Fear crawls beneath my skin like a thousand tiny insects, giving me goosebumps and making the hair on the back of my neck stand on end. I take a step back as though I'm going to make a run for it, completely forgetting that I already shut the door. My back hits the solid barrier. The blood is already pumping in my ears, a drumbeat to the rhythm of my terror. My breaths come in shallow, ragged gasps, my heart pounding against my ribs as though it's trying to break free.

"Wh-who are you?" My voice doesn't sound like my own, too shaky.

The figure doesn't move. I should take that as my opportunity to unlock the door and escape, but fear has its hold on me, its icy hand around my throat. The air feels thinner.

"Who are you?" I ask again, my voice only slightly steadier than before.

The man finally moves, leaning forward into the light. The air thins completely, sucked out of my immediate vicinity when I see his eyes. It's like they're frozen, a spine-chilling arctic blue. That chill creeps further into my bones.

"Tell me who you are," I demand.

It's either that or start pleading with the dark stranger not to hurt me, which I'm also very close to doing.

He stands. I gulp as I take in the sight of him. He's maybe an inch taller than me, but it feels like a significant inch. He's wearing dark jeans, a black T-shirt, and a black leather jacket. I can't make out much beneath the clothes, but I can tell he's at least a little bulkier than I am, broader shoulders, thicker biceps and thighs. That means any attempt to fight him probably wouldn't end well for me. He could most likely crush my skull between his legs.

His heavy stubble along his sharp jaw is dark against his pale face. His wavy black hair is pulled into a ponytail at the nape of his neck. Earrings line the edges of both his ears, and there's a tattoo on the side of his neck that I can't quite make out the details of. His icy blue eyes are cold but captivating.

If it wasn't for the breaking and entering, I might think he was attractive.

What the fuck?

Yeah...I'm never drinking again.

Yes, the man is attractive, but that is *not* where my head should be. Because what he is is extremely fucking lethal, a threatening stranger in my home. You'd think the gut-wrenching panic of this possibly hostile man in my space would've sobered me completely, but the alcohol still has me deluded, the adrenaline clouding my brain. My survival instinct is apparently zero when under the influence.

In my defense, he's definitely not soft and sweet.

Something catches the light, glinting off his left hand. No, it's not his left hand because he doesn't *have* a left hand. In its place is a hook. A very sharp, a very dangerous, *hook*.

Okay, now I feel more sober.

The seconds tick by. Or maybe time has stopped altogether. I'm not quite sure. The man stares at me, as though he's waiting for something. Probably for me to make a run for it so he has an excuse to bury his hook in me.

"You don't remember me." It's not a question. His voice is low, rough. It feels as though it rumbles right through me.

"Should I?"

He takes a step forward, and I press myself flatter against the door. He stops, puts his right hand over his heart as his lips turn down at the corners, exaggerating a frown. "I'm hurt."

I would scoff at that if I wasn't so fucking afraid. It's all I can do to keep myself from shaking. "How about you tell me who you are and what you're doing in my apartment?"

"The name's Captain James Hook. And you...you are Peter Pan."

I feel the blood rush out of my head. The temperature drops several degrees. I haven't heard that name since I was a child. It's what I told the Darlings my name was when they found me, though they were sure it wasn't my real one. The sound of it on the stranger's lips does something to me. It leaves a question in my mind.

Why does it feel more familiar than it should?

When I'm finally able to speak again, the words come out as a breath. "Where did you hear that name?"

He smirks. That's all he does. Just smirks. It's full of arrogance and malice. If I thought I couldn't feel any colder, I was dead wrong.

He's still several feet from me. I know I won't be able to unlock the door and make it outside before he's able to catch me. My only option is to run farther into the apartment. Maybe if I can make it past him, I can barricade myself in the bedroom, call the cops, and pray to whoever will listen that they show up before this man breaks down the door.

Might be the most reckless thing I've done, but I have to try *something*.

With my mind made up, I make a break for it.

I'm quick. But not quick enough.

Halfway across the living room, he catches me. His right hand grips my upper arm. Hard. He pulls me back, then shoves me. My back hits the wall beside the kitchen, and the impact forces all the air to leave my lungs. The wind instruments hanging on the wall beside me rattle. I gasp, but before I can even catch my breath, the man's hand comes up and wraps around my throat.

He squeezes and leans in, leaving little space between us. I can see the tattoo on the side of his neck now—a large shaded rose with a sparrow perched on it.

He brings his hook up right in front of my face, and my eyes go wide at the sight of it.

"You may not remember me, Peter Pan," he says, his voice even lower, even deadlier, than before, "but allow me to refresh your memory."

Before I can even think of pleading with him, his hook comes down. The sharp weapon slices right down the middle of my dress shirt, somehow managing to not carve my skin in the process. Buttons go flying across the room. Shutting my eyes tight, I wait for the feeling of metal ripping into flesh. Of pain. Of blood.

It doesn't come.

I feel his hook, but it's not stabbing. Opening my eyes, I see him dragging the tip of his hook down my heaving chest, right over the scar that's there.

"I even left you a present," Captain Crazy says, his glacial blue eyes following the trail his hook makes.

"You think *you* did that?" My brow furrows almost painfully.

"I *know* I did. I remember quite vividly."

I've had the scar on my chest for as long as I can remember, but I could never remember *how* I got it. It's mostly faded, but there's still a raised red line that runs diagonally from above my left pec to below my sternum. I watch as his hook traces it, and when I look back up at him, his eyes are on mine.

"And you still don't remember me." He tsks. "That hurts my feelings, Pan."

I don't like the way he says that name. I don't like the look in his eyes. The longer he regards me so intensely, the more I think his face is familiar. But after my brief time with the man, I don't *want* to remember him.

"Please." My voice is strained with his hand still around my throat. "Tell me what you want from me."

"Mmm." The rumble from deep in his chest hits me this time. He squeezes harder, and I can't stop myself from whimpering. "Peter Pan begging. It's like music to my ears."

"Tell me," I say, a little more forcefully.

He smirks again, raising his hook. With a deceptively gentle motion, he uses it to move the damp hair that's sticking to my forehead. The cool metal against my skin makes me shiver.

Finally, he answers, "I need you to come back to Neverland with me."

Neverland.

Neverland.

I don't know what the fuck Neverland is. So why does the name sound so familiar?

"Is that recognition I see?" He's closer now, his eyes roaming my face, his breath a ghost across my cheek. "Do you remember it? Neverland?"

Shaking my head the best I can within his hold, I say, "No."

"I think you're lying." His nose is nearly touching mine. He smells like warm leather and amber and a little like smoke.

"I think you're fucking insane," I spit back.

I don't feel brave, only stupid. This guy could kill me with his hook in a matter of seconds. He's dark and deadly. And completely out of his mind.

But…is he really out of his mind?

Is he out of his mind if his face does spark something in my brain? If something about Neverland actually sounds familiar? If it sounds like the title of a story I read as a child and just forgot the details? If I'm questioning my own sanity?

"You've grown up, Pan." His hook runs down my cheek, then over my collarbone. "But you're still an intolerable thorn in my side. You *will* remember, and you *will* return to Neverland with me."

"I'm not going anywhere with you."

I start to squirm as though I think I can actually escape him. I even go for the cheap shot and attempt to lift my knee into his crotch, but he blocks me easily. My fingers wrap around his wrist that's attached to the hand that squeezes my throat even harder. When I sink my nails into his skin as hard as I can, I'm almost offended that he makes no reaction.

"I'm going to have fun making you remember," he whispers into my ear as he drags his hook down over my scar.

And then pain explodes across my chest.

5

HOOK

Peter Pan has grown up. That fact hasn't escaped my notice. For some reason that I can't quite comprehend, I hate him even more for it.

That's why my hook is currently slicing through his sun-kissed skin, opening the old wound. It's all scar tissue there, so I know it has to hurt like fuck. But I'll give Pan credit—he doesn't scream.

Hurting Pan isn't going to bring his memories back. I know that. The only sure way to do that is with the fairy dust. I brought it, knowing it would boost his magic so he could fly us back to Neverland. Now it'll serve more than one purpose. I could take it out, throw it in his face, and he would remember everything.

But…this is more fun.

I watch as the blood wells in the cut. Instead of reflecting on the last time I did this to him like I thought I would, I watch, mesmerized, as the dark crimson spills over and drips down, a glistening stream through the subtle valleys of his abdomen.

It's kind of beautiful.

And with that thought, my anger burns hot.

I pull my hook back like Pan's the one who burned me and not my own twisted ruminations.

He's panting, a pained grimace screwing up his pretty face. There's still a boyish charm to it despite his age. I loosen my grip on his throat, and he greedily sucks in air.

"Still nothing?" I ask with a grin.

He shakes his head, his bottom lip trembling before he bites down on it.

I think I want to be the one to bite it.

Wait. No.

All I see is red. There's so much red that it's almost black. I'm sick at myself. I cannot be having those thoughts. Not here. Not now.

This is Peter fucking Pan.

I was used to him as a child; I wasn't prepared to face him as a man. It's caught me completely off guard.

But I've hated him for hundreds of years, wanted nothing more than to sink my hook into his heart and watch the life leave his eyes. No matter how badly I wanted to, how many times I nearly did it, I couldn't. I always had an inkling that he was the source of Neverland's magic. He had been there before me, and I imagined he was as ancient as the island itself.

As ancient as Neverland's star.

With those thoughts grounding me, I finally release him. I don't go far, taking only half a step back. He slumps against the wall, blood still cascading down his chest in crimson rivulets. A thin sheen of sweat gives his skin a golden glow.

"I wish I didn't have to do this." I reach into the pocket of my jacket and wrap my fingers around the vial of fairy dust. "Trust me. Bringing back Peter Pan is something I never wanted to do. Ever."

Before Pan has time to react, I pull out the vial and stick my hook in the cork. With an upward twisting motion, I pop it out.

"Goodbye, Peter Darling."

All I plan on doing is flicking my wrist so the dust lands all over Pan, but something terrible happens before I can.

He panics.

His eyes go wide at the sight of the mysterious glowing contents within the vial, and before I can make my move, he makes his first.

His arm comes up and smacks mine out of the way. I wasn't expecting it. The vial slips from my hand. It tumbles through the air, making it rain pastel dust.

"NO!"

My deafening bellow hits the instruments hanging on the walls, and the acoustics cause it to reverberate around the room. I'm frozen in absolute terror. The thought to shove Pan into the glittering rain comes too late. Most of the dust has fallen, embedded into the very fibers of the carpet. The glow of the individual particles, without the magic from them being all together, slowly fades.

Fuck fuck fuck.

This means...

I can never return to Neverland.

As I round on Pan, I can feel my entire body trembling with fury. The resulting fear is visible in his eyes.

I should kill him. It doesn't matter now, right? We can never get back to the island. We can never save it from the shadow.

My hand is back around his throat in an instant. My body presses his back into the wall so he's trapped. His blood gets on my jacket, but I don't care.

"I should end you right fucking now," I growl close to his ear. "You just signed Neverland's death sentence. And mine."

He says nothing. I'm not sure if that's a good thing or if it makes it all worse.

I need to get out of here before I really do kill him.

Before I can even move, I have to take several deep breaths. My limbs are stiff. I feel hot and cold at the same time. All I can do for the next minute is stare into Pan's forest green eyes. They remind me of Neverland, as green as its own once thriving forest. He even smells woodsy, like sandalwood and sage.

He doesn't move. He doesn't speak. I can't tell if it's out of fear that I'm about to kill him or out of defiance. My cock twitches at the thought, and that's when I'm finally able to move.

No way do I want to be fuck someone angry around *him*.

I take a step back, then two, heading for the door. I have to get out of here before I give into the beast inside me and let it do whatever it wants to Peter Pan.

Possibly the truly terrifying part is that I don't know what it would choose to do.

"You better hope I can figure out another way to get us back to Neverland, to make you remember," I tell him, neither of us ever breaking eye contact. "Because if not, I have nothing left to lose and will relish in killing you."

With that, I unlock his door and leave the apartment.

HALF AN HOUR LATER, my motel room has been razed to the ground. I walked back from Pan's apartment, hoping the fresh air would help clear my head and calm me down.

It did not.

It looks like a bomb went off in this room.

Every piece of furniture except the bed has been upended. Splinters of wood litter the stained carpet from the broken legs of the desk and chair. The sheets have been ripped from the bed and are in tatters. There are straight cuts in the wallpaper from my hook. I feel like a lion with my hair down, a mane around my face. The nightstand is upside down, the contents of its drawer spread throughout the room, pages of the Bible scattered everywhere.

Oh well. If I don't go back to Neverland, I'm going to hell anyway.

Collapsing onto the bare bed, I stare up at the ceiling, my chest heaving from the exertion the desolation caused. It barely helped. I'm still pissed. Still scared.

I have no idea how to get back to Neverland.

There has to be another way. There *has* to be. I *cannot* stay here. I'll figure something out. If I don't return to Neverland, maybe Starkey will come after me and bring more fairy dust—if he can find any—but even the chances of that are slim. This may be all on me, all on Pan. If I can get him to remember, maybe his magic will come back. I don't believe his magic ever relied on the fairy dust alone, but I don't know that for sure.

I keep racking my brain for the answer. It's the only thing I can do to keep the image of Peter Pan, all grown up, out of my head.

The way he trembled in my hold.

The way his glistening green eyes pleaded with me, knowing his life was in my hand.

The way he bled for me.

I don't want him to bleed for anyone else.

With a frustrated groan, I grab the pillow from where it landed on the edge of the bed. There's a rip in it from my hook. I feel a brief desire to bury my face into it and scream, but I'm not a fucking child. Instead, I roll onto my side and tuck the pillow under my head. I don't bother with the sheets or a blanket. I'm too heated to need covers anyway.

As much as I don't want to think about Pan as I'm falling asleep, I know I will. I have to figure out how to get him to remember. I don't even know if it's possible.

There's a small voice in my head telling me I don't want him to remember.

But he has to. Whatever the cost.

Tomorrow, I'll make a plan.

6

PAN

After the man with the hook left, I crumpled to the floor. I knew my body was in a state of shock because I couldn't stop shaking. I'm not sure how long I stayed on the ground, trying to get my panting breaths and my erratic pulse under control. I was close to hyperventilating, and I barely managed to stave it off.

As soon as the shock subsides enough, I push myself to my feet and trudge down the hallway to the bathroom.

It's small and basic, the walls painted the same cloud white as the rest of the apartment. There's no tub, just a white-tiled shower with a glass door. There are shelves and a cabinet over the toilet stocked with green towels and other toiletries.

The sight in the mirror above the small counter has me gasping. My face is pale, my chest wrecked, a clean cut right down the line of my old scar. I shrug off my ruined shirt, wincing as the motion tugs at the cut. Letting the shirt drop to the floor, I take a breath. Sweat beads on my forehead. I open the door of the cabinet over the toilet and pull out the first aid kit. Sitting on the counter beside the sink, I begin to clean the wound.

There's no telling where that hook has been.

By the time I have the wound cleaned and bandaged, I've managed to mostly calm down. I've stopped sweating, and the color has returned to my face. The cut really wasn't that deep, and there wasn't that much blood. I think it was mostly shock.

When I'm done in the bathroom, I go back into the living room to lock the door. I try not to look around and remember what happened in here.

Once in my bedroom, I kick off my shoes and pants and climb carefully into bed, lying gently on my back. All I want to do is sleep, but I can't get the image of Hook's icy blue eyes out of my head. It's like he's still right in front of me, peering straight through into my soul as though he knows everything about me.

Of course, if what he says is true, he knows more about me than I know about myself.

It can't be true though. Can it?

A place called Neverland.

A captain named Hook.

I'll bet Hook isn't even his real name, just a clever and ironic moniker that he gave himself.

Whatever the case may be, Hook's last words float around my head like a nimbus, a looming threat. He wanted to kill me tonight, I could feel it. And after he very nearly went through with it, I hated myself for those fleeting thoughts I had that he was attractive.

I wonder if this means I do have a type after all.

Not the homicidal and completely unhinged part, of course. Once I saw that side of him, those thoughts flew out the window. Before that, I think it was his rugged handsomeness, imposing presence, maybe the fact he was a little older, definitely the intense, chilling eyes with their baleful stare. He wasn't soft, sure, but that was something else entirely.

Or...maybe it really was just the alcohol.

In either case, his hook slicing open my chest managed to kill those drunken thoughts pretty damn quick.

They're gone. Dead and buried.

THE NEXT MORNING, I call into work. My chest aches like a bitch after barely managing a shower. I was supposed to be testing sound equipment today for the concert this weekend, but there's no way I'm going to be able to crawl under desks to mess with wires and climb around on the catwalk to test speakers.

So, instead, I lie in bed all day, reading, attempting to play a few songs on my favorite flute. Even the movements caused by my breaths remind me of last night.

I'm paranoid all day. Every little noise outside my apartment has me freezing, silent, straining my ears for any sound of a hook scratching at my door.

About mid-afternoon, I can't take it anymore.

I call Wendy, putting the phone on speaker as I carefully step into a pair of blue jeans. The call connects, and Wendy speaks first.

"Hey. Aren't you supposed to be at work?"

"Called in. Wasn't feeling so well this morning."

She laughs. "Let me guess. Too much French wine last night?"

I should've known she would make that assumption, but dinner feels so long ago.

"Something like that," I answer, trying to keep my voice light. "How are you feeling?"

"I had a headache this morning, but Jer made me his famous coconut water with lemon and mint. So I'm feeling much better."

"That's good. I'm feeling a little better too. I'm restless now though. I'll never understand how you can sit in one place and write all day."

She laughs again. "I'm never just in one place when I'm writing."

I roll my eyes but smile. "Right."

"So, Coastline then?"

My smile widens. Wendy gets me. "Meet you there in twenty?"

"You got it."

I hang up and finish getting ready. After changing the bandage over the cut, I choose a loose white T-shirt and slip-ons. Usually, I would wear my Converse, but there's no way I'm leaning over to tie the laces.

At the door, my hand lingers on the knob for a beat longer than necessary, as though I'm expecting to open the door and find Hook waiting for me.

I take a breath and tell myself I'm being ridiculous. I open the door, just a crack at first. No one's out there. I feel stupid. Shaking my head, I throw the door open and step outside, determined to not let that man have this kind of power over me. I lock up and try to convince myself that I'll probably never even see him again.

By the time I make it to the beach, I'm in a much better mood. I definitely let paranoia consume me while I kept myself holed up in my apartment.

As soon as I see Wendy climb out of her baby blue Volkswagen Beetle, the tension in my shoulders loosens. We hug on the sidewalk, then I hold the door to the cafe open for her. I enter behind her into a quaint space where the air is permeated by the scent of strong coffee and warm pastries and vanilla.

The Coastline Cafe is one of my favorite places. Not only because of the mouthwatering aroma and the delicious food, though that does play a part. I love the entire atmosphere. The place is small, cozy, and decorated in every corner with plants and small trees. The yellow walls are almost completely hidden behind vines that creep up and over the ceiling like a network of veins. The front of the cafe has no windows, its wall and the two perpendicular ones covered with green, the door to the kitchen barely visible to the right. But while those walls lack any windows at all, the back wall is one giant pane of glass. The view looks right out onto the beach and the expanse of the ocean.

Nothing but lush forest behind me and open waters ahead.

It reminds me of an island.

Wendy and I take our usual seat close to the back wall where we can watch the waves lapping onto the shore. After we order, I find myself staring out at the ocean, imagining I can hear the sounds of the surf on the bank. The sky is clear, the line on the horizon faint.

My thoughts are a jumbled mess inside my head. How long have I been staring out the window?

Then I realize I've been ignoring Wendy.

When I pull my mind back into the cafe and look over at her, I see her peering back beneath knitted brows, a deep crease in her forehead.

"What?" I ask.

"What's wrong?"

"What do you mean?" I ask as though I think I can get away with it.

She purses her lips and gives me that look that says she knows I'm full of shit.

I sigh and look away again. Of course. If I didn't want her to pick up on anything, I should've been more careful. This is Wendy after all. I wanted to come here as a distraction, and I hadn't been planning on telling her what happened.

"Come on, Peter." She leans forward slightly so she can lower her voice. "I know you better than you know yourself." She likes to say that a lot. "You're usually the brightest ray of sunshine in a room. You're being too quiet. Tell me what's going on."

Contemplating what and how much I want to tell her, I stare out at the ocean, biting the inside of my cheek. I don't want to scare her, but I also need to tell *somebody*.

"Someone broke into my apartment last night."

"*What?!*"

I look back at her. "I think he broke out of a loony bin or something."

"What happened?" she asks on a breath, horrified.

I shrug like it's no big deal. Meanwhile, the cut on my chest burns. "He talked a bunch of nonsense. It was all the ramblings of a madman, I'm sure."

"Why didn't you call the cops?"

Lowering my gaze to the table, I hesitate. "Because…I'm not quite sure he *was* a madman."

Wendy sighs exasperatedly. I'm being cryptic. "What does that mean?"

Looking back up at her, I frown. "I don't know. There were things about him, about the things he was saying, that were almost…fuck, this is going to sound crazy. But they were almost…familiar."

Wendy appears to freeze. She swallows, then asks, "What did he say?"

"That he needed me to come back with him to save some place called Neverland."

She doesn't move. Her eyes turn kind of glassy. "Did he tell you his name?"

"Hook," I answer slowly with a raised brow. "*Captain* Hook. Which is fitting considering he has a literal hook for a hand."

She's staring at a spot somewhere behind me. Her lips are parted. Her chin trembles. Her face pales before my eyes. There are moving cogs behind those eyes. I can always tell when they're hard at work, and right now, I can practically hear them grinding. Dread is like heavy lead in my stomach.

"Wen?"

Her focus snaps back to me. She's breathing a little heavier than before. "I-I'm sorry. I have to go."

"Wendy!"

She's already to her feet before I can react. I push my chair back, and it squeals across the wood floor. She's rushing through the cafe with quick steps, but my long legs catch up easily. I'm at her back as she pushes open the door and steps outside.

"Wendy, talk to me!"

She completely ignores me even though I'm right on her heels all the way to her car. As she approaches it, she pulls out her keys from her purse, fumbling with them like she's trying to get away from some stalker.

Totally not fair. *I'm* not the stalker; I'm the one *with* the stalker.

"Wendy, please. You know something. Tell me."

She opens the door to her car, but before she can drop into the driver seat, I grab her arm and turn her to face me. She can't seem to look at me. It's like she's seen a ghost.

Finally, her eyes find me, and all I see in them is fear, which scares *me*.

I let her go and take a step back.

"I'm sorry, Peter," she says, barely above a whisper.

I regard her for a moment, regretting telling her anything at all. She knows something, but I can't bring myself to force her to tell me, or even try to. Whatever's going on is clearly distressing to her. I hate that I'm the reason for her current state. I don't want to add to it and keep pressing her, but... my heart is racing.

All I want is the truth.

I hold her gaze and speak gently. "Please, Wendy. What do you know about Hook? Is he telling the truth?"

She shakes her head, but I can't tell if it's the answer to my question or if she's refusing to answer it at all. "I'm sorry," she repeats. "I'll tell you everything, I swear. I just...I need to figure some things out first. Please, don't hate me."

I could never hate her, but I don't tell her that. I'm too shellshocked.

This strange man attacks me in my own home. And it turns out Wendy knows him?

Taking another step back, I let Wendy get into her car. She doesn't look at me as she starts the engine and backs out of the parking space, but as she heads for the road, her eyes are on me in the rearview mirror. They're gone as she rounds the corner.

I'm left standing there, utterly confused at what just happened.

I may not know who Captain Hook is, but Wendy does.

7

HOOK

I told myself I would make a plan today, but wallowing in defeat seems like a better idea.

I'm still so fucking pissed about what happened to the fairy dust. I should've been more careful, shouldn't have let Pan surprise me like that. Now I'm stuck here with no fairy dust, no magic, and no answer as to how to get back to Neverland.

The bed is made up again, and I at least righted the furniture that I had overturned the night before. An empty takeout container lies open on the comforter beside me. The television is on, and several people are bustling around a large kitchen, preparing a three-course meal for judges who keep turning their noses up at them. But I'm not paying attention. What's on my phone is much more interesting.

I found Wendy Darling's Instagram account.

As I scroll through it, I drink straight from a bottle of rum. I still had no identification, but the guy at the counter hadn't even asked. I'm pretty obviously in my mid-thirties.

Technically older, but no one needs the exact number.

I don't know what I plan to find on the girl's social media—a term I proudly remember after learning recently. Most of the pictures are of her books, of her and her books, or of her signing her books for fans.

There are, however, a few pictures of her and Pan that lead me to his own account. I doubt this will guide me to ideas on how to make him remember, but I'm intrigued nonetheless.

First, I scroll all the way down. He doesn't seem to use the app much. He's only made a little over a hundred posts, and the oldest is about six years old. He was clearly already living here in California at the time. That's unfortunate. I was hoping to get to see a little of his life in London as that may have proved more helpful.

But when I see images of Peter Pan shirtless at the beach, I can't really complain.

The scar on his chest shines beneath the California sun in the photo, reminding me of the night before. I groan and reach down to rearrange myself.

Not the time for that.

I scroll up, stopping occasionally when I get a glimpse of his scar—*not* to eye-fuck his half naked body—or a flash of his brilliant green eyes.

It's still difficult to accept that Peter Pan has grown up. Especially that he's grown up into…well, *that.* It makes my job that much harder. And…other things harder. Even though I hate myself for it, I still can't help but imagine the rough and relentless way I would take what I want from him. I could always consider it punishment for the way he ruined my life and caused me more grief than I deserved. Get it out of my system.

No.

He's Peter Pan, and I will always hate him way too much even for hate sex.

It doesn't matter how pretty he is.

Thinking about it, it's really not fair that he grew up looking like that. It's like the universe has some sick sense of humor and is having a joke at my expense.

When a picture on his Instagram catches my attention as I scroll, it's like confirmation.

He's at the beach again. The short swim trunks he wears are tighter than before, leaving little to the imagination. His hair is wet, presumably from swimming in the ocean, and water has left glistening beads all over his tanned body. Two arms are draped over his shoulders, each of them attached to a man standing on either side of him. They're both fit, dark-haired, blue-eyed. All three of their smiles are huge, showing off their dazzling white teeth.

They're both almost as beautiful as Pan.

The universe laughs in my ear.

My hand squeezes tightly around the phone.

The caption beneath the picture reads, *The twins came for a visit!*

A winking face follows those words. I scowl at the screen.

I remember the twins, but that's not my problem. It's the fact that the three of them appear *way* too close. Images flash in my mind.

All three of their limbs tangled in a knot of bodies.

Covered in sweat and sand and salty sea drops.

The twins doing depraved things to him.

What the fuck?

I always said Pan was mine, but I didn't mean in *this* way.

Certain that my brain is broken from my trip through

the veil between worlds, I climb off the bed, deciding I need to get the fuck out of this tiny room.

After grabbing a shower and putting on clean clothes, I'm out the door.

I don't feel like ordering a car, so I walk. I'm not even sure where I'm going; all I know is I need to clear my head. Which means the direction I need to go is south because Pan's apartment is north, and that's the last place I need to be right now.

It doesn't take long before I'm downtown—a quiet square with old buildings, a library, and a courthouse. I wander around, peering into windows.

At one point, the hair on the back of my neck stands on end. Goosebumps rise on my arms. I stop in the middle of the sidewalk, and my eyes dart all around. When my gaze is drawn across the narrow road, my insides turn to ice when I see a shadowy figure lurking around the corner of the library.

Dread settles in my gut. A chill snakes down my spine.

No, I have to be wrong. It's impossible.

It's simply a person silhouetted by the sun's rays striking the side of the building at an angle. That's all. I take a step toward the curb, planning to cross the road, just to make sure. But I barely blink, and the figure is gone.

I stand there for several heartbeats as people pass by. As I light a cigarette to calm my nerves, I try to convince myself I was simply seeing things.

Or maybe I was right and traveling between worlds really did fuck with my head.

One problem at a time.

Noticing the way people slow their pace as they walk past me, I tuck my hook into the pocket of my jacket. Not out of any kind of shame. I'm just tired of the looks I keep getting.

I'm a guy with a hook for a hand. Move the fuck along, people.

Ugh. I hate them. People.

It's too crowded here.

Surprisingly, I miss my crew. Even Smee.

Okay, that's enough wallowing. I can't stay here forever, waiting until I die some horrific mortal death. I have to get back to Neverland. Which means I have to make Peter Pan remember who he is.

The only question is...*how the fuck do I do that?*

I'm going through every possible solution in my mind when I walk past a pawn shop. Something in the window catches my attention. I stop, and as though my hook has a hold of the corner of my mouth, my lips slowly form into a crooked grin.

After crushing the butt of my cigarette on the sidewalk under my boot, I step inside the store and head directly for the left wall to peruse my options.

An idea struck me outside. It's not foolproof, but it's worth a try. If I can get Pan to act more like his old self, and if I acted like my old self—though I'm sure I already did that—then maybe it'll spark something. There's a slim chance, and I have little hope. But, if anything, it'll be fun to try.

I take my time, making sure to pick out the best two. It is one of my areas of expertise, so of course I'm meticulous in my choosing.

Once I've checked out, I leave the shop, heading in the direction of Pan's apartment.

8

PAN

The state of my racing mind is a stark contrast to the serenity of the beach. While outside is calm, inside is chaos.

I decide to take a walk along the shore, soaking up the warmth of the sun, hoping that some reflection will help me make sense of what happened with Wendy. I can't imagine how she could know a man like Hook. She couldn't be having an affair—that's not like her at all. Besides, she never liked the bad boys like many women do. Jeremiah Nibs is the epitome of good, having just finished his residency last year and has a dream to open his own practice.

Had Hook hurt her once before?

The thought makes me clench my jaw so hard I fear my teeth will crack. The way Wendy reacted to hearing his name gives some plausibility to that theory.

But she would've told me. Right?

I reach mine and Wendy's favorite place on the beach—a rocky outcrop where the waves that hit it make music. After making the climb up to our spot, I sit on one of the natural steps. Staring out at the ocean, I listen to the waves on the rocks. The highs, the lows. The noise of a gentle storm growing into a louder roar before the crash of the surf. It's quite possibly my favorite song in the world.

Enough time passes while I listen to it that by the time I realize I've zoned off, the sun is making its descent toward the horizon, turning the sky a pinkish orange and leaving a golden line straight across the water.

Reluctantly, I climb down off the rocks and trudge back through the sand up the beach to the cafe. As I get on my moped and drive toward home, I have more questions than answers than when Wendy left.

The thought of going to her house instead crosses my mind, but with how she left, I doubt she's any more ready to tell me what's going on. The only thing I can do is respect the fact that she has to process whatever she's not telling me. But if I don't hear from her soon, I don't know how much longer I can go without answers.

Everything is still eating at me by the time I get home, even worse than before if that's possible.

My mind is so full.

So chaotic.

So fucked up.

I'm so unfocused on what I'm doing. Considering a dangerous stranger broke into my apartment the night before, I should be more alert.

Of course, I realize that too late.

The moment I turn the key in the lock of my door, a hand is over my mouth, a body pressed against my back. My heart leaps into my throat. All I can do is swallow it down, close my eyes, and mentally curse myself for being such a fucking idiot.

"You're going to open the door," he whispers roughly in my ear as he brings his hook up directly in front of my face as though to remind me what it's capable of. "You're not going to scream or do any of that bloody foolish shit. Unless you want a reminder of what my hook feels like. Understand?"

I nod once, the movement jerky.

"Good boy."

Okay, I wasn't expecting *that.*

And I absolutely wasn't expecting my body's response to it, to feel the urge to melt into him.

Fortunately, the stupid moan I unwillingly make is muffled by his hand.

It takes me several seconds before I can move. Finally turning the knob, I push the door open. Hook guides me inside, and as soon as we're across the threshold, he releases me and shoves me forward. I go stumbling farther into the living room. When I barely manage to steady myself and turn around, I gulp at the sight of him locking the door, his predator eyes on me. My heart races almost as fast as it did the night before.

And just like the night before, he looks like a fucking god standing there.

Or I guess devil may be more accurate.

"Get the hell out of my apartment," I demand, my tone not quite as assertive as I was going for.

He smirks wickedly, a sight that has a chill running down my spine. He removes his jacket and lets it drop to the floor by the door. "You and I have unfinished business, Pan."

I'm immobilized, a tree that's grown roots. I had genuinely believed those thoughts of finding this sinister man attractive had died.

Turns out I was wrong.

A few silent seconds trickle by as I stare into his cold blue eyes, and the chill gets worse. But then…there's a heat too. Cold blue flames.

I have to look away, but my eyes end up roaming the rest of him.

His gray T-shirt is tight enough that I can make out the definition of the perfectly sculpted muscles in his arms. His arms, that are covered in tattoos. But even with the tattoos, I can still see the veins running from his large hand and disappearing beneath the fabric of his shirt. His hair is once again tied back. His hook is fastened to his left arm with black leather straps.

Yeah, definitely a devil.

And maybe some sick, dark part of me craves his brand of evil.

I'm sure he notices me checking him out, and my face heats. I couldn't control the path my thoughts took, so I try not to be as mortified as I know I should be. I clear my throat and pretend like I wasn't just eye-fucking him and loving the way my heart races. The way adrenaline surges in my veins, threatening to make me intoxicated for the second night in a row.

Sober thoughts. Sober thoughts.

"No, I think we're quite done." I reach into my pocket and dig out my phone. "I'm calling the cops."

"And how long do you think it'll take them to get here?" he asks as he takes several steps, stalking forward like the predator he is, his arctic gaze pinned on me. "I'd probably have plenty of time to come up with some creative things to do with my hook. I can think of at least four already."

I'm reminded why I need to remember who this man is and what he's already done. I can't afford to let him distract me. Because he's right. Calling the cops now isn't going to do any good. I hadn't had much hope that it would scare him off, but it was worth a try.

"Now five," he says when I don't speak.

Resigned, I set my phone on the coffee table, not once taking my eyes off him. "So are you here to carry through with your threat and kill me?"

"Not quite yet."

"I told you I don't remember whatever past you think we share." I don't know about this whole *Neverland* thing, though I'm more inclined to believe him that there's *something* that maybe I'm not remembering. "So whatever you're going to do, just do it."

"I would love to. Trust me. Maybe I will if I can't get you to remember. But first I have to try."

"Why?"

He takes another step forward, and I step back out of instinct. "Because Neverland is dying, and you're the only one who can save it." He says it like he's angry about it.

I stare at him incredulously. That's when I notice what's hanging at his side—yeah, I was clearly distracted. They're swords. Two of them, both sheathed and hanging from his belt.

"And you're, what, some kind of pirate captain?"

He shrugs as though that should have been obvious, then grabs the hilt of one of the swords before pulling it from its scabbard.

Swallowing, I take another instinctive step back. I don't want to find out what he has planned for either of those swords. The only idea I have is to keep him talking.

"And what's Neverland?"

"A place in another world," he answers, weighing the sword in his hand, testing its balance. "A place where time doesn't move, not for humans. A place where humans live forever. A place with magic. At least it used to be. Before you left."

I take even more steps backward, shaking my head. There's something in his words that give me pause, a feeling more than a memory.

But it's wrong. It has to be.

"You're insane," I say in a shaky whisper.

He chuckles, the sound deep and menacing. Then he tosses the sword to me.

I catch it.

I actually fucking catch it. By the hilt. As though I had done it many times before. The feeling of it in my hand feels… right.

There's that adrenaline again, and I can't help but drink it in.

After I stare at the sword in my hand for several heartbeats, I finally return my focus to Hook. "Why me? What's so special about me? How am I supposed to save anything?"

"Nothing is special about you," he snarls as he pulls out the other sword. He widens his stance and holds the blade up. "But I'll answer your other questions as soon as you show me what you can do with a sword."

I swallow again, then laugh nervously. "I'm supposed to fight *you*? An old man with one hand?"

With a raised brow, he still manages to glare dangerously. "Old?"

Okay, he doesn't actually look old—no more than ten years older than me—but I'm kind of running out of material here.

He gives me no warning. Just attacks.

His sword comes down on mine, and the sound of clashing metal rings out. Jumping onto the couch that's behind me, I swing my own blade through the air. His comes back around to meet it. He moves surprisingly gracefully. I jump onto the coffee table, thankful for its sturdy construction. I have the upper hand for a few strikes of our swords before he advances enough to make me leap backward off the table, landing on my feet. But I don't have time to be surprised by my own skill before Hook comes at me again and we're moving all around the room.

The fight lasts for what feels like a long time.

And it's...*fun.*

I'm definitely drunk on adrenaline now, but I let myself enjoy it.

Hook believes he needs me, and therefore, I'm less afraid that he'll kill me as long as I don't give him a reason to. But it's not only the dwindling fear that that's how this will end. It's the exhilaration. The fight. The dance.

But then I come crashing back to reality.

When I stumble a few steps across the living room and back up into the guitars in the corner, the instruments wobble in their stands, then tip over and fall to the floor with a resounding clatter.

I hold my free hand up in surrender when Hook advances again. "Wait." Panting, I look between him and the sword in my hand. "How the hell did I do that?" I don't understand how I held my own in a sword fight with someone who claims to be a pirate.

Hook appears only slightly out of breath. "Muscle memory. You've always been incredibly skilled with a sword."

I actually grin. "Is that a compliment?"

With a scowl, he holds up his hook. "It's a *fact.*"

I'm about to ask him what he means, then it hits me when I register the way he's holding his hook in the air.

My grin vanishes. Something lodges in my throat. I step around the guitars so I can back away from him. I swear I can feel his rage rolling off him in heat waves, and I just know I'm about to get burned.

"I didn't do that," I say, shaking my head, sounding less than certain.

"You did actually." His eyes are cold blue flames again. It's too hot in this room. "Would you like to know how it happened?" As he speaks through gravel, he slowly stalks toward me. "Some of my crew and I were out exploring the island. That's all. Not up to anything especially vile. You and your Lost Boys came along. You acted like it was a game. That's all anything ever was to you. You laughed and cheered even as you cut off my hand. And then you fed it to a goddamn crocodile."

I'm breathing even heavier now than I was during our fight. My pulse surges in my ears. I don't believe him. I *can't* believe him.

Then why do I feel the urge to apologize?

I'm still holding onto the sword with a loose grip as it hangs at my side. I bring it up when Hook suddenly attacks again, the force of the hit so strong that I feel it all the way up my arm. The sword falls from my grasp and hits the wall, knocking a trumpet off its mounts and taking it with it to the floor.

The flat end of Hook's sword is at my throat. He steps forward, and I step back. Back. Back. Until I hit the wall and his body presses against mine, his sword between us, the blade against the soft skin of my neck.

We're breathing the same air. Adrenaline pumps through me in dangerous doses now. His body is pressed against mine, a little askew, his leg against my crotch. His eyes are on me.

It's those eyes.

It's his body pressed against mine.

It's the adrenaline.

The world spins, and my dick twitches to life.

I guess that settles that. My body craves his depravity after all.

He leans closer. "You have to remember who you are, Peter Pan."

My head is so muddled that I almost don't catch the desperation in his voice. "Don't call me that."

"Why? That's your name." His gruff whisper is a rough brush against my ear. "Peter Pan."

He's so close. My name on his lips goes straight to my dick. I have to look away because I know he can feel me growing hard against his thigh. My entire body feels like it's on fire. I pray he can't feel it, but I already know my prayers go unheard.

"Look at me."

His voice is so commanding that I don't hesitate to obey.

He's angry. No, he's furious. Raging mad. His left eye twitches. His nostrils flare. I may as well be a red flag in front of his face.

"That better not be what I think it is."

Yeah. He's definitely going to kill me.

I wait. For the stabbing. The gutting. The pain. The flashing of my life before my eyes. But all I ever see is the icy blueness of his, holding me hostage. The intense gaze never leaves mine, even as he removes the sword from between us and lets it fall to the ground.

His hook comes up, and now I'm sure this is it.

But instead of burying it in me, he places it on the back of my arm, the tip pressed lightly above my elbow as though he's holding onto me. He growls, animalistic.

Then I feel his large hand palm my dick through my jeans.

Wait. What the fuck?

He squeezes, and I whimper. Not out of pain. This one is different. It's desperate and needy. It's the only pleading that I can manage.

He strokes me harder, and my head falls back against the wall as I moan.

One way or another, Captain Hook is going to be the death of me.

9

HOOK

Peter Pan's moaning is an even sweeter sound than his begging.

I'm usually more of a taker than a giver, but I love the look of pleasure on his face. He's so hard beneath my hand, and there's a sheen of sweat on his temples. His head rolls to the side, and his eyelids flutter.

My hand is still between us, but I shift my hips closer, increasing the pressure for both of us, heightening the friction. My own hard cock presses into his thigh, and his eyes fly open when he feels it. I still don't stop. I let him watch me as I seal both our fates, taking us down an uncharted path with one more touch.

One more stroke.

One more thrust.

There's more lust in his eyes than I've ever seen in another man's. He wants this as much as I do—gods know why.

"What is it, Pan?" I ask, faintly breathless and genuinely

curious. Sure, I had been at half mast during the entire time our blades clashed, but I was surprised to find him hard as well. "Is it the fear? The adrenaline? The promise of pain?"

He shakes his head, the motion slow and sluggish. He's breathing hard, his warm breath surrounding me as his hips move, driving into my hand. "Please. Don't hurt me like last night."

The sounds coming out of him are a mix of moaning and begging now, and my cock strains painfully against the inside of my jeans, hard as a fucking rock. Turns out both sounds at the same time are a thousand times better than one alone.

If I go deaf, it's that sound I would miss the most.

"So I can hurt you just a little then?"

When my hook rakes down the back of his arm, pressing lightly into his flesh, he moans even louder and thrusts into my hand. "Hook..."

My name on his lips spurs me on.

Peter Pan is a little bit of a masochist.

"Fuck," I grunt at the thought as I apply more pressure with my hand and my hook.

Pan thrusts again with more fervor.

Either he really does enjoy this or...

The next thought hits me as though I just stepped off the plank into frigid waters. All the heat is gone. First, I freeze. Pan's brow creases as he looks at me with dazed confusion. Then I pull away completely, putting a few feet between us.

Pan whimpers.

While he's panting, I'm fuming.

"You're trying to distract me," I snarl.

His brow furrows deeper. His chest heaves. "What?"

I need to get the fuck out of here, figure out another way to try to make him remember, because *this* definitely isn't going to help with that. Despite the fact that Pan is no longer a child, I'm disgusted with myself. He's been my mortal enemy for hundreds of years. That's still proving to be true with the way he's purposely distracting me from what I need to do.

"Bad form, Pan."

That's all I say. I leave the swords. The only thing I make sure to grab is my jacket off the floor. Without a glance back, I'm out the door.

SOMEHOW, I'M STILL at half mast when I get back to my hotel room. I start stripping as soon as the door is closed. As I head to the bathroom, I leave a trail of clothes behind me. I turn on the shower, not waiting for the water to heat up before stepping beneath the stream. The cold shock helps sober me only briefly before the water warms and fills the small room with steam.

My walk back was brisk, not giving me much of an opportunity to catch my breath. Leaning my arm against the cool, faded tile, I bow my head, eyes closed.

Peter Pan moaning and thrusting and pleading plays on a loop in my mind like a film.

When I open my eyes again, I immediately see how hard I am.

How hard I am for *him*.

I know if I don't take care of this, I'm going to be pissed off until I do. And when I'm as pissed off as I am right now, sometimes I do things I shouldn't.

Grabbing my cock in my fist, I give it a few rough strokes, letting the water hit me in the right place. I try to think of Starkey, of the last time I was in his mouth. The memory does nothing for me.

Then Starkey's face changes to Pan's. He's staring up at me with those brilliant forest green eyes. They gleam with tears as I shove my cock deep into his throat, grabbing his messy auburn hair in my harsh grip. I pump myself faster, chasing my release, imagining his lips around me.

I come with a grunt, gasping as I watch the evidence of my sin being washed away down the drain.

When I get out of the shower, I don't bother to put clothes on. I go to bed nude, lying on my back, staring up at the ceiling. With all the lights off and it pitch black inside the room, my mind conjures up the image of Peter Pan hovering in the air above me. His green eyes stare into mine, a boyish grin on his lips, his mouth a little crooked.

Even when I close my eyes, I still see him.

I tell myself it's just my desire to see him fly so he can take us back to Neverland.

But I know better.

I'm so fucked over Peter fucking Pan.

THE NEXT MORNING, I'm awake before dawn. The satisfaction of what I did in the shower last night has faded, and now I'm pissed off again.

Peter Pan still doesn't remember, and I still don't know how to make him remember.

I almost thought it would've worked by the way he called me old like he used to and by the brief cockiness at his natural skill with a sword. Informing him about the time he cut off my hand—the worst period of my life—was another tactic. I could've sworn it was all working.

Then I felt him grow hard against my thigh.

That definitely would not have happened had he started to remember.

Now I'm back to square one.

I still believe goading Pan into doing things he used to, into acting like he used to, is my best chance. I'll keep trying that until I come up with a better idea, or at least a new one. For now, I need to research. And I'm not talking about stalking his social media again. I need to see who he is in real life. When he doesn't know I'm there.

Peter Pan can't convince me he's changed. He's older, but that's it. He's still a savage little brat, a vicious monster. It's just that now that he's not a child anymore, he can use more devious means to fight against me.

Though, I will admit I'm at fault for letting it work, if only briefly.

When I leave the hotel room, I go straight to Pan's apartment. The sun is just starting to rise as I get there. I've always loved when the sky is painted orange. Gold. Like treasure.

Yeah, I know, typical pirate.

I settle into a spot in Pan's apartment complex, a knee-high concrete wall that surrounds a garden. It offers a decent view of his door while I'm able to hide behind some shrubbery.

While I wait, I light a cigarette. Smoke swirls around my head as I stare, vigilant, at Pan's door on the second floor. It didn't seem like he went to work the day before, so I'm not sure what to expect today. My heart kind of starts ticking like a timebomb, and my stomach flutters at the thought of seeing him. I have to squash these thoughts down. I cannot let him keep distracting me like this.

I hate him like sin.

I remind myself of this, repeating it in my head like a mantra.

Then the door to his apartment opens. He cracks it at first, peering out. I smirk. Inspiring fear and paranoia is one way to make sure someone keeps thinking about you.

He steps out and locks his door—not that that's going to keep me out if I decide to get in again. But I get it. Let him have that sense of security, for now at least. I'll have it completely squashed out of him eventually. He has to learn that he can't keep me out if I'm determined to get in.

He's wearing a bottle green T-shirt today. I've noticed he's still obsessed with the color like he was when he was younger. I took a tour of his apartment the first night I was there. A few of his instruments are green. He has green bed sheets, green towels, a few simple green decorations. I want to believe there's something buried deep in his subconscious that misses Neverland and its lush forest, all the vivid green. The only deep, verdant green that I've seen that can rival it is in Pan's eyes.

When he drives away on his moped, I stand and follow. Of course, I can't keep up with him on foot. I wish I could rent a car, but I don't plan on being here long enough to try to get some form of identification.

The college is only about a mile from Pan's apartment, so that's where I start heading. I see Pan's moped turn a corner and know it's at least in the right direction.

I smoke another cigarette on the way. I'm smoking more than usual, but fuck it.

By the time I make it to the school, Pan isn't anywhere to be seen. His moped is parked in the lot. Students mill about, but I don't see Pan outside. I'm sure if he were, I would be drawn to him immediately. Only because his gravity attracts my burning hatred so strongly.

My hook remains in the pocket of my jacket as I cross campus. I don't think I stick out all that much, but the hook never fails to turn heads.

Casually, I follow a few students into the main building. I know where I'll find Pan, but I need to figure out how to get there. I follow the current of bodies through the school. It's not a huge campus, so it doesn't take long to somewhat learn my way around. When I see a sign for the music hall, I stop and switch course. The door has a tall, narrow window in it. I peer inside. Students are setting up their instruments, testing them, and the noise carries out into the hall. It's awful.

I don't see Pan inside, so I move away from the door. A young woman carrying a large instrument case nearly runs into me. I couldn't even begin to guess what's in it.

"I'm so sorry." She starts to apologize profusely while working to balance the case.

Without a word, I simply walk around her. I hear her humph in disbelief, offended that I didn't open the door for her. Not only do I not care about being chivalrous—that was never one of my traits—if Pan is in an office or somewhere in the back of the music hall, I don't want to risk him walking out and seeing me.

I decide to explore the campus a little more and maybe circle back around to check the hall again later, but as I'm making my way to the front of the building, I spot a familiar head of blond hair. It's the man I saw walking out of this building a few minutes before Pan on my first day in town. He appears to be about the same age as him and is carrying what looks like a large roll of wire.

If I'm going to find Pan, I have to follow every possible lead.

Keeping a careful distance, I follow the blond through the school until he enters through a set of double doors. I hang back even after the doors are shut behind him.

Leaning against the wall, I pull out my phone. I randomly open apps and pretend to be absorbed with what's on the screen, but I'm really staking the place out and trying not to seem too suspicious.

The double doors that the blond entered aren't the only ones. There are two more sets in the same wall, which leads me to believe it's one large room, like some kind of arena.

After a couple of minutes have passed, I push away from the wall and go to open one of the doors. I open it only enough to slink into the room in a way I hope goes unnoticed by those on both sides of it. The room I enter is vast with tall ceilings, hundreds of seats spread across the floor, and a large stage up front.

"Did you get the extra wire from the AV room?"

It's Pan's voice.

It carries through the auditorium so I can't quite tell where it's coming from. I keep to the wall, staying in the shadows of the dimly lit room.

"Shit. I forgot."

The blond is walking down one of the middle aisles between rows and rows of seats. He then turns around and looks upward with a sweeping, amused smile on his face.

I move into a corner to remain hidden, and when I follow the blond's gaze up, that's when I see him. Pan is standing on a catwalk that hangs from the ceiling. He's leaning over the railing. When he sees the other man with the roll of wire, he laughs. It's such a genuine sound, one I haven't heard from him in years. And it surprisingly doesn't remind me of back then. It's deeper, richer, but also softer, not as harsh and grating.

"You're an arse, Simon."

The man named Simon laughs back and watches as Pan lowers a piece of rope down. The blond takes it and ties it through the roll of wire.

"I just love it when you talk British to me, Peter," Simon calls up at him with a stupid flirtatious grin.

I kind of want to cut it off with my hook.

Pan laughs, a hint of embarrassment ringing through. "Get back to work."

"Hey, I was working yesterday," says Simon teasingly as he makes his way to the front of the auditorium and hops up onto the stage. He could have used the bloody stairs, but I think he's showing off. I roll my eyes. "We could've had all this done already."

Pan doesn't say anything for a beat. Then, "Do I need to get on my hands and knees and grovel for leaving you hanging?"

"That could be fun."

I seethe at his playful tone. It might be a good thing I can't see Pan's face clearly from here because if I saw him blushing, I'd find a way up there and kidnap him right the fuck out of here.

Settling into the seat farthest in the corner, I watch and listen to the two men as they work. The fact that I'm sitting in shadow has the hairs on the back of my neck standing on end. But even though it's dark, it's still nothing compared to the shadow back in Neverland.

Then there's movement in my periphery. I look over into the opposite corner of the auditorium, and I swear there's a shape there, something that casts an even darker form than the shadows around it.

A shadow darker than shadow.

It's still, unmoving. Even though I can't make out any features of it, I can almost feel it staring back. A chill sweeps up my spine.

It's as though I fucking summoned it.

But then it's gone, and I doubt myself.

About twenty minutes later, I'm thinking about leaving because I'm not learning anything new. I'm still unsettled by what I saw earlier.

But then...

"Are you almost done up there?" Simon asks Pan, facing the catwalk while he stands on the stage. "I could use some help moving this speaker."

"Yeah, just finishing up," says Pan. "Be right down."

After a few minutes, Pan disappears off the catwalk, then enters through a side door moments later. He goes up onto the stage—actually using the steps—and meets Simon where there's a large speaker. Now that they're so close, they don't have to talk as loud, and I can't hear them from where I sit. They both grab the speaker and start lugging it across the back of the stage together.

I can barely see Pan's face, but I'm certain he's grimacing. He says something, and they both set the speaker down. He leans against it, his hand on his chest. I smirk knowingly. Then the smirk vanishes while I watch Simon round the speaker and touch Pan on the arm.

I lean forward as though I'd be able to hear them, but I still can't.

And now I'm damn near shaking with rage as I watch Simon comforting Pan, speaking quietly, their faces much too close. My hand clenches into a fist, and it takes everything in me to not slam it against the back of the seat in front of me, which would only alert them to my presence.

I shouldn't be surprised that I feel so possessive over Pan. In one way or another, I always have been. Whenever we would fight, I didn't want my crew anywhere near him. He was always *mine*. If anyone was going to run him through, it was going to be me. That's how it's been for hundreds of years. I know him better than anyone else ever has.

I try to convince myself that's all it is.

When they break away, they're laughing, and Pan seems more at ease.

I should leave right now, right when I'm on the familiar fringes of severe bloodlust. For some reason, I can't look away.

Pan is all smiles and joy and light.

All because of *Simon*. I want to bury my hook in him.

Unless...it's all just an act.

I start to piece things together. Pan distracting me from hurting him last night like I really wanted to. Pan acting hurt in front of Simon to get the blond's attention and comfort. Even in Neverland, he had a way of wrapping everyone—the fairies, the Lost Boys—around his little fucking finger.

And now...he's as idealistic, as uninhibited as I could imagine him being after having grown up.

So maybe I wasn't all that wrong after all.

If anything, this has proved one thing.

Pan is still playing a game.

10

PAN

The door to the auditorium slams shut, and I snap my head up.

There's no one there.

Every little loud sound and fast movement and unexpected touch has set me on edge today. It's like I'm just waiting for Hook to come out of the shadows and finish what he started.

And I don't mean what *I* started.

Though, I am still a little disoriented, as though my world tilted on its axis and hasn't quite righted itself yet.

I mean, what the hell *was* that? I was so sure he was about to kill me. And then he does *that* instead? Talk about a total mindfuck. Every time I've thought about it today, my dick wakes up as though it too can remember his brutal touch, his perverse words, his hot breath on my face.

Fuck. Why does he have to be hot as sin?

And why do I have to be such a goddamn idiot?

These are the only two questions that are keeping my crooked, unbalanced world still spinning.

For a man as vicious and cruel as Hook, he doesn't deserve to look like that. And for that exact same reason, I should not be so attracted to him. I mean, to be fair, my brain knows that. I'm perfectly aware. However, my dick didn't seem to get the memo. When the adrenaline is rushing through my veins, that's where it all goes. Straight down, down.

"You sure you're okay, Peter?"

I look over at Simon who's taping down wire along the edge of the stage. He's asked me this several times today, and I answer with something similar each time.

"I'm just distracted."

Technically, it's not a lie. Hook's face keeps making an appearance in my thoughts, the memory of his own erection against my thigh. I thought coming to work today would be the distraction, but I guess I should've known better. Then again, it would've been even worse had I stayed home again. I was going to go crazy if I locked myself in my apartment one more day. I can't stand feeling like a caged bird.

Simon and I work well into the late afternoon and get everything pretty much completely set up with only a few loose ends to take care of over the next couple of days.

"Would you mind taking this stuff back to the AV room?" I motion to the wire we didn't use and a broken speaker. "I need to head out."

"Yeah, of course. No problem."

I nod my appreciation and head out of the auditorium, through the doors of the main building, and to the lot.

During the day when I wasn't thinking about Hook—which unfortunately wasn't very often—my mind was on Wendy. As much as I do want to respect her request for time to deal with her shit, I'm not sure how much longer I can survive Hook's visits. Not without knowing the truth, or whatever truth it is that she knows.

So that's where I go when I leave the school.

Wendy and Jeremiah's home is a cute cottage style house on a narrow street. They bought it last year to celebrate Jeremiah completing his residency program. It's recognizable by its robin egg blue door and matching shutters. When I pull up and park beside Wendy's Beetle, I see that Jeremiah's car isn't here, which is good considering the topic of the conversation Wendy and I need to have.

I walk past the perfectly trimmed hedges, up the steps of the porch, and knock on the door. Wendy answers with a polite smile. As soon as she sees me, it vanishes, replaced by a frown.

"I'm not ready, Peter."

She goes to close the door, hurting my feelings in the process. She's never, not once, shut me out like this before. I already knew this was serious, but this just heightens my anxiety.

I take a step forward so my foot is on the threshold, and I hold out my hand, laying my palm flat against the door so she can't close it.

"He showed up again last night," I tell her, my gaze fixed unwaveringly on hers to let her know I'm telling the truth. "He's not going to leave me alone, Wen. I need to know what you know."

She stares at me, then her eyes turn down.

"Wendy, *please*."

She takes a couple deep breaths before she's able to look at me again. With a tiny nod of her head, she backs up and lets me enter.

I close the door behind me and follow her through the house, our feet pattering across the hardwood floor as we pass by the alcove off the small living room. There's barely enough space in the alcove for a desk where Wendy works and a couple of small bookshelves that are filled with all the children's books she's written. The kitchen is small but cozy, with white cabinets and appliances, decorated with lots of yellow and teal.

Sitting down at the round dining table, I expect her to do the same. Instead, she goes to the stove, turns it on, and fills a kettle with water and places it on a burner. I know she's stalling, but I let her, affording her the time she needs to gather herself. She bustles about in her usual work attire—loose, pastel pajamas and bare feet.

While I wait for her to finish the tea, I can't seem to stop my leg from bouncing beneath the table. I didn't realize how nerve wracking this would be.

The kettle whistles, and she pours hot water into two mugs with loose leaves in infusers. I immediately recognize the aroma of mint and sage. It's my favorite mix. I soften and relax a bit at the gesture as she places a mug on the table in front of me.

She sits down in the chair beside me, both hands hugging her own cup, staring down at the darkening water. The ticking of the clock on the wall fills the unnerving silence.

I wait.

In a voice so quiet I almost don't hear, she says, "I'm so scared you're going to hate me."

It's then I notice how her breath is hitching, how her shoulders tremble. When she finally looks at me, her eyes are wet. My chest feels heavy. I want to tell her that there's no way I would ever hate her.

But what if Wendy did something that sicced Hook on me? What if it was something bad? My imagination had been running wild since Wendy abandoned me at the cafe yesterday. And now, it's coming up with even graver, uglier scenarios.

My wind is like a vortex of atrocious possibilities, each one worse than the last.

"Please tell me, Wendy," I say, my volume almost matching hers. "You've been my best friend for fourteen years. I love you more than anyone."

A tear slips down her cheek. I don't know how my words seem to make things worse, but they do.

She sniffs and looks back down at her tea. After taking a long, steadying breath, she meets my gaze again. "Captain Hook really is from a place called Neverland. So are you."

I'm surprised by the fact that I'm actually...*not* surprised.

I may not remember any of it, but even when Hook was telling me about it, there were small signals going off in my brain—little shocks of electricity, those neurons and synapses firing—as though they were trying to tell me it was all true. The doors to those locked-away memories were cracking open at everything that sounded and looked familiar, but then they slammed shut before any of them could seep out for me to grasp.

Wendy is quiet, like she's waiting. Probably waiting for all of my questions. There are so many. Where do I start? I sit there, sucking on my bottom lip for a while longer.

Finally, I settle on a question. "*You* remember?"

She nods. Her eyes continuously flick downward, and I can tell it's taking a lot of resolve to keep them on mine.

What do you feel so guilty about, Wendy?

That's what I want to ask, but I swallow the question back and ask another instead.

"How do you remember and I don't?"

"Because you didn't *want* to remember." She sighs and takes a sip of her tea now that it's had several minutes to steep. Setting it back down, she continues. "I didn't want you to forget, Peter. I didn't think it was healthy, but you were adamant. I don't think you genuinely forgot everything right away. I think the longer you *tried* to forget, the easier it got to keep the memories away."

She pauses to let me process everything she's saying. I'm grateful for it. Because the only thing I can think about is that I did this to *myself*. Anyone else may have laughed at Wendy and accused her of playing some joke. Maybe her and Hook were in on it.

But no...I know everything she's saying is true. I can't explain it. I just feel it.

"I don't want you to think that I've been keeping things from you," she says after a couple of minutes of silence. "I tried to bring it all up a few times as we were growing up. Every time I did, you'd get...irrationally angry. Kind of like you did back in Neverland whenever you accused me of ruining one of your games. You depend on pretending, Peter. You always have. Even in this world."

I swallow something thick that had built up in my throat. My voice sounds wrong when I'm able to speak again. "Why...why did I want to forget so bad?"

More tears well in Wendy's eyes. "It was because of Tinker Bell. She was your best friend, a fairy."

"A *fairy*?"

Wendy nods. "*She* was the one you loved more than anyone. And...she..."

"Died," I guess.

It's less a guess than it is a feeling. Like I knew. Like it was the one thing my heart never forgot.

A tear slips from her cheek and spills onto the table, acting as confirmation. "You were a mess, Peter. You had always sworn that you would never leave Neverland. That you would never grow up. Her death changed everything for you. After a while, I decided it was best if I let it go, if I just let you forget. I thought I was doing the right thing. You have to believe me."

I manage a small smile as I reach across the table to gently take her hand. I raise it to my lips and place a light kiss on the back of it, then hold it under my chin for a moment. "I do, Wen. It wasn't your fault. It was my choice."

As though the weight of the world has fallen away, her shoulders slump. She finally smiles.

Releasing her hand, I lean back in my seat and finally take my first sip of tea. It's still warm, and it helps ease some of my own tension as the heat of it travels down. I almost would've expected all my memories to come flooding back once I knew the truth, but it's not that easy apparently.

"What are you going to do about Hook?" Wendy asks tentatively.

"I'm not sure. Do you know anything about what could be going on in Neverland? Why I'm apparently the only one who can save it?"

She shakes her head. "I'm sorry. I wish I did. I mean, I may remember things that you don't, but I was still a kid when it all happened. Neverland was...well, magical, for lack of a better word. Sometimes I still have to convince myself that it wasn't all make-believe."

I nod, and Wendy lets me think for a while longer.

With a thought, I sit up, spine straight. "Nibs? The other boys?"

She smiles. "They were your Lost Boys."

"Hook mentioned them." I slowly lean back again as I work to connect dots. My thoughts are racing so fast that I can't seem to catch them and make sense of them. "Does he remember?"

Wendy nods. "We agreed to always be there for you, keep an eye on you in case you started to remember things. I know you wanted to get out of London, so I didn't try to stop you. There were always little things there that would make you scrunch your brow or flinch away, and I don't think you ever quite understood why. Not even I know exactly either, but I think it's because of all the times you and Tink visited."

"Tink."

It's a whisper, a ghost on my lips. But somehow I feel it opening a hole in my chest, a void that had always been there. I just hadn't known why. I could feel it sometimes, this deep chasm where something, or someone, once belonged. Like someone had physically ripped a piece out of me. Now it makes sense.

I'm grateful to Wendy for all the time she gives me to try to traverse this maze of new—or old—information. I don't know why I even try when I can't remember any of it, but if I don't, then I won't know how to handle Hook.

"You're afraid of him. Hook." It's not a question. I could tell by the way she reacted to his name yesterday.

"A little, I guess," she admits with a shrug. "It was more so knowing you were going to find everything out when you weren't ready. But, yeah...he's like a nightmare I had as a child and never forgot." She stares at me a little longer when I say nothing. "Are you going to be okay?"

"I have no idea," I answer honestly.

"If you want to stay..."

I consider it. Hook has shown up to my place the last two nights, and if he continues the trend, he could already be there waiting for me. As much as I could probably use a pause in our rivalry, in dealing with his hostility and intensity, the sooner I face him after knowing the truth, the sooner I can put an end to it.

"Thanks, but I can't run away from this."

She snickers.

"What?"

Shaking her head, she says, "It's nothing. It's just...you used to be quite the advocate for running away."

"I guess this is what growing up does to a person."

After we finish our tea, we both stand, and Wendy walks me to the door. I give her a tight hug, not wanting her to think I'm upset with her. I know she was afraid of that, but if she's telling the truth—and I know she is—then this was my choice, and she was simply honoring my wishes. I love her even more for it.

"I'm sorry I put you through that," I tell her when I'm standing in the open doorway. "Dealing with me forgetting everything and leaving you feeling like you had to hide things."

More relief appears to rush through her, the tension exhaled as a quiet sigh. "Thank you, Peter. I appreciate that. I had always hoped I was doing the right thing."

I hug her again and give her a kiss on the cheek. "You did, Wen. I'm grateful. And thank you for telling me everything now."

"Please be careful," she whispers before shutting the door.

Is there such thing as being careful when it comes to Captain Hook?

WHEN I GET BACK to my apartment, my mind is flooded, overflowing with everything I've learned. Somewhere in the back of my mind, I know Hook is already here. Waiting. Ready to pounce. Last night, I had been too preoccupied with my thoughts to stay alert. Tonight, I just don't care.

I open the door to my apartment, and I don't even jump when I see Hook sprawled out in the center of my sectional. His arms are extended out to the sides, resting on the back of the sofa. His dark curls are loose, sweeping his shoulders.

He looks like a goddamn angel of death.

My gaze drifts to the gold coin—it looks like an old gold doubloon—that he's rolling across his knuckles. His long fingers move dexterously, and for a moment, I can't look away. When I finally do, I find him grinning at me.

Against my better judgment, I shut the door.

11

HOOK

Peter Pan eyes me warily as I sit on his couch, and I expect him to turn around and leave, escape while he still has the door open. He doesn't, and I'm almost proud of him.

"Do you think you live here now?" he asks after the door is closed. I notice he leaves it unlocked.

"You could let me move in," I say with a shrug and plenty of sarcasm. "The motel I'm staying at doesn't ask for identification, and I pay with stolen cash. You can imagine what kind of place it is."

"Probably better than you deserve."

I chuckle as he moves into the kitchen and grabs a stool from the small bar. Bringing it around, he places it in front of the wall. After he sits down, leaning against the wall behind him, he stares at me.

That's it. Just stares.

Of course, I stare back like it's a challenge. Regarding

him closely, I stop rolling the coin and place it in my pocket. His posture is laid back, but there's a new kind of tension beneath the surface. His gaze is intense. He's trying to figure me out as much as I'm trying to figure him out.

The silence, the eye contact, it's all a bit unnerving.

"Something's different," I say, finally pointing out my observations.

While Pan doesn't move, I lean forward slightly, taking my arms off the sofa and resting my elbows on my knees. I tilt my head.

Does he remember?

"I believe you." He barely blinks as he continues our staring contest.

"Oh?"

"About Neverland. That something is happening to it. That you need my help."

My eyes narrow, a natural reflex at the idea of needing Pan's help. But denying his words would do no good considering I came all the way here just for him.

I let that slide and instead ask, "Why now?"

"Wendy remembers. She told me what she could."

Leaning back again, I feel my heart rate hitch. What all would Wendy Darling remember? What all would she tell Pan?

"I suppose you have questions for me now?" I ask even though the idea of answering Pan's questions has me rolling my eyes and feeling a headache coming on. Still, I'm desperate for him to remember and get us back to Neverland. That goal hasn't changed.

He simply shakes his head. "Not really."

"Excuse me?"

For the first time since sitting down, he looks away. "None of it matters. Whatever else you have to say, whatever else there is to know, I don't care. I don't want to hear it."

He stands and looks at me again. "I want you to leave. And I never want to see you again."

Shit. What did that girl tell him?

I'm shocked, unmoving, left staring after him as he disappears into the kitchen. I hear him open the fridge. My breathing picks up to match the pace of my thoughts as I try to figure out what went wrong and how to correct course.

Forcing myself to my feet, I follow Pan into the kitchen. He's still at the fridge. The moment he closes the door, I'm at his back, my hand snaking around to grab his throat and pulling him up against my body. He gasps, dropping the plastic container of what appears to be leftovers of some kind of Mediterranean cuisine.

He smells the same as last night, but this time with a hint of mint.

"Did you really think I was going to just leave?"

He says nothing, his body stiff.

"I would have thought you'd know better than to give me your back."

Still, he doesn't speak.

"You always loved the game, Peter Pan. I think you still do. You're just playing a different one now." Slowly, I raise my hook and trace the tip lightly down the side of his face. He shivers, and I smirk. "We're not done, Pan."

Both his hands come up and cautiously wrap around each of my wrists. He pulls them away, and surprisingly, I let him. He steps forward, away from me, and spins around. I'm taken aback by the look on his face—a kind of emptiness that I've never seen there before. I swear all the color has leached from his eyes, no longer a vivid green. Similar to the way the shadow has erased much of the forest of Neverland.

"I lost someone."

I freeze but manage to school my expression.

"That's why I left. I don't remember it, but the feeling it caused never went away. I never knew what it was—this hollowness. I got used to ignoring it, but now I recognize it for what it is. It's the same feeling I imagine I'd have if I ever lost Wendy." He closes his eyes and exhales a breath. "Shit. I shouldn't have told you that."

"No," I agree, feeling a dastardly smirk tugging at the corners of my mouth. "You shouldn't have."

"Don't you dare hurt Wendy."

"Don't give me a reason to."

He swallows, then makes his way past me. The way he leans to the side to avoid his shoulder bumping mine doesn't escape my notice. The thing we don't speak about hangs silently, heavily, in the air between us.

Turning, I follow him back into the living room. He's standing in the center of the space, his back to me, his shoulders sagging as though something heavy rests on them.

"I can't remember, Hook." He turns around. "I don't want to."

And there it is. All the rage I had been doing such a splendid job at controlling since Pan walked through that door. It rattles its cage.

I have nothing left to lose now.

So I let it loose.

Stalking closer, I want to make sure he can see my displeasure, my vehemence, my fury and my hatred, clearly in my eyes. When he takes a step back, I know he's seen it. But I don't stop. I advance further.

"I've been playing nice, Pan." I'm breathing through my nose like a fucking bull. "Do you want to see what it looks like when I'm not playing nice?"

He glances at the door that he left unlocked, then tries to run past me, and I grab him by his shirt. He's not that much smaller than me, but I'm stronger. Spinning us around, I half throw, half shove him into the wall he had been sitting against earlier. He crashes into the stool and crumples to the ground, coughing and sputtering as the wind is knocked out of him.

After tying my hair back, I go to the swords I brought yesterday that are leaning against the wall by the guitars. I pick them both up in my one hand, walk to where Pan still lies on the floor, and drop one in front of him.

"Get up."

He stares down at the blade, breathing heavily, and shakes his head.

Extending my sword, I place the tip beneath Pan's chin and lift it until he's looking at me.

This is Peter Pan at his lowest. I've never seen him as hopeless, as lost, as he is right now. I've threatened to take away all his toys—his Lost Boys, his fairy, Wendy Darling. He'd laugh, call me old, call me a codfish. No matter what I did, I could never knock him down because he'd always get right back up.

But now? It looks as though he would never rise again.

Crouching, I keep my blade beneath his chin. "You would doom Neverland?"

"What makes you even think I could save it?" His voice is just as small as he is.

"Because you have magic," I tell him, still practically snarling. "But you've locked it away with your bloody memories. The fairy dust could've brought them back, but even the fairy dust can only do so much. It's *your* magic that Neverland needs."

"Why?" he croaks.

"Without it, Neverland has no light, no sun. Your magic is what sets Neverland's star alight. In a way, you *are* Neverland's star."

Something in Pan's eyes sparks then, a flicker of that star that's been hiding in whatever dark recesses of his mind he locked it away in. Just for a moment, it peeks out, and his eyes are even greener than Neverland's forest once was. But as quick as it appeared, that spark is gone once more.

"Now get up," I demand again, standing and backing away.

Pan listens this time, doing so slowly, picking up the sword as he stands. I don't know if that look in his eyes was a sign that maybe this is the closest he's been to remembering, but that's how I'm taking it.

Which means I need to act now.

When I attack, he brings his sword up so our blades clash. I grab them both with my hook, linking them together and pulling them toward me. Pan stumbles forward until our faces are inches apart, separated only by our swords.

A grin creeps across my face when I see that spark again. "There it is, Pan. Hold onto that. The game. The fight. The adrenaline. It's everything you loved. It's what'll bring you back."

I move my hook, and he shoves me backward.

Our fighting is like a dance. It always has been. A rhythm, a push and a pull. We dance to the music of our swords as they whistle through the air and the blades strike. Our feet move to the tempo, both our reactions quick and fluid. Our movements are agile, our bodies balanced. When we fight, we're in harmony. In perfect synchronization.

Pan is just as skilled with a sword as he once was, which lets me know that his memories really are in there somewhere.

If I have to dig them out, I will.

As we continue to move around each other, our swords striking, I try not to get distracted by the way he moves. He's even more graceful now, his body lithe and nimble, all lean muscle. But I have to focus on something else, so I comb through my own memories for a story to tell, something to help him remember.

Of course, storytelling was never my strong suit. That was Pan's area of expertise.

But his were always pretend; mine will be truth.

"Did you know my pirates baked a cake once?" It sounds ridiculous coming out of my mouth, but it's also the first story that comes to mind that the old Pan would love.

Panting, Pan jumps back when I swing at him. He raises a brow. "A cake?"

"A poisoned cake."

He jumps onto the couch.

"To kill your Lost Boys."

His chest heaves, his sword aimed at me. When he scowls, it sits unnaturally on his boyish face. "And you're proud of trying to kill children?"

I shrug, my sword falling to the side with the motion. "It was a game. You started it; I was just playing it."

He jumps off the couch, and his sword comes down hard on mine. I chuckle and return the favor.

As we continue moving about the room, I tell him more stories. I tell him about the time he stole my hook and then trapped me in a cave, how my crew didn't find me until three days later. I tell him about the time he used my voice to trick my crew into freeing Tiger Lily, who I had captured to get information about him. I tell him about the time he had a bunch of fairies steal my favorite frock coat, how he practically drowned in it when he flew above my ship at night, pretending to be the ghost of the dreaded Blackbeard. My entire very superstitious crew spent the next several days throwing any artifacts that looked cursed overboard. That's how I lost my favorite dagger that I got from Blackbeard himself.

Basically, I tell him as many stories as I can where Peter Pan bested me—all the stories he would love most.

Unfortunately, I don't know if any of it's doing any good. He's still guarded. Occasionally, he slips, and I can see the delight on his face, the same satisfaction he used to get from our fighting once upon a time.

But still, it's not enough.

I hit his sword with mine. "You're not even trying!"

He hits mine back. "I told you I don't want this."

I'm so fucking pissed off that I feel like I'll never *not* be pissed off. My blood is boiling so hot that steam may as well be wafting off my skin.

I attack. Again. Again. I don't let up until Pan's sword falls from his grasp. And when it does, the tip of my blade is pressed into his panting, hitching chest.

"If you're not going to try to remember, then I may as well kill you now."

He holds his arms weakly out to his sides, offering himself to me. "Do your worst."

My shoulders slump. Whatever exhilaration Pan had been feeling while we were fighting is gone. There's a woeful sincerity in his eyes. Beads of sweat drip down the sides of his face. He raises his chin in the air, daring me. I'd say he was afraid, but I see no fear in his eyes. No, it's resignation.

Briefly, I push my sword harder against his chest. He barely winces. Then I drop the blade, letting it hit the floor. My hand replaces it, palm splayed against his chest, and I push him back. Once again, he ends up between me and the wall.

It's becoming my favorite place for him.

"Using my hook is a little more poetic, don't you think?" I bring it up, placing the tip of it below his chin. "You gave this to me, and now I'll use it to end you. Once and for all. No more games."

The only sign that he's afraid is the slight trembling of his bottom lip. I stare at it, thinking about biting it.

Other thoughts follow right behind, and I can't stop them. They tumble through my mind uncontrollably, each one more debauched and perverse than the last, moving from lips to tongue to throat to chest to lower, lower, lower.

It's a nightmare, and I can't wake myself up.

Except...I don't think I want to wake up.

I'm still staring at his lips when Pan suddenly grins, and that youthful glow is back.

"You won't do it," he says breathlessly, confidently.

My eyes snap up, meeting his, and they narrow to slits. "What makes you so sure?"

His hips shift, and he thrusts forward ever so slightly. I have no idea when I started getting hard, but he brings my attention to it with one drive of his hips.

He's flashing a full-blown smirk now. "Because you want me."

Fuck. My goddamn body has betrayed me. If I could, I'd float out of it and make it walk the plank.

But it's too late now.

I thrust back against him. He's getting hard too. I press him further into the wall, leaning forward so there's only a breath between our faces. "You're just trying to save your life."

"Maybe I am," he admits, his tongue darting out over his bottom lip. "But maybe I want you too."

His hands go to my jeans and begin to undo them. While he pulls down the zipper, my hook moves from beneath his chin to trail down his neck and over his collarbone until it rests against his chest.

He freezes, looking at me like a deer in the headlights. I can hear his heart pounding, the whooshing of the blood in his veins.

"Did I tell you to stop?"

He fumbles some more, never breaking eye contact. His bottom lip is trembling again, and it takes everything in me to not take it into my mouth and bite it. His chest rises and falls against my hook, right where I cut him the first night.

But I don't want to hurt him.

Not like that at least. Not tonight.

As he grips my hard cock, all it takes is one stroke before I'm groaning, a growl in the back of my throat. My hand finds its way into his hair and grips it tight.

"On your knees."

He listens and obeys so well, kneeling on the floor at my feet. His tongue licks up the underside of my shaft, making it jerk and pulse with need. I drop my head back, keeping my hand in his hair. His thumb smears the leaking pre-cum around as he fists my length.

Looking down at him, I moan as he strokes me again. "Have you done this before?"

His verdant eyes are practically glowing and glistening with lust as he peers up at me, stroking me agonizingly slow. "I've only ever been with men, so yeah, I've done this before."

My hand tightens in his hair as I think back to how he was with that Simon bloke earlier today. I want to erase them all, all those men he's been with, but I catch myself before saying that out loud.

Instead, I guide him to the tip of my erection. "Open your mouth."

Again, he does as I say, holding out his tongue.

I slide over it, relishing the velvety feeling and the sight of his lips around my insanely hard dick.

And then I don't take it easy on him. I've never shown any kind of generosity or mercy—especially not toward Pan—and I'm certainly not going to start now. I hit the back of his throat with one thrust and hold it there until his face turns red. I pull back, barely letting him take a breath before I drive in again.

His mouth is all perfect warmth and blissful wetness, my cock's utopia.

"This is just another one of your games, Pan," I say now that he's got a mouthful of my cock and can't speak. His hands are on my thighs, his fingers digging in almost painfully as he fights to breathe. "You think I don't know that?" I take a few slow, shallow thrusts, then plunge all the way to the back of his throat again. My voice grows increasingly rough, breathless. "I always used to indulge you. I always played along. But this time? I've got you on your knees. This isn't your game anymore."

He looks up at me, tears in his eyes from struggling to breathe, and I wonder what it is he sees.

"It's mine," I finish.

Then I fuck his mouth like a mad man who's been starved of touch, of feeling, of pleasure. His hair is softer than any other I've had my fingers tangled in, the sensation a jarring but welcome contrast to my harsh grip and brutal thrusts.

For the briefest moment, I wonder if I actually might be overdoing it. His eyes are screwed shut as though he's in pain.

It seems I can't control myself with him.

But a second later, he opens his eyes, and they find mine. There's pure desire there, bright and unmistakable. Saliva is dripping down his chin, and his own erection is straining against his jeans, threatening to burst seams.

"Fuck," I groan, thrusting harder, deeper. "Your mouth feels fucking amazing."

He moans around my cock.

"Bloody hell." I think I'm about to black out from the vibrations buzzing in his throat.

He moves one hand off my thigh to massage my balls.

His heat consumes me; his gravity pulls at me, ruining me. My star.

My balls tighten in his hand, and I nearly cry out when I shoot my release down his throat like a fucking cannon, the wave of euphoria so powerful that I actually do black out for about two seconds.

I would gladly drown in that sea of ecstasy.

Unfortunately, I'm washed ashore much too soon. I pump my softening cock once more into his mouth until Pan has sucked me dry, then tuck it back into my jeans, buttoning and zipping myself up. I crouch down to his level, brush my thumb along his lips where cum and saliva still glisten. I push my thumb into his mouth, and he sucks that dry too.

"Good boy," I whisper, grinning when he shivers.

I love that he loves my praise.

When I glance down at his erection still hard inside his jeans, I consider taking care of it. I could. I almost want to. But I won't.

Gripping him by the jaw, I make sure his eyes stay locked on mine. I keep my voice low, deceptively gentle. "We're playing my game now, Little Star. Let's see how well you follow the rules."

Standing, I walk away, leaving him there on his knees. As I open the door, I peer over my shoulder to see that his gaze has followed me. His eyes are glassy as though he's intoxicated, and there's just as much longing there as before, maybe more. And for only a second, I imagine shutting the door and taking care of him, licking every inch of him, making him come for me.

But that's not part of this game.

I walk out, closing the door behind me. I almost feel bad for leaving him like that.

Almost.

12

PAN

"Earth to Peter!"

I'm not sure how long Simon has been calling my name, but when my eyes finally focus and find him peering down at me over the railing of the catwalk, I imagine it's been quite a few times based on the look he's giving me.

Clearing my throat, I say, "Sorry. You ready?"

"Been ready."

With a shameful grimace, I finally move to quickly start flicking switches inside the sound and lighting booth at the back of the auditorium. Lights flicker on and off all around the large room.

"Okay, hold it. There's one at the end not working."

As I shut off the lights, Simon walks across the catwalk to one of the stage lights at the far end. He crouches to check its wiring, and while I'm waiting, my mind wanders for the umpteenth time that day.

We spent all morning testing the speakers and sound equipment. It's been awhile since any kind of concert or other production has been hosted in this room, so there's been a lot of work to do. Unfortunately, Simon could probably get away with saying he did all the work today himself.

I don't know where I was, but it definitely wasn't here.

All I know is it was somewhere between a Neverland I don't remember and my apartment last night. I keep trying to imagine Hook in another place, some magical land with fairies and mermaids, dressed in some eighteenth century pirate outfit. I can almost do it, but then my mind takes me right back to the memory of last night, the one rooted in reality, the one where he's just some hot as hell guy, rough around the edges, knows exactly how to give me the perfect amount of pain and pleasure. The one where Hook smells like leather, amber, and smoke.

The one where I want to run my hands through his long hair.

It looks like it would be soft.

"Try it again!"

This time, I don't fall deep enough down the rabbit hole to where it takes me ages to resurface. I don't make Simon wait this time, flicking the switch for the lights right away.

"We're all good," he confirms. "Anything else I need to do up here?"

I suck on my bottom lip. I tend to do that when I'm thinking, but right now it just reminds me of how Hook tasted. A little salty, a little sweet. Not to mention his size. *Big*. Bigger than any other guy I've been with. Long and thick and perfect.

I'd be lying if I said I didn't love it.

"Peter?"

"No, you're good," I call back up to him.

I hadn't managed to think of anything, and Simon was

starting to sound irritated. Not that I blame him. I don't feel like myself. I haven't been able to concentrate for the past couple of days, and I'm probably being more of a burden than anything else.

Once again, my thoughts are interrupted, but this time by a crash from above.

My head snaps up to see Simon's legs dangling off the edge of the catwalk. My heart jumps into my throat. I leap over the wall of the sound booth. I have no idea what I'm going to do, but I have to do *something*.

Before I can, something moves in the corner of my vision, up high, as though it's flying across the room. When I turn to follow it with my eyes, it's like I'm teleported to another place, but I don't know where because everything is dark. So dark. Darker than anything I've ever experienced. It's suffocating, crushing. And cold.

An icy shiver travels through my body, reaching my bones, my soul.

When I come back from wherever I went, everything is back to normal. I squint in the low lights of the auditorium. It's always a little chilly in this room, but it's nothing compared to the frigid temperatures of that darkness.

"Fuck," Simon grumbles.

I look up to see him climbing to his feet. My heart is pounding so loudly in my ears I can barely hear his movements against the metal grating.

"Simon, are you okay? What happened?"

"I'm good," he says as he continues on his way to the door for the catwalk. He's limping. "Just tripped."

We meet downstairs, and I kind of check him over. "Are you sure you're all right?"

He winces when he puts weight on his left foot. "I think I twisted my ankle."

"You should get it looked at. Just in case. We have a big concert to work in two days. Want me to take you to the doctor?"

"On your moped?" He raises a brow at me. "I should probably not test fate right now."

I snort.

"It's my left foot. I can drive myself. Thanks though."

We're done here anyway, so I go ahead and help him to his car. I try not to look back into the auditorium as we're leaving, but I think whatever had been in there follows me because I never quite shake the chills, even after Simon is in his car and I'm sitting in the mostly empty parking lot on my moped.

Taking out my phone, I navigate to my messages with Wendy. My fingers hover over the keys, hesitating. My plan was to ask if she wants to meet at the cafe because I could use a distraction, but I'm second guessing myself. Wendy is too damn perceptive. She'd undoubtedly see right through me, and then she'd hound me until I told her about the depraved things that Hook has done to me and made me do to him.

And she'd know I didn't hate it. Not even a little.

With a sigh, I shove my phone back into my pocket and speed off out of the lot.

I decide to go to the cafe by myself, fully expecting Hook to be waiting for me at home, like he's a stray cat that I fed and won't leave. But I'm not ready to face him, not ready to fall back into his orbit. Just…not yet.

He's so intense, and one of the things that scares me is that I *like* his intensity. Not quite the death threats and the carving up my chest kind, of course. It's the intensity in the way he looks at me with those glacial eyes, like they could flash freeze me at any moment. The way he touches me like he has to hold himself back. He says it's me who always loved the game, the fight, the adrenaline. If he believes it's one-sided, he's fooling himself. Maybe it didn't always used to be that way for him—I wouldn't remember—but it definitely is now.

Once I park outside the cafe, I go in and order one of my usuals—a fresh mint iced coffee with pistachio milk. It's delivered to me in a to-go cup, and I take it outside.

I don't walk all the way to mine and Wendy's spot. It's not that far, but my energy is simply drained today. Instead, I walk a little ways down the beach and find a mostly secluded spot to plop down in the sand. Taking off my shoes, I let my toes wiggle into the sand while I sigh contentedly.

I never cared for being alone; I simply got used to it after a while. And now it makes a little more sense. Wendy told me about the Lost Boys, about Tink. Without them all in my life like I imagine they once were, I understand the hole in my chest a little better.

Not that that makes it easy to deal with or to accept.

But right now, with the view of the sun setting over the horizon, I'm at peace—with being alone at least. With not remembering. I imagine if I remembered, that loneliness would crush me. That hole inside my chest would open up and eat me alive.

I'd be a black hole instead of a star.

That thought takes me back to when Hook told me that. That I'm a star. I wanted to laugh, but deep down I knew it was true. I can't explain why. Ever since Hook first arrived, I can't really explain much of anything.

And now I'm thinking of all the other things he said. Not necessarily *what* he was saying. Just the memory of his voice—rough and husky and lethal—leaves me needing to rearrange and sip my coffee as a distraction.

Last night, I had to take care of myself. It's not that I expected anything from him, but I ached for his touch. I had never been used in that way before. Used, sure. But that was on a whole other level. I got myself off right there where he left me, his scent still enveloping me, the proof of his orgasm still on my tongue. I imagined my hand as his, rings on every finger. I imagined his warm breath on my neck, his low voice in my ear.

So much for escaping Hook for even a few hours.

I try to let my mind rest, not think of anything but the setting sun, the gentle waves leaving their seafoam on the beach, my toes in the sand.

Eventually, it works and my mind is a little calmer. I stay long enough to watch the sun disappear over the horizon, as if it's slowly sinking into the water. The sky darkens as I sit there long after my drink is gone. Stars start blinking into existence as though waking up for the night, a few at first and then many. There's an entire school of twinkling fish reflected in the ocean by the time I finally stand to leave.

As I drive away on Lily toward home, I'm still not sure I'm ready to see Hook, like I haven't recovered from the last time.

But it turns out I didn't need to worry. Hook isn't there when I get to my apartment. I even spend the first few minutes checking the other rooms to make sure, not putting it past him to wait until I'm in the shower to attack.

No, he's not here.

Why am I disappointed?

Did he finally realize that I'm not going to remember without fairy dust and give up? I did tell him I never wanted to see him again. Maybe he took that to heart and already left town. As I eat a quick microwave dinner and then get a shower, I try to tell myself that it's for the best. I couldn't give Hook what he wanted.

The mirror is fogged over when I step out of the shower.

Wiping it away with my hand, I ignore the sight of my wild hair that's sticking up in every direction to look instead at the dark red, diagonal line across my chest. The clean cut has scabbed over. It itches, and I barely resist the urge to scratch at it. My eyes are always drawn to it every time I'm without a shirt in front of a mirror. I remember how utterly terrified I was when it happened. How badly I shook as I cleaned and dressed it.

It shouldn't. It really shouldn't. But knowing that Hook wanted me last night makes me hate him a little less for what he did.

Oh well. It doesn't matter if I hate him or not.

I hope he's gone. He makes everything too damn complicated.

As I climb into bed, I repeat those words to myself over and over.

I hope Hook is gone.

I hope he doesn't come back.

I don't crave his voice in my ear, his eyes piercing me like ice, his hand and his hook on me. The way he terrifies and excites me.

Groaning, I roll over onto my side. When that becomes uncomfortable, I return to my back with my fingers interlaced behind my head. I stare up into the darkness between me and the ceiling. I feel more alone tonight than I have in quite some time. My apartment feels more empty.

When my eyelids finally begin to grow heavy and they start to slowly shut, they're jerked back open. Not by a noise or movement. By a feeling.

Cold.

It's fucking freezing.

Maybe I'm already asleep and dreaming. Because as I stare up, shivering, the darkness is darker than before.

Blacker than black. Pressing. Suffocating. Like I have a pillow over my head.

No matter how much I try to move, I can't. I've never experienced sleep paralysis before, but this is what I imagine it would feel like.

I can't move. Can't cry out. My throat is tight. My heart is racing.

I'm still so cold.

All I can do is keep staring up into the dark until this passes. *If* it passes. It feels like it never will.

Then something erupts from within the darkness, and it's bright. Like stars. Or glittering rain. It drifts down over me like sparkling snow. It lands on my body and melts into me, winking out like dying stars.

When it's all gone, I can move. I sit upright, panting. Something moves in the darkness, but I'm too freaked to pay it any attention. The darkness fades to a more normal kind of black. The coldness passes too, and I'm flooded with warmth and relief and...*memories.*

It's like the neurons and synapses in my brain are on fire.

And then...

I remember.

13

HOOK

I didn't stalk Pan today. I'm not going to his apartment tonight. I don't even know why I'm still here. I officially have no idea how to make him remember. I should kill him and leave.

Or...just leave.

But I can't.

I can't give up on Neverland and live out the rest of my mortal existence in this place. I came here to do a job—to make Pan remember and return to Neverland so he can save it. I won't let myself give up until one of us is dead. Only then will I admit defeat.

For now, let's call this a temporary ceasefire.

Pan may be getting a day off from my tormenting, my prodding and poking to try to force him to remember, but it has nothing to do with benevolence on my part and everything to do with my need for a break.

I shouldn't have let last night happen. I shouldn't have,

yet I can't make myself regret it. Because it's the last time it'll ever happen. I can't get wrapped up in Peter Pan, can't forget like he did. I have to remember why I'm here. Remember who I am and who he is.

I have to remember how I hate him, how I will always hate him.

The sun set some time ago. It's late, and I've spent most of the day pacing across the motel room. Sitting on the edge of the bed, I put my head in my hand. I'm tense tonight, and I know exactly why.

I'm still craving Pan's touch, like he's a drug and I'm already addicted. But I have to get clean. If that means several nights of staying away, then so be it.

The television is on, the volume low. I have no interest in whatever's on the screen. The bed is unmade since I didn't let housekeeping in today. Other than the television, there's only one light on in the room—the dim bulb of the lamp on the bedside table. I got a shower earlier, and there's still steam wafting throughout the room like fog drifting along the ceiling.

I'm wearing only a pair of jeans, and my hair is down, still dripping on my shoulders. It feels too hot in this room. Maybe I'll open the window and get some fresh night air through here.

Before I can even move, there's a knock.

Frozen in place, I stare at the door. Housekeeping isn't here this late. No one from the front desk ever bothers me since I stay paid up. I have a feeling I know who's on the other side of that door and I'm not going to like it.

There's another knock, louder, more violent.

Pushing off the bed, I then cross the room. Another knock comes just as I open the door, cutting off the sound.

And I was right.

Peter Pan stands on the other side.

Before I can take in the sight of him or make some quip about him being here, joke about him missing me, his fist is flying at my face. It's the last thing I'm expecting, so I don't react fast enough to stop him. His fist hits its target, and I stumble back a few steps, more out of shock than from the blow itself.

Okay, maybe he didn't miss me.

"What the fuck?"

When we had fought countless times back in Neverland, the occasional punch or kick would be thrown among the sword fighting, but his had felt like little more than mosquito bites. But he had been a scrawny twelve-year-old back then.

Now...*fuck, that hurt.*

Pressing my thumb to the corner of my mouth, I wince before glancing down at the blood. "Nice sucker punch, Pan."

The door closes, and I look up to see him leaning his back against it with his arms crossed.

"It's been awhile, Captain Hook."

All the air leaves my lungs. He's not smiling. He's not doing anything, his expression stoic. Everything he's not saying is in his eyes. It all swims around in those emerald pools—rage, resentment, remorse. But behind all of that is what I'm used to seeing when I look at Peter Pan.

Arrogance, cockiness, naivety.

He's back.

"Aye. It has, Peter Pan. You remember." It's not a question.

"I do." His gaze rakes over my half naked body.

I don't react. I know that's not where this conversation is heading. Instead, I take a step forward, prepared this time in case he decides to strike again.

He holds up a hand. "Stay the fuck away from me."

"You're the one who came here," I say with another step. I've never been scared of Peter Pan, but right now, he looks lethal. I'd be lying if I said it didn't make my heart race and send the blood straight to my cock. "How did you find me?"

"I just looked for the shittiest motel," he says with a shrug. "And bribed the front desk clerk for your room number."

"So *why* are you here?" I ask, already knowing the answer.

His jaw clenches, and I can see it working, his teeth grinding. Then, "You killed Tinker Bell."

Again, I don't react. I'm too busy trying to follow the flow of my thoughts, debating with myself on how I want to handle this. I was supposed to be there when he remembered. I had a plan for this...kind of. Now I feel like I've been thrown into choppy waters with hungry sharks.

"How did you remember?" I ask to buy myself some time.

"It doesn't matter."

My eyes narrow. "I think it does."

He says nothing.

I sigh, realizing he's not going to tell me. "Fine. So what? Are you here to avenge your fairy's death?"

Scowling, he finally moves away from the door. "*My fairy?* You mean my best fucking friend?"

He shoves me. I let him, taking a single step back.

"I was a child, Hook. Playing games. Everything was just make-believe. That's what I thought. Foolish, ignorant little Peter Pan." He laughs, but it's short, derisive. "And then you took her from me. My best friend!"

When he goes to hit me again, I stop him, knocking away his arm and punching him instead. I aim for his gut, the hit landing hard. He doubles over, coughing and gasping for air. Guiding him back toward the bed, I push him down on it. As he's still trying to catch his breath, I climb on top of him.

Then he's thrashing beneath me, trying to slap me, punch me, kick me, whatever he can. His nails scratch down my arm. It stings, and I know he's drawn blood.

When I see it, that's all I see.

Just red.

I grab his throat and squeeze. His face turns red too as he claws at my wrist. I press my body harder into his. He's bucking beneath me, which only awakens my cock, making it stir.

"Get off me," he chokes out, his body still flailing.

"Calm. The fuck. Down." I growl the words into his ear, then lift up enough to stare into his eyes. His face is damn near purple, but he won't stop fighting. "Unless you want to find out how long you can go without air."

Gradually, he settles, and his arms drop to his sides on the mattress. I ease my grip on his throat, and he gasps, greedily gulping in air as though I had been holding him under water. His reddish-brown hair is damp with sweat. He scowls up at me, and there's more malice, more resentment in his eyes than I've ever seen. It doesn't waver even as he pants heavily, his chest only able to rise so much with me pinned on top of him.

"Fuck you," he spits.

My nose skims along the side of his face. "I usually like being the one doing the fucking."

He starts writhing beneath me again.

"Go ahead." I grind my hips against his, making sure his dick feels how hard mine is. "Feel what your struggling does to me."

He stops immediately but not before a whimper escapes his lips. When I pull back to look down at him again, he's biting his bottom lip. Every bit of his hatred is still there in his eyes, but now it's clouded by lust.

It hangs in the air between us. Thick and heady.

Fuck. He has to hate me.

He can't want me as badly as I want him. We're toxic, explosive. Might as well stick our heads in a loaded cannon.

I was supposed to have distance from him, clear my head, remember all the reasons to hate him, the reasons I shouldn't want him like this, replace these urges with the more familiar loathing. I haven't had the time to do that, and now that he's here...

My head swims, my cock aches.

Why does he have to be so goddamn beautiful?

"Don't let me stop you," I say against my better judgment. "Keep fighting me. We both know how much you love it."

We *both* do.

Pan frowns. "You said this was your game now, but it has been from the beginning, hasn't it?" He's still glaring at me, but his voice is despondent, hopeless. "What was it? To make me want you so that you could hurt me? Hurt me before you kill me? Would that make it more satisfying for you? If so, then go ahead. You've succeeded."

My jaw clenches. My fingers around his throat flex, but I don't release him. I'm having to resist the urge to squeeze harder. I feel like punishing him for always thinking he knows everything, always thinking he's the cleverest of them all. For pulling a thread he should have left alone, a thread that's frayed and tangled and weak, tied to something I thought was long gone.

"I didn't lie to you about Neverland, Pan. I have no intent to kill you when you're the only one who can save it. But I won't deny everything else."

I won't deny everything else because I need him to hate me.

We can't be anything but what we are.

We're a bad moon rising.

So I can't comfort him, even if it was in me to do so. Instead, I grind against him again. He moans, and I can feel his length harden through our jeans.

I can't comfort him, but there is one thing I can do. I can make him feel good, even if it's for the first and last time.

14

PAN

What the fuck is wrong with me? I have to be broken. That's the only explanation for this.

I remember everything now. I remember who I was, who Hook was. I remember all the fights we had, every single one. All the fights me and my Lost Boys had with him and his pirates. I remember bringing Wendy to Neverland. I remember Hook threatening everyone I cared about. The Lost Boys, Wendy, Tink.

Tink.

My best friend.

Who Hook killed.

I remember like it was yesterday. I found her. Tinker Bell. On the ground by her nest. Her tiny body cold, gray, lifeless. Hook finding me on my knees, sobbing. Him boasting about what he had done.

So why the fuck is my body reacting to him like this?

His hand is still around my throat. He's still grinding

against me, each thrust making my dick harder and harder. His knee presses into the mattress between my legs, and I widen them on instinct. His damp hair hangs around his face, curtaining both of us as we share the same air. I'm aware of every inch of him that's pressed against me, every inch of hard muscle and inked skin.

There's a heat, a heaviness, that has settled deep in my gut, and no matter how hard I try, it won't go away. My erection is straining against my jeans, desperate to be free, aching for release. If only I could close my eyes. Maybe I could pretend it's not him, but I can't even do that because his arctic eyes have mine frozen on his.

"Why are you doing this?" My voice trembles as he thrusts against me.

"Do you want me to stop?"

I could say yes, but just the idea of his body leaving mine makes me feel empty inside. His presence confuses me. I hate him, but I need him. I need him to satisfy a part of me that I wasn't aware existed.

So I don't answer. I don't say yes, but I don't say no.

"I need you to hate me, Pan." His hand leaves my throat. I almost protest but stop short when it goes to the button of my jeans instead, his weight lifting enough so he can maneuver. His hook comes up, the curved metal cool against the skin beneath my chin. "I'm going to make you feel good so that you hate me even more."

His logic shouldn't make sense, but it does. I'll hate him for making me feel good, for making me want him after what he's done.

Except...I won't just hate *him*. I'll hate myself too.

Oh well. A problem for another day.

I'm already too far gone.

"Tell me you hate me." His lips are so close to mine as

he unzips my jeans and reaches into my boxer briefs to grip my painfully hard cock.

I throw my head back, making unintelligible noises. The curve of his hook glides down my neck, causing me to shiver, before coming to rest against my collar bone.

"Tell me," he demands as he smears pre-cum around the head of my dick.

"I do," I say on the back of another moan. "I hate you so fucking much."

"Good boy." Those words make me harden even more in his fist as he slowly starts to stroke. "Give me all your hate, Little Star, and I'll give you mine."

And then he's stroking me hard and fast, the bulky rings on his fingers feeling surprisingly good, driving me wild. All sense of time and space escapes me. I'm here with Hook, but we have no past. He never hurt me. He's simply this devastatingly gorgeous man who ignites my entire body on fire with one touch while simultaneously keeping me frozen with one look.

It's so intense. Why is he so goddamn intense?

I have to look away.

The moment I finally do, he snarls, "Look at me."

He gives me no choice, his voice fierce, his mere presence ruthless and dominating in the best way. Staring up into his eyes, I want to touch him. Anywhere. I want to put my hands on his face, feel his dark chest hair against my palms, tangle my fingers in his long, damp hair. But I don't. I leave them on the mattress at my sides, clutching the sheets with white knuckles. It's bad enough that I'm pistoning my hips, about to come in Hook's fist.

"I want your eyes on me as I make you come." His voice is rough, his gaze holding mine hostage again. "I want to make sure you don't forget *this*."

I mumble more curses and incoherent sounds followed by, "I fucking hate you."

"Good. Don't forget that either."

While he strokes me with a perfect rhythm, he's still thrusting his hips, his erection so hard as it hits my thigh that I think it might bruise.

Fuck it. Let it.

His hook moves lower and snags the hem of my shirt, slowly lifting it to expose my torso. He stares down at the mark he gave me and bites his lip, then lowers his face until there's only a whisper between us. His hair is soft against my cheek.

"Break for me, Pan."

That sends me over the edge.

"Oh, fuck," I groan as I come undone.

My cum shoots out over my bare abdomen as I throw my head back onto the bed, eyes shut tight, chest heaving with ragged breaths. I'm still panting when I look back at Hook, and when I do, I see that he has his own dick in his hand now as mine lies spent. I can practically see it throbbing as he strokes himself.

"You're so fucking perfect when you fall apart for me."

I can't help the whimper that escapes my lips, the waves of my orgasm still rolling through me.

Hook comes, his own release coating my abdomen alongside mine. We both stare down at the mess we made, the painting of our pleasure on my body. We stay like that for a moment, breathing heavily, savoring the last few seconds before we're once again Peter Pan and Captain Hook. Sworn enemies. No matter what world we're in, or how much time has passed, or whether I remember it or not, that will always be true.

Stealing one last moment, Hook lowers his head and

brushes his tongue in a path up my abdomen, sweeping both our cum into his mouth. His eyes meet mine, and he licks his lips.

"Your hate tastes so good, Little Star."

And then the moment is shattered. Hook's body leaves mine, and I feel it. The emptiness, the vacuum that he leaves behind.

I fucking hate it because it's there at all.

He grabs a towel from the back of a chair and tosses it to me before giving me his back.

The towel smells like him. Clean, masculine. I try to ignore the scent as I clean our cum from my body, wiping down my abdomen. Lowering my shirt, I stand as I button my jeans. I don't look at Hook as I cross the room to the door and open it.

"Pan."

I stop in the open doorway but don't turn around.

"I'll give you time," he says, his voice surprisingly steady after what we just did. "But we *will* be going back to Neverland."

Without responding, I walk out of the room and close the door behind me.

THE NEXT MORNING, I lie in bed for much longer than I should. I don't even care that I'm going to be late for work. I barely slept. When I got home last night, I took another shower. A long one. I scrubbed my entire body like I could undo what Hook had done to me.

Because I was right. I hate myself almost as much as I hate him.

Hook killed Tinker Bell. He murdered my best friend and drove me away from Neverland, away from my home. And yet he did exactly what he said he was going to do. He made me want him. He made me feel good.

Even though I may have been able to wash him from my body, I couldn't erase him from my mind—the memory of him on top of me, of his perfect, sure strokes getting me off, of his voice in my ear. It had been even better than what I imagined the night before when he left me on my own.

If only things were different...

But they're *not*.

I have to remember that. I have to accept that. Hook and I *do* have a past, one I can't forget again, and I can't forgive him for what he's done. Which means I can't be with him in the way I was last night. Not anymore. Not ever.

There's an ache in my chest as I get out of bed and get ready for work. It's been there since I left Hook's motel room. If I thought I could claw it out, I'd do it. I'm tempted to try.

I want to go back to before I remembered everything.

Yes, Hook was still a vicious, callous dickhead, but I saw so much more beneath that mask. I was determined to coax it out. With how badly he seemed to want me, I believed I could do it. Because when he touched me, his gaze turned a little less icy. When he spoke to me, his voice held a hint of vulnerability. When he forced me to sword fight with him, I saw as much exhilaration in his cunning smile that I felt in myself.

But with my memories back, that illusion of him has been shattered.

He's simply Captain Hook again—ruthless, cutthroat pirate. The villain of all my stories. The perfect adversary I always loved to fight.

Except that was when I was a child. Now, after having grown up, I don't want to fight anymore. If I can't have what I truly wanted with Hook a day ago, then I don't want anything else with him. I don't want the quarreling, the hostility, the rivalry. Not with him.

As I head to work, I try to convince myself that I have a choice. Even though it isn't what I want, maybe it'll be best to return to that.

I'll want him less if I hate him more.

Fortunately, work helps distract me from thoughts about Hook this time.

There are several instruments in the music hall that need repairs, so I do those. I also do a few individual instructional sessions with students who need a little extra work before the concert tomorrow.

I spend some time in one of the soundproof practice rooms by myself, playing the flute. I don't follow any sheet music; I just play whatever comes to me. Music has always been my safe place. Even though I forgot my life in Neverland, that was one thing that never changed.

Even while I'm working and playing music alone, the question of what I'm doing and what I plan on doing nags at me.

The reason I came to work is because I needed to feel normal, and my life for the last fourteen years is what's normal to me now. It still feels that way, even though I remember who I am and where I came from, even though I can once again feel my magic. It hums just below the surface, beneath my skin, in my bones. A vibration that's always there. I haven't reached for it, haven't tried to grasp it and use it. Am I even going to be able to control it after spending so long ignoring it?

However, if Hook is telling the truth and Neverland is in trouble—after what I saw in my bedroom last night, I believe him—then I don't have a choice.

I have to return to Neverland.

But Hook said he'd give me time. I suppose he knew I'd need it.

I'm sure returning will bring memories of Tink rushing back. I'm sure it'll hurt like a bitch. It hurts *now*, remembering her, remembering losing her. But Neverland was her home too. I can't see it gone.

There will be memories of Tinker Bell everywhere. I'll see her in every fairy on the island, and they will either make me want to stay or run away again.

Leaving here is going to be hard too, but maybe I don't have to stay away. Maybe I can come back. I don't know how I'll feel once I'm back in Neverland, if Neverland will even give me the choice. I may have left, but not only is Neverland my home, it's so much more than that. It's a part of me, and I'm a part of it. It let me go once. Would it let me go again?

Toward the end of the day, I pull my phone out and see I have a text from Jeremiah.

Curly is in town visiting. He's only here for tonight. Meet us at Marooners' after work?

A smile tugs at my stiff facial muscles. I'm not surprised that I've been frowning all day. The thought of seeing a couple of my Lost Boys now that I remember helps to somewhat lift my spirits. I don't get to see them much, besides Nibs. I see one—or two in the case of the twins—every couple of years maybe.

My smile fades when I think about how badly I fucked up with them all. Yeah, they were orphans when I found them, but I was selfish. I took them for no other reason than because I was lonely in Neverland. I made them forget all about who they were and where they came from so they'd never want to leave.

I'm surprised they don't all hate me for it.

I text back, *Sure! I have to do something after work real quick, but I'll be there after.*

Simon enters the music hall after I send another text and go to put my phone back in my pocket. He didn't need a cast on his foot, but he's still limping slightly. He's carrying a couple of music stands and walks a bit too close to several cases of tubas as he crosses the room.

"Watch it!"

Stopping, he swerves just in time before he ends up knocking them all over like dominos. He grins sheepishly at me. "Thanks."

"Have you heard anything from USC?" I ask as I go to help him with the stands.

He frowns and shakes his head. "I was hoping I'd hear something before this weekend."

I look up at the clock on the wall and shrug. "It's still a quarter till five."

"Yeah, thanks," he says with a scoff.

"Don't give up." I put a comforting hand on his shoulder. "You're brilliant."

He beams at me. "Thanks, Peter."

I nod and backstep toward the door. "I'm out of here. See you tomorrow at the concert?"

"Yeah, see ya."

I head out of the building and to the lot. I'm really not looking forward to what I have to do next, what I spent all day convincing myself I need to do.

At least I'm meeting Nibs and Curly at a bar afterward. I'm definitely going to need a drink.

15

HOOK

I almost didn't let Pan leave last night. I almost told him the truth, all of it.

I'm not convinced I did the right thing—making him hate me as much as I'm sure he does now. To be honest, I'm a little surprised he didn't hate me that much before. Then again, Peter Pan has always had a thing for the danger, the chaos, the thrill. I'm sure I check all those boxes for him.

But Neverland is dying. That is what I need to remember, what I need all my focus on. Maybe now I'll have the time to distance myself from all the other thoughts that haunt me.

The fate of Neverland is bigger than Peter Pan and Captain Hook.

I told Pan I'd give him time, so that's what I plan on doing. Even if I go crazy in this small room.

Fortunately, I do need to get out today. I'm running out of cash. I could also use another bottle of rum considering I drank the rest of mine last night. And as I'm walking out the door, I open my pack of cigarettes to see there's one left. So, I need more smokes too.

Heading away from the motel, I light my last cigarette and take a deep puff. I don't remember much from the time after Pan left. Half a bottle of rum was enough to get me where I needed to be—a little unaware, a little numb. I had to have smoked nearly half a pack too, but at least I didn't have to deal with the aftermath last night.

Of course, present me is a little pissed at past me because now *I'm* the one having to sort through what the fuck happened. And that's difficult to do when I can't stop thinking about last night—the way he writhed beneath me, the way he came undone for me. All of it so fucking beautiful.

For the life of me, I can't figure out how we ended up here. I think it's probably best if I try not to think about it too hard. If I do, I'm going to want to find him, spill everything, and do whatever I want with him like I've been dying to do.

So I don't think about it.

I head into the heart of town on foot and duck into the first convenience store I see to buy a fresh pack of cigarettes. As I light up another one, I start scoping out potential victims on the street.

It's godawful hot. The sun is high in the sky already since I slept in so late. I'm still a little hungover. The protein bar I had for breakfast sits heavy in my stomach. My hair is tied back, but I'm still sweating. I reek of rum.

Fuck, I'm pathetic.

As I pass by a couple standing in front of a shop window, I not-so-accidentally bump into the man. My hand slips into his back pocket and pulls out his wallet as we both stumble around each other. Apologizing profusely, I slip his wallet into the pocket of my jacket. He gives me a kind, forgiving smile and waves it off.

Dullard.

Once I'm out of sight, I bring the wallet back out and peek inside. I curse when I find only a twenty dollar bill. Hardly anyone carries cash on them, so I'm going to have to snatch quite a few wallets today. I could probably get a couple uses out of the man's card before he realizes it's gone and shuts it off. I've had plenty of experience by now to learn that's what eventually happens.

I spend the rest of the day picking a few more pockets, using cards to buy lunch and another bottle of rum that I stash in the inner pocket of my jacket. I'm tired by the time the sun disappears behind buildings, leaving only shadows.

After checking the contents of the last wallet I'll be swiping for the day, I go to put it in my pocket, but when someone bumps into my back, I drop it on the ground instead. The person—no, the *kid*—who hit me quickly plucks it from the sidewalk and runs off with it.

"Hey!" I shout after the boy before giving chase.

That wallet has a couple hundred dollar bills, which would be enough to pay my room for the next few nights. I *need* to get it back.

The boy looks over his shoulder and appears surprised to see that I'm following him. He ducks into an alley, and I chase after him.

As soon as I round the corner, I come to a stop and smirk. The narrow lane between the two buildings is a dead end. No sunlight reaches here, and the alley is shrouded in shadow. The boy looks to be maybe fifteen or sixteen and is frantically searching for a way out. He jumps, reaching for the fire escape ladder hanging from the building on the left.

I stalk forward. He peers at me, eyes wide with panic. He jumps again, his fingers managing to grab the bottom rung.

Before he can pull himself up, I grab the back of his shirt

and yank him down. Spinning him around, I back him into the wall, the front of his shirt balled in my fist.

"You should know better than to steal from a thief." I raise my hook in front of his face.

"I'm s-sorry. I'm sorry." He starts rambling and sweating profusely. "Please don't hurt me. I'm s-so sorry. Here. Take it back. I'm sorry."

He drops the wallet on the ground at our feet. I chuckle. I'm not really all that angry. My blood isn't boiling. I'm not seeing red. This kid is lucky I'm only interested in scaring him and not hurting him.

I'm briefly reminded of all the times I fought with the Lost Boys back in Neverland, the times I had one of them in my clutches. It makes me feel strangely nostalgic.

Maybe I did have more fun playing Peter Pan's games than I let myself believe.

No, I didn't just think that.

"What did you need the money for?" I ask.

His bottom lip trembles, and his eyes grow a little wet.

"Answer me," I demand, shoving him harder into the wall.

"B-beer."

Laughing again, I release him. "If you had said medicine for your sick mother, I may have let you keep it. Get the fuck out of here."

He does. Without hesitation, he bolts back down the alley.

"Make better choices!" I call after him.

Shaking my head at my own hypocrisy, I bend down and pick up the wallet. When I stand again, I swear my heart jumps into my throat.

"Bloody fucking hell."

I stumble back a step. Steadying myself, I stare at Pan, clutching my heaving chest. He stands a little further in the alley. He's still, silent, just a darker silhouette in the darkness. I can tell by his shape that it's him.

"How the fuck did you get here?" I ask, considering he seemingly came out of nowhere.

"I flew," he says dryly, taking a step forward. "I can fly now."

"Okay." I speak slowly, finding his impassive voice suspicious. "*Why* are you here?"

When he takes another step forward, I can make out his features a bit more clearly. There are dark circles under his eyes as though he didn't sleep at all last night. Everything about him seems a little...grayed out. In the dark, his hair is a little dull, his eyes a little less green. It shouldn't strike me as odd, but it does.

"To tell you that I'm returning to Neverland," he says in that same stilted voice.

"Great. When?"

"Tomorrow."

Placing the wallet in my pocket, I nod. "Tell me where to meet you."

He slowly shakes his head. "I'm leaving without you."

And just like that, I'm at the end of my fuse.

"Like hell you are."

He says nothing, still motionless. My jaw clenches until it aches, until I swear I'll crack teeth. My left eye twitches. My fuse ignites.

I rush forward, ready to grab him, to hurt him, to crush him, to cut him.

But I don't get the chance. He leaps back into the air before I can get to him. By then, he's hovering high, out of my reach. He smirks down at me, the line of his mouth a little crooked. It's *almost* classic Peter Pan. Except it doesn't quite reach his eyes.

Something is off about him, but I can't quite put my hook on it.

"You are *not* leaving without me, Pan," I snarl up at him.

"I'm sorry, Captain Hook. The games have been fun."

"Wait!" I swallow. Time ticks by slowly, and I can almost hear it. I have to make a decision, and I have to make it now. Finally, I say, "I didn't kill Tinker Bell."

He blinks. "You're lying."

And then he's gone. Doesn't even give me a chance to explain.

Watching him fly away, I'm left feeling a murderous rage I can't remember ever feeling—not since Pan cut off my hand. Everything is so red it's black. My entire body is shaking violently. My vision is a blur. I stumble back until I feel the cool wall behind me. The alley is a tunnel that keeps getting longer and longer.

Pan cannot leave me here. I have to do something.

But what?

Slowly, things start to come back into focus. The alley is almost pitch black now, but I'm able to think a little clearer. To form a plan. On such short notice, it's certainly not the greatest, but it's all I have.

It's a good thing I already made Pan hate me.

If he didn't already, he will after tonight.

16

PAN

I've been pacing in front of Wendy's door for the last five minutes. She needs to know that I remember. She needs to know that I have to go back to Neverland. But it's not any of that that I'm scared to tell her. I know she'll be able to sense what I'm *not* telling her.

"How long are you going to stay out here?"

I stop pacing to look at Wendy standing in the doorway, having not even heard the door open. Too wrapped up in my damn racing thoughts, swimming in them, drowning in them.

"Until I have the guts to come inside," I say honestly.

"Okay." She nods, then grins. "How long will that be? I kind of have a deadline."

I laugh nervously, then finally make my way up the porch to the front door. I stop a few feet away, staring at Wendy for a moment before saying softly, "I remember."

Her face falls. "Oh." She steps to the side. "Do you want to come in?"

After I step inside the house, Wendy closes the door behind me. Once again, she's in her work pajamas.

I move into the cozy living room and plop down on her seafoam green couch. Leaning back, I stare at the opposite wall where photographs printed on canvas hang to form an abstract shape. The photographs are mostly of Wendy and Jeremiah, but there are a few with me, Wendy's parents and brothers, and Jeremiah's adoptive family. It all feels so *normal.*

Wendy sits on the couch beside me. "Do you want some tea?"

"No, thank you. I told Jer I'd meet him and Curly at Marooners'."

"Right. He told me Curly was in town. He said I could join you guys, but I really do have a deadline."

"I won't keep you long."

"It's fine," she says quickly. She curls one leg beneath her so she can turn her whole body toward me. Her brows knit. "Are you okay?"

I consider her question for a minute, then slowly nod. "I guess. I should've had fourteen years to mourn Tinker Bell, but I was too afraid to and decided to forget her instead." I sigh and put my head in my hands. "I'm a terrible person."

"Hey." Wendy scooches closer to me and pulls at my arms until I look up at her. "You are not a terrible person. You were a boy who didn't know how to handle grief."

"I don't think I know how to handle it any better now that I'm grown up."

She shrugs. "None of us do."

It's silent for several seconds. She's being patient with me, and I appreciate that more than she knows. But it's time to rip this off like a Band-Aid.

"Anyway," I start slowly, "I just wanted to let you know that I remember. And that...I have to go back to Neverland."

"You believe Hook?"

I wince. *Fuck*. "Yeah, I do."

She raises a brow. "And?"

"And what?"

"Peter Pan, you are exceptional at pretending, but you are bloody awful at lying when you're actually trying to."

Shaking my head, I chuckle. "I'm pretty sure it's only you I can't lie to."

She watches me, her gaze sharp, her lips pursed. She waits.

"I kind of like you calling me Peter Pan," I say, grinning. "I missed that."

"Don't change the subject."

Damn. She caught me.

"I remembered something else," I finally say with a sigh. I look away, avoiding her gaze. "Hook was the one who killed Tink."

"Oh." Her voice is quiet. "I guess I can't say I'm surprised."

"You can't?"

Why am I so shocked? Hook had always fought with me and my Lost Boys, threatened us even. But if he and his pirates actually wanted us dead, wouldn't they have killed us? We were only boys. They were bloody pirates with guns and cannons. Through all the fighting, all the threats, Hook had never killed any of us. Back then, I thought it was because we were just that good, just that clever. Now? After all of it, Hook killing Tinker Bell surprised me.

But Wendy didn't share that sentiment.

"He's always been the villain of your story, Peter," she says. "The bad guy. The enemy. Your nemesis. The antagonist."

"Okay, I get it." I roll my eyes.

She sits back and tilts her head. "There's something else you're not telling me."

My stomach churns. Shit.

Like a Band-Aid, I remind myself. She's going to get it out of me one way or another. I always had a feeling that she knew me better than I knew myself, and it turns out I was right. I can draw out the dread and anxiety or simply spill it all now.

I choose the latter.

"I may have...kind of...definitely...fooled around with Hook."

"*Excuse me?!*"

Oh, now *that* surprises her?

Yeah, that tracks.

Wincing, I look away again. "In my defense, I didn't remember who he was. Well...except for the last time."

"How many times have there been? Never mind. Don't answer that." Pressing the heels of her palms into her eyes, she lets out an exasperated breath. She looks back at me, her face scrunched. "Do you care about him?"

"What? No. Absolutely not." I shake my head, trying to convince myself as much as Wendy. "Especially not now that I remember. It's just...I guess we had fun. There was the challenge, the adrenaline, the sword fighting."

"Ew. Gross."

My eyes widen, and I feel my face heat. "*Actual* sword fighting, Wendy!"

"Oh. Right." She grins, her own cheeks pink. "When I said gross, I didn't mean because...you know. I only meant because he's Captain Arsehole."

"I know." I never had to worry about that with Wendy. Sighing, I lean back. "Tell me I'm insane."

"You're insane," she says easily.

We both laugh. Despite her agreeing with me, there's very little judgment coming from her. I don't know why I was so nervous to tell her. It's probably just my dramatic arse always expecting the worst. But I definitely needed this. I needed to get the weight of it off my shoulders.

"But I still love you, Peter Pan."

Then that weight is right back on, settling like it's returned home. Something lodges in my throat, but I give her the best smile I can. I've always told her I love her, whether I'm the first one to say it or saying it back. For fourteen years, it came so easy. But...after remembering, knowing the truth of my existence now, I don't trust myself to get the word out, so I don't even try. Fortunately, she doesn't seem to notice that I don't reciprocate.

And now I need that drink more than ever.

"I should head over to Marooners'," I say, standing.

Wendy does too and walks me to the door. "You have my blessing to get completely sloshed. Just don't drive after."

"I promise."

After giving her a tight hug, I leave to meet up with Nibs and Curly.

Two of my Lost Boys.

I smile at the thought as I climb onto my moped.

THE BAR IS PACKED, even for a Friday night. It's filled with the heat of bodies and the buzz of voices, but it doesn't take long for me to spot Nibs and Curly. Nibs is wearing a lime green tie today, and Curly's hair is as blond and frizzy as ever.

Of course, Curly's legal name in this world is Curtis Cuthbertson. And he's never lived it down.

As I move through the bar, the bass of music pumps through the crowded building. Someone yells, "Let's do shots!" There's cheering. A waitress moves in front of me carrying a tray of a dozen drinks, and I pause to let her pass. The walls are covered in vintage beer signs and neon lights that glare down in every direction. I approach the round bar table at the opposite edge of the room that Nibs and Curly are standing at. There's already a steaming pizza with two slices taken from it and three bottles of beer all on the table. The aroma of freshly baked dough and melty cheese hits me, and I realize how hungry I am.

"Hello, boys." I grin widely as they both look at me from the other side of the table. "How are my two favorite Lost Boys?"

Their eyes go big. They glance at each other, then back to me. Their jaws go slack. At the same time, they say, "Peter?"

I hold my arms out to my sides. "Peter Pan's back, bitches."

They both round the table and attack me from both sides, throwing their arms around me. We're all laughing as we group hug. I feel the urge to crow, but I squash it down. I'm not some savage child in the woods. I'm a grown adult in a very crowded bar full of drunk people.

Actually...I might fit right in.

"How did you remember?" Curly asks as we break apart.

"Kind of a long story," I answer, not wanting to get into details.

Nibs hands me the third beer from the table and takes a drink of his own. "Have you told Wendy?"

"Yeah, I went over there after work."

"I'm surprised she didn't make you stay so she could

give you shit." He grins. "She still won't let the whole floating leaf thing go."

"Still?" Curly asks with a laugh.

Nibs shrugs. "It's not like she even got that far. She woke up and was able to swim back."

"I have no idea how she fell for you." I shake my head and chuckle. Then another thought hits me, and I lower my head. "Tinker Bell convinced you all to do that."

They're both looking at me apprehensively when I lift my head again. I understand why. I couldn't handle Tink's death back then, and it was so bad to the point that I forced myself to forget. To forget everything, including my Lost Boys. I fucked up bad. I didn't mourn Tinker Bell when she deserved someone to mourn her, and since I didn't mourn her back then, I know I'm making up for lost time.

"I'm sorry I forgot you lot," I say, frowning, hoping they forgive me.

"We understood, Peter." Curly slaps my arm affectionately. "You loved Tink more than anyone."

There's that word again. *Love.*

"Are you going to be okay?" Nibs asks.

"I'll be fine, guys. Really. I'm not gonna go off the deep end. Swear." I hold up my bottle of beer. "Besides, Mother gave me her permission to get hammered."

Nibs groans and puts his head in his hand. "Don't call her that. It's bad enough we all called her that when we were kids."

"You sure you don't have an Oedipus complex?" Curly ducks to the side as Nibs goes to shove him. Beer sloshes out of his bottle.

Curly and I both laugh while Nibs broods.

It's not quite like old times, but for a little while, it feels a little less like we're all so grown up.

Nibs eventually lets the joke go, and we end up reminiscing about Neverland more. I don't tell them about Hook or the fact that I'm going to have to go back, not wanting to ruin the night considering we're having so much fun. It feels good to relax and let go and enjoy the time I have with two of my Lost Boys.

We drink several more beers and order a second pizza. The conversation skirts around Tink a little too much for my liking. I know they're worried about me, but I don't mind talking about her. It feels good to talk about her.

However, I do clam up when Hook is mentioned. If they notice, they don't say anything.

I'm right there on the verge of drunk when my phone vibrates in my pocket. Pulling it out, I open the text message. It's from Wendy.

I have to talk to you. It's important. Can you come over? Please don't tell Jer.

My brow furrows, but I type back a quick, *Be there soon.*

"Well, boys." I return my phone to my pocket. "I think I'm gonna have to call it a night. I need to get an Uber."

"You could crash with us if you want," offers Curly.

"He's staying at the motel next door," Nibs explains. "I already told Wendy I was probably going to stay there tonight so I don't have to worry about getting a ride home so late."

"Thanks for the offer. But I have to work that concert tomorrow, so I should get home."

We exchange handshakes and hugs. As I leave the bar, I order an Uber. I could've waited inside, but I needed the fresh air. I lean against the wall of the building, enjoying the cool nighttime breeze against my face, hoping it sobers me at least a little.

Once I'm in the car and we're heading to Wendy's, my stomach is doing flops. And it's not *just* because of the beer.

I'm a little nervous to find out what Wendy needs to talk to me about so badly that she ended my night with Nibs and Curly a bit early. It hadn't hit me back at the bar, but now that I've had a little time to process it and wonder, my nerves are kind of frayed.

I get out of the car in Wendy's driveway. Fortunately, the driver pulls off before he can see me stumble up the walkway to the front door of the house. I knock.

"Come in."

Wendy's voice is muffled, shaky.

I open the door.

Sobriety hits me like a fucking freight train. All the air is expelled from my lungs. My heart drops into my stomach like a lead weight. My chest tightens, and I'm paralyzed.

Hook stands just inside the living room. He has Wendy, his hand with a fistful of her long hair, his hook at her throat.

"Close the door, Pan."

17

HOOK

Pan closes the door, his movements slow, stiff.

"I'm sorry, Peter," Wendy whispers.

I have to hand it to her. She put up a fight, which made it that much harder to get her to do what I said without hurting her. I'm not sure why, but I had a strong desire *not* to hurt her. It took me threatening both Pan and her fiancé before she finally cooperated and sent that text.

Now...one of the Lost Boys I wouldn't mind sinking my hook into as much.

But Wendy was not only more convenient after I managed to find her address, but I suspect she means the most to Pan.

Judging by the look on his face, I was right.

What I was *not* expecting, however, was the look of pure betrayal on his face and what it does to me. I was prepared for the fear that's there too, but beneath it, it's like...I've let him down, disappointed him. The anguish in his eyes pulls at that thread that he had started unraveling from its tangled state last night.

I should really cut the damn thing out.

"What are you doing, Hook?" Pan asks, voice shaking.

"You know exactly what I'm doing." I grip Wendy's hair tighter, and she whimpers. The sound does nothing for me. It's not as sweet a sound as Pan's soft cries. "Wendy Darling has grown up too. No less fierce than I remember. Sure would be a shame if she doesn't get to grow up more."

Pan looks as though I just struck him. Hurt screws up his face even as it turns red from anger. "You really want to take everything from me, don't you?"

"I told you I did not kill Tinker Bell."

His jaw falls slack, and his eyes widen. I can see the whites of them. Did he not hear me earlier in the alley?

No, he *did*. He said I was lying.

Another one of his games?

He shakes his head. "What?"

Now I'm angry again.

"I'm not playing this fucking game with you, Pan," I snarl.

Wendy hisses when the tip of my hook digs into the skin of her neck a little more than I mean it to.

"Okay, okay." Pan holds his hands in the air. He swallows. "No games. I swear. I don't remember you telling me that."

I narrow my eyes. Then, as though to refresh his memory, I repeat what he told me after I let him know the truth. "You're lying." When he still appears just as confused, I scoff. "Come on, Pan. I know your memory is shit, but you couldn't have possibly made yourself forget after only a few hours."

"A few hours?" His face screws up even more. "Hook, I haven't seen you all day."

That's enough to shock me into silence. He appears genuinely certain and sincere, but that doesn't mean anything. He lived for hundreds of years on make-believe. Wouldn't it be a difficult habit to break? I shouldn't trust him for that reason alone. I don't know what to believe, but I know I didn't make up that conversation. Either he's lying or his memory has taken another hit. Those are the only possible explanations.

He swallows again. "If this is about Neverland, you said you'd give me time."

My mind is reeling. My breathing is heavy. "You said you were leaving without me. A few hours ago."

"He was *here* a few hours ago," Wendy says. She sounds a lot calmer than I do despite my hook still at her throat.

"Hook..." Pan takes a cautious step forward, his hands in the air again. "You saw me?"

All I can do is nod.

What is he playing at? I can't make sense of any of this.

But then I think back to when I saw him in that alley. How all his color seemed muted, how he appeared to be shrouded in shadows darker than those around him. His hair more brown than reddish-brown, his eyes more gray than green.

All the air leaves Pan's lungs, his face falls, his shoulders slump. He shakes his head. "That wasn't me."

"What the bloody hell do you mean that wasn't you?" I'm even more pissed because I don't understand.

For a third time, he swallows. "It was my shadow."

His words hit me like a punch to the gut, a razor to my veins.

His shadow? Could that be...*the* shadow?

It's almost enough to make me release Wendy, but I force myself to hold onto her until I know what the fuck is going on. Right now, she's the only leverage I have.

"I didn't know he could manifest himself to look like a convincing version of me," Pan says, his cautious eyes still on me. "If I did, I swear I would've told you. I knew he was here because he's the reason I remembered. He made me remember."

"Why?" My mind is still struggling to wrap itself around it all. "Why would he do that? And why would he come to me?"

"To do this to us," he answers simply, and that hits me too. "He needs us on opposite sides. Because he's the one killing Neverland, isn't he?"

I nod. Again, it's all I can do. I know he's right; I just don't know how.

Pan sighs. "Hook..." He hesitates, then, "Please let Wendy go. We'll talk about this."

Wendy's hair is still wrapped tightly around my fist, and I don't let it go. I lower my voice and force it to not shake this time. "All we need to talk about is going back to Neverland. Do you have any intention of leaving me behind like the shadow said?"

Pan actually smiles. It's a ghost of one, a whisper on his lips, but it's still there. "What's Neverland without Captain Hook?"

I expect the weight in my chest to lift, but instead it grows heavier. It aches as I stare at Pan. I don't know why, but I believe him without question. He was never planning on leaving me behind. He's not going to leave me behind even after I threatened Wendy.

He's too fucking good for me.

"I'm sorry, Wendy Darling," I whisper in her ear before releasing her.

That may be the first time I've ever apologized to someone, at least in recent history. But it doesn't matter. Not to her. I know that the moment she rounds on me and slaps me across the face. *Hard.* Enough to snap my head to the side. I feel my lip cut into my tooth.

When I turn my head back, I scowl at her, my top lip curling. She stands, arms cross, defiant. I admire her fire.

Slowly, I bow my head without taking my eyes off her. I wouldn't put it past her to attack me again. I'd deserve it.

"A pleasure as always, Wendy Darling."

"Go fuck yourself," she sneers.

I grin back at her. Then, without another word, I make my way to the front door. I don't look back at Wendy. I don't look in Pan's direction. I close the door behind me. Despite my desire for answers, to know about Pan's shadow, I have to get out of here. My heart is drumming a beat in my chest that won't stop feeling so damn heavy.

I can't help but think I fucked up.

That's a feeling I haven't had in a long time, and I don't fucking like it.

I'm halfway across the lawn when I hear the door open again and Pan shout my name. Stopping, I turn to see him standing in the light of the open doorway with Wendy.

"I'll be right back, I swear," he says. She whisper-hisses something back to him, and he replies, "He won't hurt me. Just stay inside."

Wendy slams the door, making Pan flinch. I smirk.

I think I like Wendy Darling.

Pan hops down the steps of the porch and crosses the lawn. He stops a few feet from me, then falters back a step. He runs his hand through his hair, and I kind of want to do the same to it.

Instead, I clear my throat. "What do you want?"

"I have to know," he finally says. "Did you mean it when you said you didn't kill Tink?"

Now it's my turn to hesitate. Eventually, I nod. "I meant it."

"I want to believe you."

He frowns. I can barely make it out in the dim light of the streetlamps, but I don't like the way it sits on his face. He should be smiling. He should always be smiling.

His voice turns desperate. "God, I want to believe you."

"It's the truth. I did not kill Tinker Bell. I give you my word."

"Then why did you make me think you did?"

"Because I wanted to hurt you," I say as though that should've been obvious—because it should've been. "All I ever wanted was to hurt you. You know that."

"And Wendy?" The unease is clear in his voice. "Would you have hurt her?"

My jaw clenches, and I see red in the edges of my vision. At first, I think I'm angry because he clearly wants to believe that I wouldn't hurt her. But then I realize it's because...I don't think I would have.

I cross the distance between us so that I can get in his face, scowling. My voice comes out gravelly. "Do not make the mistake of thinking that I'm a good person."

"Is that your answer?" he asks, quiet.

"You underestimate how determined I am to return to Neverland."

"Is *that* your answer?"

My jaw hurts.

Fuck.

I bring my hand up, place it on the side of his face, holding him there, staring into his eyes. The green of them sparkles like stars in the night. I could get lost in them and then use them to find my way home.

I think they'd probably guide me right back to him.

If tonight's the night for truths, then...

"You just remembered you lost a friend." My voice quakes like the earth is cracking, opening up beneath my feet. I hate it—the vulnerability. "I was not going to take another one from you." I release him quickly as though simply touching him burns. "Not so soon at least."

That smile ghosts across his face again. "Does this mean you don't need me to hate you anymore?"

My breath hitches. That feeling in my chest is so heavy. That thread is pulled taut, stronger than I thought it was. He's not unraveling it so much as he's adding stitches, mending it. My heart beats once, so hard that it feels as though I've been brought back to life. I nearly gasp.

"I don't know what I need from you," I say honestly.

I watch his throat as he swallows. I want to bite it. I want to mark him. My cock twitches at the thought, and I'm about to give into it. Before I can, Pan reaches up and touches his thumb gently to the corner of my mouth. When he pulls it away, there's a spot of blood there. I remember feeling my lip cut into my tooth when Wendy slapped me, but I didn't think it had been hard enough to make me bleed. I'm even more impressed now.

I stare at Pan as he stares at the blood as though he's mesmerized by the sight.

Looking up at me again, he grins. "You deserved that, you know."

"I deserve worse. Including the other two slaps she gave me before you even showed up."

Pan chuckles. I love the sound.

Fuck. I have to get out of here.

"Goodnight, Pan." I turn around and make it a couple of steps.

"Hook."

I stop, take a breath, and look back at him over my shoulder.

Opening his mouth, he falters, closes it. The wrinkles between his brows are so deep. I want to smooth them out with my lips.

"I'll find you when I'm ready," he finally says.

Nodding, I shove my hand into the pocket of my jacket, then walk away into the night.

18

PAN

As I watch Hook walk away, I worry my bottom lip. I don't realize I'm doing it until I taste blood. I don't care. I keep staring after Hook until he disappears into the darkness.

I don't know what I was going to say to him, but I wanted to say *something*. That I understood why he had done what he did? I'm not sure that's true. I know he honestly believed it was me who told him that I was returning to Neverland without him. But Hook threatened Wendy.

How can I understand that?

How can I forgive that?

I could've told him I believe him about Tink. Because oddly enough, I do.

But does it even matter?

Even after Hook has vanished, I continue standing there, looking in the direction he left. Part of me isn't ready to go back inside.

Wendy is pissed, and I'm kind of scared. I know I'll take whatever she dishes out. After the night she had, she's allowed to be in whatever mood she needs to be in. She's tough; she always has been. Hook was right. She's fierce, but I know this had to have shaken her. She just never would've let Hook see.

So I'm not surprised to find her on the couch, wrapped in her favorite weighted blanket, staring off at nothing.

I close the door slowly, quietly, not wanting to spook her since she doesn't look like she's completely here. I take a few steps into the living room so she can see me before saying, "Hey. I'm gonna make us some tea, okay?"

She nods but doesn't look at me.

Going into the kitchen, I fill the kettle with water before putting it on the stove. I make some chamomile tea, hoping it'll help calm her.

When I hand her the warm mug, she takes it, finally pulling her focus back to the present. "Thank you," she says in a small voice as she holds the cup in both hands in front of her face, letting the steam drift up to her nose.

Leaving some space between us, I sit down on the opposite end of the couch with my own tea. "I'm sorry Hook brought you into this."

She looks at me and sighs. "It's not your fault." Leaning back against the couch, she studies me, letting several seconds pass in silence. Her brows are drawn together, and I can almost see the gears moving in her brain. Then, "You have feelings for him, don't you?"

Her words momentarily give me pause as I feel a profound sorrow. But I hide it, instead covering it up with a snort. The expelled air blows the steam away from my tea.

"I'm sorry, *what?* No. No, I do not have feelings for him. He's Captain Hook for fuck's sake."

Wendy's eyes are bug-eyed. Her brows shoot up toward

her hairline. "Wow. I didn't actually think you did, but...well, your face proves otherwise."

"What are you talking about?"

I can feel the heat crawling up my neck, like something under my shirt is on fire. My face is burning, but that does *not* mean I have feelings for Hook. Because...I *can't*. For the same reason I couldn't tell her I love her earlier. However, I can't tell her the truth. But the moment I avert my gaze, I realize I fucked up.

"Ah ha!" she exclaims, pointing an accusing finger at me. "Avoiding eye contact."

I look at her once more with an exaggerated, wide-eyed stare. "Someone must be over being threatened, huh?"

She glares at me. If it wasn't for the hot tea in her hands, I'm sure she would've kicked me by now. "Captain Hook used to star in my nightmares as a child. Yes, seeing him shook me up a little. But..." Pursing her lips, she looks down at her tea.

"But what?"

She says nothing.

"Wen?"

She huffs, then looks back up at me with what I'm pretty sure is reluctance. "He didn't hurt me. I actually got the feeling like he was actively trying *not* to. I'm pretty sure I know why."

"Don't say it."

"Because he didn't want to hurt *you*."

I roll my eyes and shake my head. "That doesn't matter, Wendy. He still came here and *threatened* to hurt you. Wait." Setting my mug down on the coffee table, I prop one leg up on the couch so I can turn my entire body toward her. "Are you *defending* him after what he did?"

She shrugs, the corner of her mouth tipped up. "I'm just trying to make it easier on you."

"What do you mean?"

"So you don't feel bad for feeling whatever it is you feel for him."

Closing my eyes, I slump back into the couch. I think about Hook's hand on my face, that goddamn intense way he stared at me. Despite how icy his eyes are, I felt nothing but warmth when he held my face. When he confessed he wouldn't have hurt Wendy, I wasn't sure I believed him at that moment, but the fact that Wendy believes it is almost enough for me.

"I honestly don't know what I feel for him," I say with my eyes still closed. "I think he's so used to being the villain that he can't see the good he has in him too."

"Well, *that* might be a leap."

I open my eyes to see Wendy grinning.

"I'm just saying. Be careful. He's still a pirate. He's still volatile, but...I don't know. Maybe all these years without anyone to fight with softened him up."

Before I can stop myself, I snort. "I think it might be the opposite."

"Peter Pan!"

Wendy's face turns beet red, and we burst into laughter.

After some of the tension has abated, I tell Wendy a little of what I can about my shadow. Admittedly, it's not much. Then she picks out a movie while I make us more tea. She gets a text from Jer to let her know that he and Curly made it safely to his hotel room, so I decide to crash here for the night. Wendy and I curl up on the couch together and pass out about halfway through the movie. In the morning, I call an Uber to take me to get Lily before Jer gets home so I don't have to explain why I didn't go home like I said I was going to.

Wendy and I agree not to tell him what happened the night before, at least until Hook and I have gone back to Neverland.

THE AUDITORIUM IS PACKED. The noise of the crowd reaches backstage as I run around helping the students who need last minute tweaks to their instruments. There's so much nervous energy back here that it becomes contagious and starts infecting even me.

By the time I make my way to the sound booth at the back of the auditorium, I'm sweating profusely—thankful that I chose my darkest green dress shirt for this occasion so any sweat stains aren't as noticeable—and trying not to make eye contact with anyone in the audience. Most of them are already in their seats, facing the stage where there are dozens of chairs and instruments set up and waiting for their musicians. We're a small community college, so the auditorium isn't as big as some. However, it looks like most of the seats will be filled, which is still pretty impressive. And a little intimidating.

Simon is at the lighting console when I approach. "Dude, we have a front light out."

"Seriously?" I look up at the catwalk, and sure enough, one of the lights is out. "Fuck."

"You want me to—"

"Nah, I got it," I say as I'm already walking away, not about to make the man with the sprained ankle go up there.

Glancing up at the catwalk, I think how easy it would be to fly up there. Well...once upon a time it would have been easy. I still haven't tried to fly since I got my memories back—or use my magic at all. I'm sure I'll be rusty. Or maybe

I can't fly at all anymore. Though, if that's the case, I'm going to have a much bigger problem than a light being out.

Like my shadow devouring all of Neverland.

Yeah, that would be a much bigger problem.

A long time ago, my shadow was a part of me. I always kept it close. Because it was the darkest parts of me turned flesh...well, almost. Not quite flesh. He's made of darkness and shadow and smoke. He started pulling away from me little by little without my notice until he got too out of hand. Neverland banished him. It was my fault, I'll admit to that. I had one responsibility as a child. One. Keep my shadow on a short leash. Because I knew what it was capable of. I knew if given the chance, it could grow more powerful than me. It could kill Neverland's star and swallow everything in darkness.

I don't know how he escaped whatever prison Neverland made for him, but it seems that's exactly his plan.

I can't let that happen. I only hope I remember how to fly.

After taking the stairs up to the catwalk, I go over to the light that's out. I check it, and I'm pretty sure it's the bulb. There are some extra bulbs at the end of the catwalk, so I go get one. As I'm walking back to the light, something catches my eye from below.

There's a bright glint in my periphery. It's brief, like a flash of lightning. Looking down, I freeze when I see the source.

Hook is standing by the double doors on the far right of the auditorium, the light catching on his hook. He's staring up at me, and all of the movement, all of the racket from down below fades into the background like white noise. I'm suddenly aware of my heart beating in my chest as something gets lodged in my throat.

I can't explain my reaction to seeing him here. Maybe it's because I don't know *why* he's here.

But no...I know it's more than that.

I turn away from him. It's the only thing I can do. I wish he wasn't here. I have a job to do, and now that I know he's here, his presence alone is going to distract me.

As soon as I get back downstairs and enter through the door into the auditorium, he's right there, leaning against the wall on the other side. When I round the corner, I have to stop short before I run into him. I assume this isn't his first time here since he knows where I was going to show back up.

The thought of him having watched me has the hairs on the back of my neck standing and my stomach doing flips.

"What are you doing here?" I attempt to keep my voice curt, but I can't stop it from sounding breathy from being so close to him. "This is my job. You can't be here."

He looks around the crowded auditorium, one brow raised. "This looks like a pretty public concert." He scratches at the long stubble on his chin as his eyes zero back on me, his gaze as intense as ever. "Now why shouldn't I be allowed to stay?"

I cross my arms. "Because I haven't forgiven you for the shit you pulled last night."

Shrugging, he leans a little closer, his chest brushing against my arms, eliciting goosebumps. "I have an answer to your question," he starts in that husky voice that always shoots straight to my dick. He lowers his head, looking at me through surprisingly dark and thick lashes.

He may be dangerous, lethal even, cruel, savage, but... *fuck*. He's beautiful too. I kind of want to stare into his eyes forever.

"I don't need you to hate me, Little Star," he continues, casting a shiver down my spine. "But you can if you need to.

You can hate me all you want, but that's not going to stop me."

I realize how heavy I'm breathing when my arms continuously brush against his shirt. The room spins. I swallow. "Stop you from what?"

The grin he gives me is wolfish, downright erotic. "Doing whatever the fuck I want."

The air between us thins. Everything except the two of us blurs. And now I'm standing in a crowded theater rocking a semi because Hook won't stop staring at me as though he wants to dig out a piece of me like buried treasure.

I just might let him.

"I have to get back to work," I say a second before I force myself to walk away.

What the fuck?

Where the hell did that come from?

Two nights ago, Hook was determined to make me hate him. Last night, he certainly didn't seem to care what I thought considering he threatened Wendy. Though, I'll admit that while I haven't fully forgiven him for it, I do somewhat understand why he did it now. He came here so that I could save Neverland. I would've been upset too had I been told I wasn't going back.

So then what changed? Or is this still some kind of game?

Neither one of those questions matter. Not when the bigger question is—what do I do about it?

By the time I return to the sound booth, my breathing has only minimally evened out. My heart is still beating somewhere in my throat.

"You good, Peter?" Simon asks as I enter the booth.

"Yeah. Why?"

"You look a little zoned out. Who was that man?"

Shit. Of course Simon saw. In a large room full of people,

I should probably be flattered that he had his eyes on me enough to notice my conversation with Hook, but I'm too busy trying to come up with a convincing lie.

"Just an old friend."

"Really?" Simon's brow raises skeptically. "He didn't look all that friendly."

I laugh, hoping it sounds natural. "Old enemy then," I offer, trusting the half-truth to sound more convincing while still coming across playful. "But don't worry. It's fine. Promise."

He seems to believe me well enough.

We each take a seat behind the sound and lighting boards and wait for the concert to start.

19

HOOK

I couldn't sleep last night. Not that I'm surprised. Not with Pan's eyes full of stars and Neverland's forest seared into my mind, the feel of his face against my palm burned into my flesh, the sound of his laugh still ringing in my ears. I used to hate it, his laugh. Now, it's deep and charming and alluring.

While I was awake in the dead of night, I made a decision. I can't leave Pan alone. I *won't*. Even if that means I damn myself to Davy Jones's Locker, so be it.

I haven't forgotten anything. Not who I am, not who he is. It just…it doesn't matter to me anymore. I needed him to hate me so that he wouldn't distract me, but now I know we're going back to Neverland. I believe Pan when he said he wouldn't leave me behind. So now that my job is done—Pan remembers and he's taking us both back—why not let myself have what it is I really want?

Even if it's only here in this world.

The moment I saw him on that catwalk, I knew I made the right decision. The moment he invaded my space—or rather I invaded his—I knew there was no going back.

Of course, I'm assuming Pan even still wants me. However, that's not difficult to do with the way his body reacts to me. A moment ago, he was breathless from me simply getting close, his heaving chest straining at the buttons of his dress shirt.

He may be thinking about fighting whatever it is that's between us, but I'd rather it be me he fights before we end up in his bed.

That thought has my cock twitching as I find a seat.

I sit in the back of the auditorium where I can see the place Pan is working with only having to turn my head to the side.

The students begin filing out onto the stage at the front of the room, taking their seats in chairs set up for them. Most of the larger instruments are already out there, while some students carry their smaller ones with them. Once all the students are in their place, a woman steps to the front of the stage to address the audience. I don't pay attention to a damn thing she says. My eyes are already on Pan again.

Just like that, everything goes red.

Pan and that Simon guy are sitting close, *too* close, heads together, speaking in whispers. Simon laughs at something Pan says, then bumps his shoulder into his. They both try to hide their snickering behind their hands.

The woman on stage moves to the conductor's podium before the orchestra. There's silence in the auditorium before the music starts, but it's so loud inside my head. Loud and hot, like a cannon just went off.

I see red. Blood. My hook anchored in Simon's chest.

Screaming. Pleading.

So much blood.

The music starts, and I'm snapped out of my daydream.

Everything is still a little red as the color lingers. My jaw hurts from clenching. My nails bite into my palm. The tip of my hook is pressed a little too hard against my leg.

I've always been obsessed with Peter Pan, but that obsession has morphed into something even more dangerous.

Possessive.

Salacious.

The old Peter Pan has died, and a new one's risen from his ashes. He's a star—Neverland's sun—and I don't care if I get burned.

Peter Pan is mine.

Those words repeat over and over in my head as the concert carries on. I don't listen to the music, but that doesn't mean it doesn't reach my ears. All it succeeds in doing is giving a rhythm to Pan's name that echoes within my skull.

Peter Pan. Peter Pan. Peter Pan.

It's like a song, mellifluous, and it helps to calm me. Somewhat.

I look over at the booth he's in a few more times. Fortunately, with the concert hitting its peak, both he and the blond are hard at work.

At one point, Pan's gaze meets mine, and he looks almost surprised. I wonder if he can tell I'm still pissed off. I feel more composed than I did, but every time I catch sight of Simon, my jaw aches.

The concert lasts for what feels like much longer than necessary. By then, I've had enough of the noise, the music, the applauding, the people. Even when it's over, I have to wait for all those people to leave. And they do it slowly, taking their bloody time. My rage has been on a steady simmer since the thing started, and as I'm waiting for the place to clear, I can feel it threatening to boil over. All I want is to snatch Pan away and take him somewhere where I can finally have him alone.

Whatever patience I have has pretty much run its course by the time the last of the audience leaves. Some of the students are still here, socializing on and around the stage, but the only ones at the back of the auditorium now are me, Pan, and Simon.

Then when they leave, it's just me.

My eyes bore into Pan's back as he walks down the aisle toward the stage with Simon right beside him. They're talking and laughing, and I know Pan is aware that I'm watching. He doesn't even glance over his shoulder at me, as though he thinks ignoring me will make me leave.

He's dead wrong.

After he and Simon talk to some of the students on stage, they both disappear behind the curtain together.

There's my breaking point.

Leaving my seat, I head to the stage. I receive a few looks from the lingering students, but no one stops me. I pass through the curtain to an empty backstage.

At that point, I'm definitely ready to kill someone.

Then I hear voices from around the corner.

"So, I need to tell you something," I hear Simon say.

Taking a quiet step forward, I peer around a wall into a mostly empty hallway. Pan and Simon exit out of what appears to be one of the doors into the music hall.

"What's up?" Pan asks.

"I was going to tell you before the concert, but I…well, I figured I might get a bit emotional. I didn't want to make things awkward."

Pan chuckles casually, though I can hear a nervous undertone to it. "Okay?"

"I want to let you know how much it means to me that

you've believed in me. I think if it wasn't for you pushing me toward USC, then I wouldn't have had the guts to try. But it turns out you were right. I got the call Friday evening." He appears to pause for dramatic effect.

"And?" Pan presses.

"I got in."

"I fucking told you!"

Simon throws his arms around Pan.

I black out.

The next thing I know, I'm ripping the blond away from Pan and shoving him back against the nearest wall. Fisting the front of his shirt in my hand, I bring my hook up in front of his face, relishing the way his eyes nearly pop out of his head.

"Hook! What the hell are you doing?"

Pan is beside me. I can't bring myself to look at him. His own anger seems to tangle with mine in the air between us. I can feel it, along with fear and concern for the man on the other side of my hook.

"Hook!"

All I can do is stare at the blond in front of me. The blond with the blue eyes and the kind face—the kind of person Pan should probably be with. Because I can't even answer his question. I don't know what I'm doing. I blacked out before I realized what was happening. I think I was ready to kill this man. I still might.

I want to. I *really* fucking want to.

"Hook," Pan says again, quieter. "Please let him go."

I do. For some reason, I do exactly what Pan asks of me.

Letting Simon go, I give him one last scowl, then turn and stalk off. I don't look back. I can't. I don't want to see the look I know is on Pan's face. That same look of betrayal and disappointment that I saw last night.

Maybe now he'll fucking understand that I'm not the kind of man he should be with.

So much for thinking I could still have him.

WHEN THE DOOR TO Pan's apartment opens, I'm sitting in the corner of his sofa in the shadows. My gold coin is in my hand, rolling across my knuckles. I can't tell if he senses my presence or not. He closes the door behind him, and when he flicks on the lamp, his eyes are already on me, as though he knew exactly where to look for me. He doesn't look surprised that I beat him here, or that I'm here at all.

I know I shouldn't be here. I keep fucking things up whenever I'm around him, but I can't stay away. I'm no good for him, yet my feet carried me here of their volition.

"You have to go," he says. He doesn't look happy, but I can't blame him.

Unmoving, I grin. "I've heard that before."

"I mean it." Throwing his keys onto a table, he takes a step into the room. "You need to leave. Now."

Still, I don't move from the couch, continuing to roll the doubloon across my knuckles. My gaze roams his body, my cock twitching to life at the thought of ripping open that dress shirt with my hook like last time.

This time though, I'd only hurt him in the ways he'd love.

"Stop eye-fucking me." He crosses his arms like that will stop me.

I let my gaze drift slowly back to his face, then raise a brow. "Would you like me to do it for real?"

"No." Despite that one word, his cheeks flush, telling. "I can't do this with you, Hook. You don't get to threaten everyone I care about and then expect anything from me."

"Well, that doesn't seem fair." Still grinning, I pocket my coin, stand, and slowly cross the room, stopping when there's a few feet left between us. "I threaten a couple of people, and I get nothing. But when you thought I killed Tinker Bell..."

"One, that's never going to happen again."

The sincerity in his words causes my left eye to twitch.

"Two, do you think it just doesn't matter? That you can go around threatening my friends and that I'll forgive you every time?"

"I've told you before that I'm not a good person," I say, lowering my voice. "And if you expected anything more from me, then that's *your* fault. I'm the villain, remember? Not even Peter fucking Pan will ever change that."

His expression falls, and there it is again. He's looking at me as though I just clawed out his heart with my hook.

It makes me want to dig out my own and give it to him.

Slowly, Pan nods, then takes a step to his right and picks up one of the two swords leaning against the wall. He raises it, the tip of the blade inches from my chest. "Then maybe I should run you through," he says, his tone sincere and crestfallen, his mouth pulled down in a frown. "If you're the villain, isn't that what I'm supposed to do?"

"Maybe you should. That would be very *Peter Pan* of you." I take a step forward, the blade digging into my chest. "Except *he* would be smiling while doing it."

I want to tell him to smile, that I need to see it. Because I'm tired of fucking up and erasing that smile from his face, shrouding his light with my darkness. He doesn't deserve it. I wish I knew of another way to be, to exist, to live in his light without losing myself.

Pan shakes his head. His bottom lip trembles the smallest bit, and my eyes are drawn to it as he says, "I'm not that same boy you knew back in Neverland, Hook."

Silence. Heartbeats. The air crackles.

After staring at him a moment longer, I release a breath. "Thank the gods for that."

I don't think, just act. I hit his sword away with my hook and close the distance between us. My hand is on the nape of his neck, pulling his face toward mine.

And then my lips are on his.

20

PAN

Hook is kissing me. And fuck if it isn't the best I've ever been kissed in my life.

It's crushing, consuming, captivating.

The sword falls from my hand. I'm shocked into stillness for only a moment before I'm moving, pushing his jacket off his shoulders and letting it drop to the floor. He doesn't stop kissing me. It's so intense, like he'll die if his lips leave mine. I swear my own lips are going to be bruised and my face beard-burned, but I don't even care.

I take it all.

All lips, tongue, and teeth.

Time seems to move on around us forever and crawl to a stop at the same time. I don't know how long we kiss before we come up for air.

We're both panting, staring into each other's eyes. There's electricity between and around us, like lightning arcing—lightning an icy shade of blue.

Then his hook is under my chin, and his lips are coming at mine again.

"Wait." My voice is breathless, my vision a little dizzy. "There's something I've been wanting to do."

He leaves his hook beneath my chin, but I don't complain. It makes my dick strain harder against my dress pants as I reach for the nape of his neck and undo the leather tie around his hair. Letting it drop to the floor on top of his jacket, I run my fingers through his wavy black hair. I can't help but grin at the way his eyelids flutter.

"Do you like that?" I ask. I sure as fuck do. It's as soft as I imagined it'd be.

"I just like you touching me," he says before his lips are on mine again.

He takes a step forward, and I take a step back. I'm not sure where we are in the room, my sense of space completely obliterated. I don't even remember what we were talking about before this, like kissing Hook may be the only thing I've ever known. When I try to remember, a voice in the back of my head tells me not to.

It's familiar, that voice. The one that told me to forget before.

That makes me pull away. I *can't* forget again.

I don't know if the anguish and the doubt are clear on my face, but something makes Hook speak before I can, as though he's assuming my affliction is his fault.

"I'm sorry."

My eyes widen almost painfully. The only time I've ever heard Captain Hook utter those words was to Wendy the night before. I was shocked then, and I'm more shocked now that they're directed toward me.

He swallows and tries to catch his breath. "For what I did to Wendy."

"You mean that, don't you?"

"I do. If I had known that was your shadow and not you, I never would have gone that far." Then his eyes darken, and the next time he speaks, his voice is a growl. "I won't apologize for Simon though. He touched you, and you're mine."

"Hook, I'm not—"

"Only here."

When I search his eyes, I can't be certain what it is I see. It's like ice and flames, the coldest blue and the hottest desire. Behind it though, I don't know...desperation?

I feel a pang of guilt.

His hand goes to my hair, and he yanks on it until my head tilts back so I'm looking at the ceiling instead of him. Maybe he knows what it is I'd see on his face if I looked long and hard enough. His teeth scrape against my jaw, his lips brush down to my throat. He bites me, and I let out a whine.

"What do you think, Little Star?" His breath is warm against my neck. "We can always go back to being enemies in Neverland."

I consider asking him if that's what he wants, but the thought of him saying yes, that it's exactly what he wants, threatens to turn me inside out. I'd rather pretend that's what we both want.

I can do that. I'm a master of pretend.

It would be for the best anyway. For both of us.

Moaning as he thrusts his hips, I can feel how hard he is, his cock rubbing against mine through the layers of fabric between us. A heavy heat settles in the bottom of my stomach.

"Answer the question," he demands, voice low, lips sweeping against my throat.

"Okay," I barely manage to whisper.

"Say it."

I have to swallow before I can get another word out. "I'm yours. Only here."

"Good boy."

And then he's all over me while I ignite from his praise, every inch of him on every inch of me, burning me further. He brings my face back down to his so that he can ravage my mouth, sliding his tongue against mine. His hook skims slowly down my throat, leaving me shivering. Then buttons are flying everywhere as he slices right down the middle of my shirt.

Yanking my mouth away from his, I glare. "I'm going to run out of shirts at this rate."

"Shut up."

The command isn't necessary considering his mouth is on mine again less than a second later, swallowing any objection I attempt to make.

He backs me up again, and the back of my legs hit the chaise of the sectional. Hook's hand leaves my hair to push against my chest until I fall back onto the sofa. He brings his knees down on either side of me so that he's straddling me, then grabs my left wrist with his right hand and my right wrist with his hook. Bringing them together, he holds them in his hand, then raises them above my head on the couch. He leans over me, looming like the dark and gorgeous angel of death I once thought of him as.

My chest rises and falls with each of my quick, shallow breaths, and his eyes are pinned right on my scar. His hook grazes over the cut he made, and I can't help the involuntary twitch that goes through me.

"Don't worry, Little Star," he breathes as he leans further down. "I won't hurt you unless you want me to."

His lips brush over the cut, kissing me there, his hair sweeping over my chest. I arch my back into his touch, and he grinds against me.

I need the layers between us gone like yesterday.

"Hook," I moan. "Please." I wiggle my hands that he's still holding above my head. "Please. I want to touch you."

The moment he lets go of my wrists, my hands are at his shirt, gripping the hem and pulling it up and over his head. I toss it away, then rub my hands up his abdomen to his chest, over the hard ridges of muscle, the dusting of dark hair beneath my palms. It doesn't fully cover his tattoos, and I can see them clearly now. There's a large ship—what I assume to be the Jolly Roger. A couple of skulls. An anchor. A mermaid with a bare chest. I lightly graze my fingertips over each piece of art. I hadn't been paying attention the last time I saw him without a shirt, too preoccupied by my misery. The memory of our fighting has my dick straining painfully against my pants, making me wince.

When I look up into Hook's face, I'm surprised to see him staring at me. I stare back, wishing I could read what's going on behind those eyes.

"Do you want to hurt me?" I ask in a whisper, trying to distract myself from whatever is in that look that he's giving me.

He grinds against me again as his hand goes to my throat. "Do you want me to hurt you?"

I rake my teeth over my bottom lip. "Maybe a little."

"I'll give you as much pain and pleasure as you want, Little Star." His hand squeezes around my throat, and little flashes of light explode in my vision like mini supernovas as he cuts off my oxygen. "And you'll take it all, won't you? Only from me. Because you're *mine*."

Then his lips are on mine again, swallowing my eager agreement, and I close my eyes as his tongue darts inside my mouth. The cool, sharp touch of metal skates down my chest. When it grazes over my nipple, I moan into Hook's warm mouth.

He presses the tip of his hook a little harder into my flesh, and I swear my dick is about to burst through the material of my pants. But then it's gone, both the cool metal and the heat from his body and his mouth. For the second while my eyes are still closed, I feel cold and rejected. Then my eyelids flutter open as I suck in air, and I see him undoing my pants. He tugs them down along with my boxer briefs, causing my insanely hard erection to spring free against my abdomen.

Without his cool gaze leaving mine, he lowers and runs his velvety tongue up the underside of my shaft from base to tip. It has me throwing my head back on the cushion and making more embarrassing, unintelligible noises.

His warm breath caresses my length as he says, "Fuck, you taste amazing."

And when he takes me whole into his mouth, I'm fucking gone.

I never want this rapture to end.

It lasts a little while longer, and after sucking me until I'm damn near ready to explode, he pops off, having to practically pry my fingers from where they were grasping his hair.

Our eyes meet again as he stands and his hand goes to his own jeans. He moves agonizingly slow as he releases his cock and lazily strokes it while staring down at me, our eyes searching each other's as I lie there panting.

"You've always driven me mad, Pan. But *this* madness?" He shakes his head, his tone husky, *hungry*. "This is a madness I'm happy to suffer."

Right now, *he's* the one driving *me* to the brink of insanity. I'm practically writhing on the couch as I watch his hand move up and down his thick length, dying for him to touch me. I'm close to begging when his knees hit the sofa again and he's straddling my legs.

When his dick meets mine and he rubs them together,

smearing our pre-cum all around and slicking us with it, I throw my head back.

"*Fuck*," I groan. "Fuck yes."

I move my hips in time with his. His hand is around both of us, increasing the friction as we thrust against each other. The bulky rings on his fingers are once again adding an extra sensation—hard metal contrasting with soft flesh—that has me quickly reaching a peak.

"Look at us," he growls.

My eyelids flutter listlessly as my gaze stops and lingers for a beat on his face, at the possessive, animalistic look in his eyes. It's so intense and visceral and turns me on even more. Then I peer down at both of us in his hand, moving together between his ringed fingers.

And…it's the single hottest thing I've ever seen in my life.

I can't really explain why. I wouldn't say I've engaged in *lots* of sex and foreplay, but I've had my fair share. I mean, it's not like I get hard for every gorgeous psychotic man who breaks into my apartment.

Okay, I guess I do.

But this…this feels kinkier somehow. Dirtier. More erotic. Or maybe it's just because it's Hook.

Either way, I've never been more turned on in my life. I want to burn the image of us together in his hand in my mind.

"I want you to always watch, Pan," he says breathlessly, earnestly as though reading my thoughts. "Watch as I make us both feel good. And never fucking forget it."

"Oh, fuck," I whine, unable to look away even if I wanted to.

"You forgot me once before, but this time, I'll sear myself onto your fucking soul. You'll never be able to fucking forget again."

"Fuck, Hook," I moan. "I'm gonna come."

"Come for me, Little Star. I'll follow you over the edge."

A strangled cry escapes me as warm cum shoots onto my abdomen, and true to his word, Hook joins me, his own release adding more to the canvas.

I could get used to both of us painting me up like this. Our collective masterpiece.

Reaching for him, I tangle my fingers in his hair and pull his face down to mine. I kiss him, then rasp against his lips, "That was so fucking hot."

"I meant it when I said I'd give you time," Hook says, still breathless. "If we're enemies when we're back in Neverland, then I'm going to need a little time too." His hand grips my hip, his fingers digging into the skin of my arse. A hint. Or a warning. "I'm not done with you yet."

My eyes would shoot wide open if it wasn't for how drowsy I suddenly am. And a little cum drunk. Still, my stomach does a nervous flip.

Slurring a little, I ask, "You promise?"

"Promise, Little Star."

WHEN I WAKE UP the next morning, I'm still on the sectional, curled up on the chaise with…a blanket over me?

I don't remember falling asleep. I don't remember grabbing a blanket. Would Hook have done that? The thought has me feeling all kinds of strange things while I'm still in that groggy state between awake and asleep.

A crash in the kitchen jolts me to full consciousness.

Throwing the blanket off me, I notice my pants are back on and I'm still wearing my dress shirt that has no buttons, my chest exposed. I swear I can still feel Hook's lips there. My abdomen is clean of any evidence from last night, and I can feel the ghost of his lips on my forehead.

I try not to imagine Hook taking care of me as I fall asleep, but I fail.

There's a warm tingling in my gut, a flutter in my chest, as I round the corner into the small dining area. The feeling vanishes in an instant as I stop short at the sight of my kitchen.

There are pots and pans scattered everywhere, each containing what appears to be some kind of yellow cake in different stages of the baking process. Some are still runny, like uncooked batter. Others are burnt with dark, hardened crust on top. Broken eggshells litter the counters, and it looks like a bag of flour may have exploded at some point.

The crash that woke me must have been the still smoking cake that has probably made a permanent home of the pan it's in. It's on the floor right by the oven. Hook stands there, face red, glaring down at the charred dessert as though it's personally insulted him.

I stand there, completely frozen in shock, somewhere between laughing until I can't breathe and maybe calling an exorcist.

Captain Hook, rogue pirate and villain of Neverland, is baking a cake in my kitchen.

Or at least trying to.

Hook senses my presence I guess, and his glare moves from the cake to me. I must look like I'm closer to laughing than anything else because he snarls angrily. "Say something and I'll gut you."

I hold up my hands innocently, but I can feel my smile spreading across my face. It's taking everything in me not to start cackling. Hook's hair is tied back again, and there's flour dotting his face like powdered freckles. I'm pretty sure there's egg on his gray T-shirt. I cross my arms and lean my shoulder against the wall, taking in the scene and burning it to memory.

I can't stop myself.

"All that's missing is the apron that says 'Got cake? 'Cause I can *hook* you up.'"

Hook slams the oven door shut and scowls at me. His expression is downright lethal, like he really does have the urge to kill me. It only makes me have to work harder to not laugh. My cheeks ache from grinning so damn big, like my face is going to split in half.

"Say something else. I dare you."

My heart rate spikes at the challenge, and I wonder what he would do to me if I did. I kind of want to find out, but a different curiosity gets the better of me instead.

"Why are you baking a cake, Hook?"

He sighs heavily, taking the oven mitt off his hand and throws it down onto an empty egg carton on the counter. "I thought..."

When he hesitates for a beat too long, huffing like a raging, frustrated bull, I manage to put things together myself.

"Wendy." My face falls a little but not completely, amusement making way for awe and something softer. "You mentioned cakes the other night. Wendy was the one who kept taking the pirates' poisonous cakes away from the Lost Boys." After a moment, my eyes narrow. "Wait. Are you trying to poison her?"

He laughs, but there's little humor in it. "We both know she's too smart to fall for that. No, I...I thought it could be a peace offering."

Okay...*what?*

Captain Hook. A cake. A peace offering.

Three things that absolutely do not go together.

But I'm not stupid. I'm pretty sure I know where his true motivations lie. I saw something in his eyes last night that I never would have dreamed of seeing. *Remorse*. And that shook me, like my world was suddenly upside now. He was regretful for what he did—because it hurt *me*. I could tell he was scared I wouldn't want him anymore. I really shouldn't want him. Hasn't he given me reason enough?

I guess if this is the way he's chosen to redeem himself, well…it might be working.

Only because it's kind of funny too.

"Who are you and what have you done with Captain Hook?"

After stepping over the blackened remains of the cake on the floor, Hook strides right up to me. He places his hand on the side of my neck, gripping me possessively, and kisses me. I almost melt into him. He bites my lower lip before pulling away slightly, drawing a whimper from me. He stays in my space.

"Not enemies here, remember?"

I'm breathless from his kiss as I say, "Oh, I don't know. I think we're still enemies. Just enemies with benefits."

He grins, but there's a flicker of something in his eyes that I can't quite translate, there and gone again in an instant. "Does that mean you won't help me with this bloody cake?"

"Oh, no." I shake my head as I take a step back, Hook's hand falling from my face as I go. "You're the one making the peace offering. It wouldn't mean shit if I did your job. That would be cheating."

Hook scowls again. "You're right. Still enemies."

I finally laugh, shaking my head. I take one last look at my kitchen that's going to take all day to clean, then sigh and turn away. “I’m going to get a shower. Please don’t burn down my apartment.”

Hook calls after me as I head down the hallway. “I make no promises.”

21

HOOK

Fuck this goddamn cake!

I fully intend to make Pan help once he's out of the shower. Or rather, I'll *convince* him to.

When I was rummaging around in his bedroom last night, I found some interesting things. No, I don't have any shame. And now seems like the perfect time to let him know how little shame I have.

As I move down the hallway, I strip off my clothes that are covered in flour and eggs and let them fall to the floor. I stop in his bedroom before heading to the bathroom. The door is unlocked, and I can't help but smirk while wondering if Pan did that purposefully.

Consciously or subconsciously, he was hoping I'd join.

The door doesn't make a sound when I open it, so Pan is unaware of my presence as I step into the room. I don't make it far. My feet plant roots when I catch sight of him behind the clear glass door of the shower.

His back is to me, and I take in my fill of the view of his defined, toned muscles, his shoulders, his sun-kissed skin, his perfectly round arse. His body is soapy, his reddish-brown hair wet. There's a tattoo on the back of his left shoulder that I'm seeing for the first time—a tribal tattoo of a sun. I wonder if he knew on some subconscious level what he was even when he had no memories of it.

When he turns around, our gazes meet. Then his lowers. Mine follows, and I see that I'm well past half mast. Not that I'm surprised. Peter Pan is a work of art.

A work of art that I want to dirty. Ruin. Corrupt.

I stalk forward, noting how Pan's cock is already growing hard too. Using my hook since I'm holding something in my hand behind my back, I slide the glass door to the side and step into the shower. Pan appears frozen in shock.

"What are you doing?" he asks in an unsteady whisper.

I close the door behind me, the spray of the shower raining down between us and misting all around. Placing my hook on his bare, wet chest, I push him backward until his back hits the tiled wall. He lets out a shuddering hiss from the cold.

The warm water hits my back as I bring my hand around and hold up the treasure I had dug up last night. I tilt my head and ask in the most innocent manner I can, "What's this?"

Of course, I know exactly what it is. I may not have been to this world in a hundred years, but I'm not stupid. The thing that I'm holding in front of his face is a black silicone butt plug. I can't help but grin at the way Pan's cheeks turn a beautiful shade of pink. The color looks glorious on him.

"Considering you found that in my nightstand, I think you know exactly what it is."

I brush the tip of the plug against his lips. "Open your mouth."

He obeys so well, and I push the toy past his lips. He sucks on it, and my cock jerks.

"Such a good boy for me."

He makes a noise that's a cross between a moan and a whimper.

After I pop the plug out of his mouth, I move my hook off his chest and stab it into the flat bottom of the silicone toy.

"Hey! That's—"

I don't give him a chance to finish. Grabbing his arm, I spin him around to face the wall. With my right arm, I hold him to me around his waist, my hard cock pressing against the globe of his arse. While teasing the plug against his hole, I kiss up his shoulder to the back of his neck. I move around to the side of his throat and bite. At the same time, I slowly push the plug into Pan's entrance.

He lets out a harsh cry, placing his hands on the shower wall to steady himself.

Once the toy is fully seated, I pull it out just a little, then push it back in. I tighten my hold around him as he arches his back, and I'm sure I hit that perfect little spot inside him judging by the way he throws his head backward onto my shoulder and pants.

Lowering my arm, I wrap my hand around his cock that's rock hard and give it a few strokes. He makes unintelligible noises and muffled cries.

"Oh, fuck. Hook."

"Do you want to come?" I whisper roughly in his ear, still stroking him.

"Yes. Please."

I loosen my grip on him, and he whimpers. He thrusts his hips, trying to chase the friction of my hand as I deny him, all the while fucking himself on the toy that's pinned on my hook.

Biting his earlobe, I draw another cry from his lips. "Beg for it, Little Star. I love to hear you beg."

"Please, Hook. Please. I want to come."

Fuck, I love that sound. The begging, the moaning, the raspy, husky, gravelly tone of his voice. The words carried on a breath. Right now, it all belongs to me. And while I may have an ulterior motive for being in here, I savor this all the same. I actually nearly forgot why I came in here to begin with.

But then I remember.

"You'll owe me a favor."

He only nods.

"Say it."

"I'll owe you a favor." He says it without hesitation. "Fuck, please. I'll do whatever, I swear. Please just let me come."

I can't help but chuckle, imagining how mad he's going to be at both of us for this later.

But he did what I asked, so I oblige and tighten my fist again. He pumps himself into it while I stroke him. He rolls his head on my shoulder until his slick forehead is pressed against the side of my face, his warm breath sweeping across my cheek as he pants.

"Does it feel good, Little Star?"

"So fucking good," he moans.

As I stare down into his beautiful face, I realize that I've never had anything as intimate as this before. My own pleasure has always been the driving force behind anything I do, but this…this is different. It shocks me, excites me, terrifies me. All I want is to see the look in his eyes as he reaches the peak of pleasure.

But then I realize his eyes are closed.

"Open your fucking eyes," I growl.

He does.

When I look into the depths of those green pools and

feel the tug of that thread in my chest, I know I'm irrevocably fucked.

"What the fuck did I tell you about that?" My voice doesn't sound as angry as I intend.

"I'm s-sorry."

"Your pleasure belongs to me, Pan, and I want to fucking see it in your eyes. If I don't, I swear I'll stop."

His brows dip down. "No. Please. Please, Hook. Don't st-stop."

I wasn't going to. There's no way I could.

"Then come for me, Little Star. Let me see it."

He groans, and his body shudders as his release shoots out onto the tiled wall.

I let go of him, then grab his face to turn it toward me for a forceful, merciless kiss. As my lips move against his and my tongue darts into his mouth, I lower my hand so that I can put a finger on either side of my hook. I gently pull my hook out of the plug but leave the toy inside him. He whimpers into my mouth. Then my hand goes to my own pulsing, needy cock and begins to stroke.

Pan pulls away, and my brows draw together as I watch him get on his knees in front of me. His hand wraps around mine like he's asking for permission.

"That's not the favor I had in mind."

"Then it won't count as the favor," he says breathlessly as he peels my hand away from my length and places a kiss to the underside of my head that has my eyes nearly rolling backward into my skull. "Can I? Please? I want to."

As if I could deny that request.

My hand goes to the back of his head, fingers tangling in his wet hair, holding him so his mouth is just a breath away from my dick, only for a moment. I gently graze my hook down the side of his face, making sure his eyes stay on me.

"You're so fucking perfect."

There's a spark in his eyes as I guide his lips to my cock. He takes me into his mouth, and a groan rumbles in my throat.

Pan's words from earlier come back to me.

Who are you and what have you done with Captain Hook?

I'm asking myself that same question now because I don't have the urge to keep control as Pan takes it for himself instead. He wraps one hand around the base of my shaft and strokes as he sucks me, cheeks hollow. His other hand comes up and massages my balls. I could slam my cock into the back of his throat like last time, take away his ability to breathe.

But…I don't want him to stop doing what he's doing.

Unfortunately, *because* he's doing what he's doing, I'm not going to last long.

I feel my balls tighten in Pan's hand a moment before I'm coming into his mouth. He sucks me dry before I haul him to his feet and press him between me and the wall of the shower to give him another punishing—but really *rewarding*—kiss, tasting myself on his tongue.

My hand snakes around and grabs his arse before pushing against the butt plug. "Leave this in for the rest of the day," I growl against his lips. "It'll make it easier on you later."

When I step back, I smirk at the stunned, woozy look on his face.

He doesn't even ask.

WHEN WE GET OUT of the shower, I cash in my favor and make Pan help me with Wendy's cake. Just as I expected, he's pissed.

For some reason…it's fucking adorable.

He moves around mixing ingredients, throwing dirty dishes into the sink, and mumbling curses, bitching about how I destroyed his kitchen. I'm tempted to tell him that this is nothing and he should've seen my motel room the night of our first encounter. But I decide not to remind him of that night. He may be displeased at the state of his kitchen and angry with me for manipulating him into helping with the cake, but right now…I don't think he hates me.

And I don't want to remind him of the time he did.

I'm leaning against the counter when Pan picks up the can of frosting for the cake that's currently in the oven.

"You even bought frosting?" he asks, raising a brow.

I shrug. "It's not a cake without frosting."

His expression softens for the first time since we left the shower. Setting the can back down, he continues to regard me with scrutinizing eyes.

"Don't look at me like that." Moving away from the counter, I cross the kitchen in two strides.

"Like what?"

I trap him between me and the opposite counter, then place my hook beneath his chin and tilt his head up. "Like you still expect the best of me."

I don't want him to look at me like that. Not because I'll only ever keep disappointing him if he does, but because I think I may want to be the best of me for him. Because that thread that he keeps tugging on is connected to a black heart that I thought was long dead. However, after being with him the last several days, I think there may actually be a spark of life in it after all, the thread a little less frayed, a little less at risk of unraveling.

But I'm too scared to let him think otherwise.

"You can't expect anything of me," I tell him.

He frowns. "I don't."

I'm not sure if I believe him.

Slowly, I move my hook until the sharp tip is pressed against the soft skin of his neck. I gently glide it down, running it over his jugular, staring at his pulse point that throbs with every beat of his heart. I get a little lost in the rhythm. His chest heaves, and then all I want to do is rip his T-shirt open like I do his dress shirts.

"Hook," he breathes in a shuddering whisper. "I—"

I don't give him a chance to say whatever he was planning to. I trade my hook for my hand and wrap it around his throat before crushing my lips against his.

I fucking love kissing him.

He tastes a little earthy and a little sweet. His lips are so soft and compliant as I open them with my tongue and slide into his mouth, massaging his tongue with mine. I'm sure my beard is rough against his clean-shaven face, but he doesn't complain even when my kiss turns rougher, like I'm determined to leave him in ruins. My hook skims down the front of his shirt as we kiss, and I'm having to once again fight the urge to rip it off him.

The oven dings.

I tear my mouth away from Pan's, turn, and walk out of the kitchen into the small dining area, needing to put space between us. Not surprised to find myself with a semi, I rearrange before turning back to see Pan pulling the cake from the oven.

Now that the cake is baked, Pan makes me frost it myself. I don't argue. When he jumps onto the counter to sit and lets out a muffled cry from the toy still inside him, I can't help but smirk while I smooth out the white frosting the best

I can. I'm no baker, so it's not going to be pretty. Especially when Pan's mere presence is such a distraction.

Once the cake is finished and covered with foil in its pan, I carry it to the front door, balancing it on my left arm. Before I turn the knob, I peer back to see Pan leaning against the wall.

I'm tempted to toss the cake to the floor and forget my entire peace offering mission in lieu of stripping Pan bare.

"Are you sure you don't want to come?" I ask instead, trying not to sound too uneasy.

Judging by Pan's grin, I don't think I succeeded.

I'll admit this entire gesture is for Pan. Wendy's alive. She's fine. I didn't hurt her. She probably deserves an apology, and I'm not the kind of man who usually gives one. But this is all for Pan because of all the times he's looked at me as though I caused the destruction of his very soul, like I stabbed him in the back a thousand times with my hook.

Attempting to bake a cake and present it to his best friend as an apology is a single step short of carving out my own heart and dropping it at his feet.

Actually, the latter may have been less painful.

Now that I actually have to deliver the bloody thing, my nerves are in tatters.

Still grinning, Pan says, "I don't expect you to get on your knees and beg for Wendy's forgiveness, but I at least trust you not to hurt her." His face screws up as though something interrupted his train of thought. "How are you going to get there? How do you get around?"

"Something called Uber."

Pan chuckles. "Yeah, I've heard of it. How do you afford it?"

I look at him as though the answer should be obvious. "I steal."

His jaw goes slack, and he makes a disappointed noise. It's okay. I'd much rather he be disappointed about me being a thief than because I betrayed him.

You can't be betrayed by your enemies.

The thought comes and goes, but it leaves me feeling a little unbalanced.

I roll my eyes, then deadpan, "Pirate."

He sighs but flashes a smile that damn near has my heart stopping. "Get going then, pirate."

TWENTY MINUTES LATER, I'm stepping out of the Uber in front of Wendy Darling's house. I tell the driver to give me ten minutes, not expecting to be here any longer than that. If she invites me inside, it's because she plans on killing me. I'll be lucky if she even talks to me from the porch. My bet is that it takes her two minutes before she's throwing the cake in my face.

I ring her doorbell, then step back onto the stairs. It seems safer to keep my distance lest she make me bleed again.

The door opens, and Wendy immediately refuses to crack it more than a few inches. Her expression goes through several different emotions in a very short amount of time. First shock. Then hatred. Then something that's a lot more like suspicion.

Without a word, she slams the door shut.

"Wendy, please!"

She opens the door again, again only a few inches. She spits venom at me, her tone full to the brim of animosity. "What the hell are you doing here, Hook?"

I hold up the cake. "Giving you an apology."

Her eyes narrow. "What is it?"

"Cake."

Goddammit, I feel so fucking awkward. I don't recognize myself. I curse my insatiable obsession with Peter Pan. This is all his fault, the fact that I have some semblance of a conscience now. I'll be thoroughly punishing him as soon as I get back to his apartment in an attempt to prove otherwise.

That thought, of hurting him the way he likes, gives me a small boost of confidence.

"You know," Wendy starts, cracking the door open two more inches. "If you had your way, the Lost Boys would've died a long time ago."

"It's not poisoned."

"Prove it."

After taking the last couple of steps down until I'm standing on the walkway, I place the pan on her porch. I lift the foil and stick my hook into the cake. Bringing it back out, perfectly balancing a small bite on the tip, I bring it to my mouth. A hundred years with the thing has given me plenty of time to practice.

"And how the hell do I know where that thing's been?" Wendy asks, nodding at my hook.

In Peter Pan's arse.

"It's clean," I promise her.

It's the truth. I've washed it many times since.

Wendy's lips purse, but she opens the door a little more. "Captain Hook baking a nonpoisonous cake as an apology? We really are far from Neverland, aren't we?"

"Considering I'm here to apologize, I should be transparent with you. Pan mostly baked it. I frosted it though."

Wendy's eyebrows shoot up toward her hairline, then a slow smile starts to spread across her face. "You two are baking cakes together?"

I clear my throat and shift on my feet awkwardly.

She grins brighter. "This isn't for me, is it?"

Bloody hell. She's perceptive.

But I don't answer the question. She already knows anyway.

"I truly am sorry, Wendy Darling," I say with an amount of sincerity that surprises me. I bow my head, then turn to head to the car.

"Hook."

When I look back, I see Wendy picking up the cake.

"Don't you dare hurt him." Her tone is stern, her eyes burning a hole right through me.

I give her a small smile, reminded of how she had always been so tenacious and protective of Pan and the Lost Boys, like a damn mama bear. Or a guardian angel. I'm almost envious of Pan.

What I say next might be the most shocking thing I've done today. Or of all time.

"That used to be all I ever wanted to do. Now...I'd rather cut off my other hand."

And I know it's true.

22

PAN

As soon as Hook is gone and the door is closed behind him, I sink onto the couch, gasping when I'm reminded of the butt plug. My head is spinning and swimming and somersaulting. The past couple of days don't feel real. And yet…they feel more real to me than anything else ever has.

I glance over at the chaise where Hook had me laid out last night. The memory practically plays out in front of my eyes. My dick instantly throbs in my jeans.

Yeah, I can't sit here right now.

Forcing myself up and back into the kitchen, I look around, knowing I have my work cut out for me as far as cleaning goes. I have no idea how Hook managed to get egg on the ceiling.

This should be fun.

At least it's Sunday, so it's not like I have anything better to do.

While I clean, my thoughts keep racing, never slowing down, a vortex that just keeps spinning, spinning, spinning.

Now that all the truths have come out into the open since I regained my memories and things have somewhat calmed, I'm surprised by the fact that I wasn't disgusted with myself for what I had done with Hook. We may have known each other when I was a boy, but we're both so different now, like completely different people. At least I am, and at least my perception of Hook is. Not to mention now I realize he's not just a figment of my imagination.

Hook really isn't who he used to be, or who I thought he was. Maybe *I* was the villain and had made him that way.

No, I won't go down that road. Hook enjoys being the villain, I know it.

Wendy may not have been the type to fall for the bad boy, but apparently I am.

I sigh heavily while scrubbing down the counter.

But he's also not as monstrous as he once was. At least, I don't think he is. Sinful, yes, but for different reasons. Maybe his time in Neverland without an adversary did change him. Or maybe it was his time in this world. How long had he been here before finding me? It could've been awhile.

Or maybe what changed him was…*me*.

The thought that I could've been responsible for the change I've seen in Hook hits me and makes the air a little thin. I have to pause what I'm doing and lean back against the counter to catch my breath.

I shouldn't think that. That's a dangerous path to go down.

Hook hasn't changed, I try to convince myself. Nothing's changed. It's all in my head.

Because if he *has* changed then I'd have to admit to myself that he's changed me too, and I can't do that. Not when it would hurt too damn bad when we go back to being enemies once we return to Neverland as agreed. Not when I haven't even decided if I'm going to stay in Neverland. If there's a way to defeat my shadow and keep it gone forever, why stay? There's no Wendy there, no Lost Boys, no Tinker Bell. I'd be all alone.

Not that that's too much different from now, but still...

Only when I feel a sting behind my eyes do I start to move again. I spend the next half hour cleaning flour off the counters and floor, taking a mop to the ceiling, washing dishes. I throw out the pan with Hook's last cake in it instead of attempting to excise it from its shell.

When I'm finished, I fall onto the couch again—a little more gingerly—this time with my favorite flute. I play a little bit, letting the music whisk me away to a place where my thoughts aren't so loud and large and intrusive. It works for a while before Hook's face pops back into my mind and swims around behind my eyelids as I play.

A knock at the door cuts the melody off with a sharp note.

It feels too soon for Hook to be back. I wonder if he changed his mind.

But when I open the door to my apartment, I find that it's not Hook standing on the other side.

It's...*me*.

Well, shadow me.

Hook was right. He does look like my twin.

However, despite the sun still being out, the sky a cloudless blue, my shadow is shrouded in darkness as though it's night. Everything about him is lackluster, his colors muted, almost gray. It's such a strange phenomenon.

As eerie as his appearance is, I quickly get over that fact as my heart begins to race and a chill creeps up my spine. It sneaks up on me, then I'm practically shivering from the cold.

"What the fuck are you doing here?" I manage, my teeth almost chattering.

"It would appear my plan didn't work, so I'm moving to plan B."

He even sounds like me.

"You're not gonna do shit."

I go to slam the door in his face, but he stops it with his hand. He stalks forward, and I take a step back. My shadow clearly has magic if he can manifest himself like this. But how much magic? And how much do *I* have? Chances are my shadow is going to have the upper hand here.

Turns out I assume right.

After he closes the door, he's in the air. He rises, tilts back, and kicks both his feet into my chest. I go flying backward across the living room, crashing into my guitars and crumpling to the floor.

"You were supposed to fight," he says, malice dripping from his tongue. "Decide not to go back to Neverland at all. Give up. Maybe kill each other. Not end up in bed together."

I cough as I scramble to my feet. "We haven't been to bed yet."

Without giving him the opportunity to predict my move, I hurl my fist at him, catching him in the jaw. He barely even stumbles back, his head briefly cutting to the side before his eyes are back on me.

"Too bad you won't get the chance," he taunts.

He raises a fist to copy my move, but I see it coming, duck, and catch him in the gut. This time, he staggers back as the air abandons his lungs. I'm hoping it's a sign that he's using too much power to keep himself in this form. He's much too corporeal to be a shadow. Maybe he's growing weak from the effort.

"Why are you even doing this?" I ask, wanting to keep

him talking as I come up with a plan to gain an advantage. "What's the point of all this?"

"The sun has reigned over Neverland long enough, keeping me confined, trapped, in my small corner of darkness. It's not enough. It never has been. You'll find out what I'm talking about soon enough."

"Why make me remember then? You could have had Neverland to yourself. I wouldn't have been able to return at all had you left it alone."

"You were going to remember eventually, going to try to stop me. It was just a matter of time. Unfortunately, I had to speed things up a bit. See, I would like to return to my dark, dark Neverland. It's too damn bright here."

"It's California, dickhead," I spit back before aiming another punch.

This time, he ducks, and I have to circle around him. My mind and the room are spinning in opposing directions, and I fear the floor is going to be pulled out from under me. I've tried to grasp onto my magic that's humming weakly somewhere within me several times. Maybe it's because I abandoned it for so long, but it keeps slipping through my fingers.

"So what's plan B?" I ask, sure I already know the answer.

"To remove you from the equation."

"You can't kill me without killing yourself. Light and dark can't exist without the other."

We both know this is the truth. It's the only reason my shadow still exists. After dealing with the many times it used to escape, wreaking havoc anywhere and everywhere, I wished I could just be done with it. End it like it wanted to end me. But neither one of us ever could without dooming Neverland completely. And the shadow still wants Neverland for itself. Only it wants that world to know darkness like it's known darkness its entire life.

He sneers. "I don't have to kill you."

I'll be damned if I go down without a fight.

I rush at him, but I never make it.

Everything goes dark.

And cold.

So fucking cold.

I'm pretty sure I collapse onto the floor, but I feel nothing solid beneath me, like maybe I'm falling and I'll never stop. Falling into a chasm so deep it's endless. An abyss, a black hole. My senses have been stripped bare.

All I can see is darkness.

All I can feel is cold.

All I can hear is the deafening silence of nothingness.

Even time doesn't exist. Seconds could be passing. Or years. It could be fucking years. Eons. It feels like fucking forever. It's eternity, that's what it is. It's an infinite amount of time of nothing but darkness, cold, fear, and loneliness. Everyone and everything I ever knew, ever cared about, is dead and gone.

Nothing exists, nothing but me and this void.

I'm alone.

I was meant to live forever, forever in Neverland. That's why I existed. But now...now I'll live forever in the dark and the cold and the nothing.

It creeps inside me, becoming me, until I'm one with it.

This black oblivion is all I know now. All I'll ever know.

23

HOOK

Before heading back to Pan's place—I don't even consider returning to my motel room instead—I ask the driver if he knows any good Mediterranean restaurants, thinking back to the leftovers of Pan's that I ruined the other night. Since I don't know exactly what he likes, I get a little bit of everything.

Fuck, today's a weird day.

Baking a cake and apologizing to Wendy Darling.

Fucking Pan with a butt plug in the shower.

Now picking up food for him.

I really need to get back to Neverland and the Jolly Roger and my crew so that I can feel like a damn pirate again. Right now, I'm barely a pathetic excuse for one.

I carry the large bag full of takeout food to Pan's front door. I don't knock. The door is unlocked. One foot makes it over the threshold before I come to a sudden halt. Ice drips down my spine to the ticking of a clock as time slows to a crawl.

Pan is crumpled on the floor on the other side of the living room, curled into a small ball. He rocks back and forth, his eyes wide open, tears streaking down his face.

The bag of food falls off my hook onto the floor.

"Pan!"

Before I can rush over to him, I see who's responsible for Pan's state—a figure, almost a silhouette, standing in the shadows of the room.

"What did you do to him?" I demand, spittle flying between my teeth.

"What needed to be done," he answers in Pan's voice, only more monotone, like he lacks a soul.

After slamming the door shut, I pick up one of the swords leaning against the wall.

Let's see if I still remember how to be a pirate.

I surge forward, swinging my blade around. It slices right through the shadow's middle. However, his body—or form or whatever it should be called—simply parts around it like smoke. Frustration claws its way up my throat as I roar. I swing my sword again.

This time, a sword materializes in the shadow's hand, and it meets mine in midair between us.

The shadow tilts his head as he stares at me between our crossed blades. Then he gives me a wicked grin. "You're too late, Captain Hook. Peter Pan is gone. I've won."

My eyes narrow as I regard him carefully. Even though he's the embodiment of shadow, he appears almost…pale. His eyelids are heavy. His chest heaves ever so faintly.

He's growing weak.

Smirking right back at him, I say with confidence I don't completely feel, "It's not over."

Moving my blade, I swing it through the air once more, and he's not quick enough to stop me this time. I swing it back and forth like a pendulum, cutting through his form over and over and over. Each time, it parts, leaving behind a trail of whisps, until he appears like a sheer, black veil that's been razor cut a hundred times. He becomes thinner and thinner.

And then he wanes, slowly shrinking back into natural shadow until he's completely vanished.

I stare at the spot where he disappeared, waiting, watching.

Nothing moves.

My sword falls to the ground, and I rush over to Pan. I drop to my knees in front of him, holding out my hand but not touching him. He's in the same state as before—eyes wide, tears constantly flowing, swaying on the floor. How would he react to me touching him? Would he react at all?

"Pan?" I say, my tone urgent.

There's no change.

It's like he's not here.

I put my hand on his shoulder, and when he doesn't react, I shake him cautiously. "Pan?"

He gasps. He sucks in lungfuls of air as though he hasn't breathed in days. His eyes are still a bit out of focus, but something tells me that he's *here* now. I don't know where he went, where he was before, but I know he's back.

At least, somewhat.

He starts to hyperventilate, sobs wracking his body. He still hasn't looked at me. Does he even know I'm here despite touching him?

I try again, this time a little softer. "Pan?"

Fresh tears cascade down his soft cheeks. He's so pale, drenched in sweat. His lips are blue like they're covered in a layer of frost, and his teeth are chattering.

What the fuck do I do?

I move my hand to the side of his face. Fuck, he's freezing. Like a goddamn ice cube. My heart races faster.

What if he's not going to be okay?

He *has* to be okay.

I try to reach him again. "Peter?"

His gaze snaps to mine. He stops breathing, stops crying. He looks at me for a long time.

In that span of time, I realize I called him by only his first name for what may have been the first time. I like the way it tumbled from my lips.

I like that his name was what reached him.

He launches at me, knocking me back onto my arse and curling into my body, molding against me. He's so fucking cold that I'm instantly shivering, but I don't care. I hold him close, offering him my body heat. His shirt is drenched with sweat, and I'm surprised it's not frozen to his skin. He clings to me, my own shirt held tight in his fist.

"Peter, talk to me," I whisper. "Tell me you're okay."

He shakes his head against my chest.

I hold him tighter. "You're not okay?"

Again, he shakes his head. When he finally speaks, his voice is raspy, quivering. "It was s-so dark. And c-cold. I was all alone. I was s-so empty. Alone."

"You're not alone now." Placing my hand on the back of his head, I run my fingers through his damp hair.

"It f-felt like forever. An eternity. It was n-never going to end."

"It did end," I insist strongly. "I promise you it did. You're not alone. I'm here, Little Star."

He tightens his hold on me, grasping my shirt until his knuckles are more white than the rest of him, and that's saying something considering how ashen his skin is. How cold. Fuck, he's still *so* cold. His entire body still trembles. I know I need to do something to get his temperature up because my body heat isn't cutting it.

"Don't let go, Peter."

Holding him securely, I manage to get to my feet with him in my arms. He's not as heavy as I imagined he'd be, but it's still a chore.

I pad across the living room and down the hallway to his bathroom. Thankfully, the door is open. Once inside, I carefully set him down on the closed toilet. He's still holding onto my shirt with a death grip, and when I try to get him to release me, he whines and sobs again.

My chest aches heavily as I stare at him.

I think he's stitched that frayed thread connected to my black heart so thoroughly that it's now a strong leash, and he could rip the organ out of me if that's what he wanted.

I don't make him let go, instead reaching over to the glass door and sliding it open. Then I pick him up again and carry him into the shower, setting him down on the tiled floor. Again, I have to reach instead of making him let go. My fingers barely manage to curl around the shower handle to turn it on. I don't turn the temperature up too hot, not wanting to shock Pan's body by moving from cold to hot too fast.

Even on warm, it feels like the difference between ice and fire.

Sitting down beside him, I pull him into my lap again. The water hits us both around our legs as we sit there fully clothed. I hold Pan to me as he buries his face in the crook of my neck, my hand rubbing comforting patterns across his back.

He's barely calmed down, still breathing heavily, still crying, still trembling. At least he's stopped sobbing. And as the steam from the water fills the shower, he starts feeling warmer too.

I think about how close I came to losing him, and the moment I do, I feel something foreign, a kind of sharp prick behind my eyes. I blink until it's gone. I realize that my chest is moving in tandem with his, and it takes me a moment to figure out if his breathing has slowed down or if mine has picked up. I think it's a bit of both.

Our clothes are now plastered to our bodies like a second skin. Pan is motionless except for the occasional shiver. I wonder if he fell asleep.

I give him a few more minutes until I'm more than satisfied with how warm his body is. Then I move him enough to brush my lips against his forehead, testing if he's awake. He sighs, and his hold on my shirt begins to gradually loosen until some color returns to his knuckles.

"I'm going to get these wet clothes off you," I say softly. "Is that okay?"

Pan nods and leans back.

Removing his T-shirt, I toss it over into the corner of the shower. It lands with a wet splat. I then go for the zipper of his jeans. If this evening had gone how it was meant to, I'd be enjoying this moment instead of being too goddamn scared of spooking him or hurting him further with the state he's in. He lifts himself so I can get the jeans off, and I see that he still has the butt plug in. I consider removing it, but again, I don't want to overstimulate him, so I leave it.

After his clothes are off, I take off my own shirt, throwing it over with his clothes. I can't get to my jeans since he's still on my lap.

"Can you stand if I help you up?"

"I think so," he answers in a weak voice.

He moves off my lap, and I stand and shut off the water. After I remove my jeans, I turn back and offer him my hand. He takes it, and I haul him to his feet. His legs nearly buckle beneath him, but I catch him under his arms. Our slick chests meet, and our gazes lock.

His eyes are wet and bloodshot and swollen. He grabs onto my biceps for stability and licks his dry lips. He opens his mouth but quickly closes it again.

"Come on, Little Star. Let's get you into bed."

He grips my arms tighter, his eyes widening. "Please, d-don't leave."

Goddammit.

Even if I attempted to rip myself away, something would end up left behind in shreds.

"I wouldn't dream of it."

I help him out of the shower, and we both drip water on the rug as I grab two of the sage green towels from the shelf above the toilet. I dry us both off, then wrap towels around each of our lower halves. Since Pan is still shaky on his legs, I don't trust him enough to walk. I pick him up once more, and he clings to me again, wrapping his arms around my neck. I shouldn't enjoy that as much as I do.

In Pan's bedroom, I lay him on the bed. His eyes are open, watching me, and I can tell he's still afraid that I'll leave. But I don't. I lie down on my back beside him and bring the covers up over both of us. Moving into the crook of my arm, he curls into my right side of his own volition, his arm over my waist and his cheek against my chest, warming me inside and out.

For a moment, I'm a little dazed. I can't remember ever sleeping in the same bed with another person. I've never been sentimental toward my partners, never cared about their wellbeing.

Not like how I care for Pan.

Peter.

He sniffs, then says in a quiet, hoarse voice, "I don't want to go to sleep. It was dark for so long. I don't want it to be dark again."

I glance back at the window to the left of his bed, grateful for the amber glow from the apartment lights peeking in through the blinds. I don't blame him for being frightened to go to sleep. I've spent years living close to the shadow. And while I may prefer darkness and clouds and storms, getting too near to it always left me feeling the worst I had ever felt. Hopeless. Lonely. Full of despair. That's why I always sent others to map its growth. I hated going near it.

"It won't be dark," I try to reassure him. "You'll dream."

"What will I dream about?" he asks as though asking for ideas.

Smiling, I stroke his back. "Neverland. How it was, not how it is now. The way you remember it before you left. Warm and sunny. The trees as green and beautiful as your eyes. Everything so bright and full of life. Mermaids singing. Fairies flying all around. Sword fighting with bloodthirsty pirates."

I think I feel him smile against my skin. His body relaxes into me, and a few minutes later, he's breathing steadily, peacefully.

I'm exhausted as well, so I allow myself to follow him down.

Before I fall too deep, I realize something. I think I realized it some time ago, but only now do I let myself think it.

I'm not sure I want to go back to being enemies with Peter Pan.

24

PAN

It's warm.

That's my first thought as I'm gradually rising out of the pit of unconsciousness. It wasn't as dark as I had feared. I dreamed of Neverland. I think that was because of Hook.

Hook.

My eyes fly open.

Now I know why I'm so warm. Because my body is pressed against another, my arm thrown over him. He smells like amber and spice, and I inhale a deep breath just so I can fill myself with his scent, ground myself, know that this is real.

Judging by the amount of light in the room, it's still night, the middle of the night or early morning, only the glow of the lights from outside barely keeping the darkness at bay.

The darkness.

Memories of tonight—last night?—come back to me in an overwhelming rush. Shutting my eyes tight, I press my face into the side of Hook's chest, breathe him in again. If it wasn't for him, where would I be right now? Still in that darkness? Where it was so dark and cold and empty and lonely.

I felt as though I had left Earth. I don't know where I was, but I'm pretty sure that place is my worst nightmare.

If that's the darkness my shadow has had to endure for hundreds of years, I almost feel sorry for it. *Almost.*

Slowly opening my eyes again, I peer up at Hook without trying to move too much. His own eyes are closed, and his chest moves beneath my head with each measured breath. He looks so much different than I've ever seen him. There's no scowl on his face. He's peaceful. Comfortable.

He called me Peter.

He chased away my shadow.

He took care of me.

I think he saved my life.

It all hits me at once, like a powerful blow, crushing my lungs, and I'm suffocating under the weight of something I can't comprehend. I jolt up into a sitting position with my back facing him, trying to catch my breath. Putting my elbows on my knees and my face in my hands, I press my palms into my eyes until I see stars. Hook stirs behind me.

"Peter?" His voice is thick with sleep, but the effect my name on his lips has on me is as potent as it was earlier. "Are you okay?"

I think I know what it was that hit me.

I lift my head, my eyes staring at an empty spot on the wall, my heart pounding in my ears. It's so loud that I can barely hear myself when I say, "You need to leave."

"What?" I feel his heat at my back when he sits up. "Tell me why."

"I just...I can't...I can't do this."

"Do what?" he practically growls. "Don't tell me that damn shadow scared you from fighting him."

I shake my head. "No. No, of course not. I want to save Neverland as much as you do, but...whatever's going on between us...I can't do it."

The silence that follows cuts nearly as deep as my own words. I hate what I'm saying. I hate the words that spew from my lips, like they're poison darts aiming at both of us. Because I *want* to do this, whatever it is between us. But I *can't*.

When I thought it was only about sex, I was okay with it, but the last couple of days...

Fuck. I wasn't prepared for this.

Hook barged into my life when I didn't even know who he was. But he knew *me*. He had an advantage. I saw him as this dark and dangerous and dreamy man, and my dick wanted him almost instantly. Why did he have to give into it? He knows who I am, what I am. Did he forget that part like I forgot everything else?

I sniff when I realize all the emotion got to me and I've got tears in my eyes.

There's a humming in my ears that I ignore.

"I'm grateful that you saved me," I say with a shaky, croaky voice when he's said nothing. "I really am. But I won't do this to either of us."

"What are you talking about?" He moves closer to me, and I can feel his breath on the back of my neck. "Do what, Peter?"

A tear slips past my lashes when I close my eyes. "Don't call me that."

"I'll call you whatever I want." He kisses the side of my neck, and I break out in goosebumps. His lips brush my skin as he whispers, "Peter."

I let my head roll to the side and take a shuddering breath. Then I force myself to pull away from him. Twisting around, I back away, putting two feet between us. Before I can stop myself, I blurt out, "I'm not real!"

His body jerks back as if I've just slapped him. Again, brief silence, and then, "What?"

"I'm not real," I say again. "Not like you are anyway. Surely you knew that?"

He furrows his brow so deeply that a crease forms between them, then runs a hand through his wavy black hair that hangs down around his beautiful face. "You have magic..."

"Yes. Because I was born from Neverland. Neverland needed me. It needed my shadow, like night and day. So it created us. I'm not real like you because I was conceived from magic—for a purpose. And because of that, I..." I choke on the truth.

Hook reaches for my hand and grasps it tightly in his. "But you left Neverland, and you grew up. I think you're more real than you think you are. You feel pretty damn real to me."

I frown, and I feel it weighing down the rest of my face. "I grew up and I'm corporeal, yes. But I don't...feel things like a normal person. I can't..." I have to look away. "I can't love."

Silence.

For a long moment, all I hear are our breaths and our heartbeats.

Then he says, "Look at me."

As always, I do.

There's something etched across his face that I can't quite translate. Hurt, maybe. Maybe disappointment. Maybe anger.

When he speaks, it's with what I can only translate as malice. "I never asked you to."

I look away again immediately, shame and rejection bringing a fresh wave of tears to my eyes that I barely manage to hold back behind a weak dam. I bite down hard on my lip and sniff. "I'm sorry. I thought...I don't know what I thought. You took care of me last night."

Not that I gave him much of a choice with the way I leaped into his arms like he was my knight in shining armor.

Yeah, I remember that. I'm a fucking moron.

Hook's a pirate, not a knight.

I guess I let myself forget again.

His hand leaves mine, grabs my chin, and forces my face back toward his. He grips hard, causing me to wince. "Do you love Wendy?"

"I...I care about her."

"You love her. Don't try to tell me you don't. You loved Tinker Bell too. You loved her so much that her death wrecked you and drove you out of Neverland, out of your home."

He pulls me closer until I can feel his warm breath fanning my face. My own breathing hitches. Even in the yellow glow of the outdoor lights through the blinds, his ice-blue eyes still manage to penetrate whatever wall I keep up, the one that I convince myself is doing its job. His grip on my chin never falters. All the sensations, the way he touches me, the way he's everywhere, all around me—it all has my dick threatening to tent the towel that's still wrapped around my waist.

"You cannot make me believe that Peter Pan is incapable of love." His voice is still rough but no longer angry. "I've seen it for your friends. As for me, I never asked for it. Because you *shouldn't* love me."

He's wrong. He has to be. I've spent my entire existence—minus the fourteen years I forgot who I was—believing that I wasn't capable of love. It was innate knowledge, simply part of my existence. I had accepted it. That fact had never hurt me.

Not like it hurts now.

Because if I *could* love, I think I would love James Hook.

And that realization hurts worse than anything.

The humming gets louder.

"Then we really should end this," I say even though I don't want to. "One of us is going to get hurt. Especially once we return to Neverland and go back to how things used to be."

Hook's jaw clenches, and I can see the muscles at work as he continues staring deep into my eyes, holding me in place. "What if I don't want to go back to how things used to be?"

That makes me jerk my head out of his grasp. "We may not have a choice."

"And what does *that* mean?"

"That Neverland has its own magic. What if it has its own plan for us? What if it doesn't give us any options other than what *it* wants?"

His hand goes to the nape of my neck, and he pulls me close once more. His eyes narrow, and his voice drips with venom. "Now you're just looking for excuses."

"No, I'm not." Pressing my palms against his chest, I attempt to push him away. His grip on my neck tightens, and I wince. "Let me go, Hook."

The moment I start to struggle, my dick decides it wants to make a tent after all. I only realized recently that this side of me exists, but I think it may exist for Hook alone. The side of me that wants to fight him, that wants him to hurt me, that wants him to own me, ruin me. I want all of that, so I keep struggling, keep trying to writhe away.

When his hook comes to rest beneath my chin, I still. My dick strains against the cotton fabric of my towel, and it takes everything in me not to thrust my hips in search of friction.

Does this make me fucked up? Yeah, maybe a little.

"Is that what this was all about, Peter?" That venom in Hook's voice licks at my skin as the smooth metal of his hook glides down my throat. "Did you just miss the fight? Is this what you wanted? Because we both know if there's one thing you *do* love, it's the fight. The adrenaline. The pain."

His hook grazes over the healing cut on my chest, and I'm left trembling, my breaths quick and shallow.

Did I plan this when I decided to open up to him, to tell him my secret that I've kept from everyone? No. I really am terrified.

Of not being able to love Hook.

Of *loving* Hook.

Of returning to Neverland and becoming enemies again. *Real* enemies like we once were.

Because right now? He's right. I do fucking love this.

Hook smirks wickedly as though he can hear my confession. "You could've just asked."

Then his lips are on mine, bruising, punishing. His beard scratches and sears my face like it's made of white hot flames. His hand moves from the back of my neck into my hair, yanking my head exactly where he wants it so that he can assault my mouth with his tongue, his teeth, his hot breath.

My lips move against his, trying to keep the pace while my hands reach for his towel. Beneath it, he's as hard as I am. I pull the towel off him, and as soon as I wrap my hand around his thick length, we both moan into each other's mouths.

His hand goes to my throat. Then the room flips as I'm thrown onto my back on the bed.

"I was going to be gentle on you," Hook says into my ear as his body blankets mine. He squeezes my throat deliciously, then runs his tongue along my jaw. "That was my plan after what happened last night. But you don't want gentle, do you, Little Star?"

I shake my head.

No, I don't want gentle. Not right now. Not after last night. Not after seeing that look in his eyes—the concern, the care, what I thought might have been love, or the start of it. It scared me too damn bad.

Almost as much as the darkness, the cold, and the loneliness.

Right now, what I need is what he's so good at giving me.

He skates the sharp point of his hook down my chest, pulling a whimper from me. His hook catches on the towel, and he tugs it away from my body. Our dicks touch, both of us leaking pre-cum, and the feel of him drives me crazy that I instantly shut my eyes and start rutting against him. His hand squeezes my throat a little harder, and I'm not sure if it's meant as a warning to stop or as encouragement to keep going. It has the effect of the latter.

I'm writhing and moaning beneath him pathetically when I feel a pressure in my arse and an intense spark of pleasure. I gasp and stop moving. Opening my eyes, I look up to see a devilish smirk on Hook's face. His hook is pressing against the toy that I nearly forgot was there.

"I should punish you every time you close those beautiful eyes." *His* eyes look dangerous as he glares down at me. "Keep them open, Peter. Or I *will* stop."

His hand leaves my throat, and I suck in air. He lowers his body, and his hot breath is against the head of my dick before his mouth envelops me.

"Oh, fuck," I groan.

He sucks vigorously. I don't close my eyes even though my eyelids are heavy with pleasure. I watch him as he sucks and laps and worships.

His mouth leaves me, and his words rumble against my

cock. "I can't get enough of you. You're my new fucking addiction. Now I want *all* of you."

My hands go to his hair as his mouth returns to me. I tangle my fingers in the dark wavy locks and moan as his hand fists the base of my shaft and he takes the rest of me deeper until I feel the back of his throat. His hook pushes against the plug in a steady rhythm, making my body squirm and my hold on his hair tighten.

"Fuck, Hook, I'm gonna—"

He pops off, causing me to whine. "Don't you dare."

With his hand, he slowly removes the toy from my arse, then tosses it aside. He spreads my legs and lifts them, and when I feel his warm breath against my hole, I buck my hips in shock. With his arm beneath my leg, his hand grips my hip, holding me in place, and his hook rests against my other hip like a warning.

"Stay still, Little Star," he says, his breath against my balls. "I don't want to hurt you. Not *that* bad."

Then his tongue is against my hole, and the cry that escapes my lips is pitiful and desperate. He swirls his tongue around the ring of muscle, then pushes it inside.

I'm fucking gone. I've never felt this good in my life.

Everything is rose-colored. There's pure bliss in my brain. Rhapsody in my bones. Euphoria in my veins.

After he fucks me with his tongue, he pushes a finger inside me, slick with saliva. Two fingers. I wrap my hand around my hard dick, not sure how much longer I can survive this.

Then his fingers are gone, and Hook grabs my wrist before I can stroke even once. I practically sob as he pulls my hand away. I need friction. I need release. Every nerve ending in my body is on fire, and Hook is the only one who can put it out.

"You can come when I tell you to."

I peer at him through my lashes, pleading with my eyes. He holds my gaze as he sits up and spits into his hand. He works it over his cock, and I'm mesmerized as he strokes himself that I nearly forget that I have lube in my nightstand. Condoms too, but, well…I'm both clean and immortal.

"Wait."

My tone is still imploring, and that works in my favor because when I reach over to grab the lube out of my nightstand drawer and go to hand it to him, he scowls down at the small bottle as though I've offended him. But by his size alone, I know—I just *know*—he's going to hurt me. And that's not including the *deliberate* brand of hurting.

So I know I have to beg.

"Please, Hook," I plead desperately. "It's…been awhile for me."

He glares at the bottle for a few more beats, the vein in his temple throbbing. Then, "I prefer olive oil."

I barely manage to mask a grin. "You really are old."

He growls. Literally fucking growls.

After snatching the bottle, he pours a generous amount over himself and my hole. The way he works his hand furiously lets me know I pissed him off, the look in his eyes conveying a desire to hurt me, to break me.

I buzz with the thrill.

"You didn't want gentle, Peter," he reminds me as he presses the crown of his cock against my entrance. "You're especially not getting it now after that."

His hand comes back to my throat, squeezing close enough to cut off my air. My eyelids flutter, threaten to close, but I force them to stay open. He already looks and sounds lethal enough as it is.

I fucking love it.

The look in his icy eyes hits peak intensity as he pushes against the rim. "You're going to take what I give you, come when I tell you, scream if you need to."

I nearly come from his words alone.

And then he's inside me.

My moan fills the otherwise quiet room. Despite the toy inside me all day and the lube he didn't want to use, it fucking hurts. But it also feels so fucking good. I try to thrust against him, to take more of him in, drowning in the pain and the pleasure, but he doesn't let me, pulling back to keep just his head inside. I groan when it's not quite where I need him.

"Hook, please," I beg.

He gives me another inch, but it's still not enough.

So I beg some more. "Fuck. Please, Hook. Please. I need you."

"You know I love the sound of you begging, Little Star."

He thrusts all the way in to the hilt, giving me what I earned, and all I see is stars again as he hits that magical spot inside of me just right. I cry out and expect him to finally start fucking me.

But he doesn't. He doesn't move at all.

I try to do it instead, but he's still holding me in place. Squeezing my throat a little tighter, he leans over me and brushes his lips against mine. It's almost too tender.

"You should know that I don't give a fuck what Neverland wants," he whispers against my lips. "I don't give a fuck what you think you're capable or incapable of. All that matters is that you're mine."

I nod emphatically, hoping it's enough for him to give me more.

"Say it."

"I'm yours."

"Good boy."

His mouth inhales my resulting moan as he kisses me and starts to fuck me relentlessly.

I knew what he could do to me, but I wasn't prepared for it.

His tongue strikes against mine, then his teeth bite into my bottom lip. Hard. I taste the coppery tang of blood, but I don't even care. It mixes with the taste of him, which is succulent and inviting. His lips take a brief journey down to my chin, along my jaw, nipping back along the same path before his mouth returns to mine. It makes me delirious. It's all so intoxicating. As is his hand around my throat and the way his cock hits my prostate perfectly with every goddamn thrust.

"Fuck, you feel so fucking perfect," he growls against my lips. "Like fucking *mine*."

If Death were to decide it wanted to take my immortal life *right now*, I would sell my soul for one more minute of this. I'd go to hell for just a few more seconds of heaven.

But this isn't going to last as long as I wish it could. Hook and I are a force of nature.

"Hook," I say on a breath shared between us. "I can't…"

No one can stop a force of nature.

"Go ahead, Little Star."

His permission is all I need to come, totally untouched. My release spurts out onto my slick abdomen as I unravel.

I'm an exploding star, a fucking supernova.

Hook follows me seconds later, filling me with his release. I've never felt so full in my life, so complete.

He hovers over me while he catches his breath. His hand on my throat relaxes and moves down, his palm placed tenderly, possessively, over my hitching chest.

I wish this moment could last longer too.

When he pulls out of me, I whimper from the loss of him. He takes one of the towels and cleans us both off, then tosses the towel onto the floor before falling to the bed beside me. He grabs me and pulls me toward him until I'm in the crook of his arm. Our chests are both still a little slick, heaving.

I shut my eyes tight, suddenly scared again as I realize how badly I want him. Not just in this way. But how badly I want to *keep* him.

"Get some more rest, Peter," he says, his lips against my forehead. "You're going to need it because I'm still far from done with you."

My whole body tingles at his promise. I haven't gotten enough of him either, and I'm terrified I may never get enough. I like having him in my bed. I like having his body beside mine. I like the way he feels inside of me, the power he has over me, the way he's under my skin, in my bones.

I may even *love* it all.

But could I love *him*? Or is this going to break us both?

25

HOOK

I wake up in Peter Pan's bed, and for a brief moment, I'm faintly disoriented. Like everything that's happened in the last twenty-four hours has been a dream.

Peter's warm body pressed against mine helps to ground me. His legs entwined with mine is something I never thought I'd like as much as I do. I instinctively hold him a little tighter, and he begins to stir. His auburn hair looks a little more red than brown in the morning sun rays that are filtering in through the blinds.

His eyelids flutter open, and the greenest eyes I've ever seen greet me.

Fuck, he's beautiful.

That thought pours out before I can stop it.

"You're so fucking beautiful."

I clench my jaw out of instinct because I've never been one to be so vulnerable.

But the moment that Peter smiles, wide and brilliant,

the tension leaves me. It surprises me that I don't care how vulnerable I am around him. He brought my cold, dead heart back to life and now controls the leash around it, the one he somehow mended from tattered remains.

Not that I'd ever tell him that.

His fingertips trail lightly over my jaw, my hairline, before his fingers comb through my hair. Then he whispers with that same smile, "So are you."

I blink several times, taken aback. No one has ever called me beautiful before.

Needing an excuse to evade the compliment, I roll over onto my back but keep an arm around Peter, holding him close. I stretch my body beneath the covers and am reminded that he and I are both completely naked.

I fucked Peter Pan last night, and now we're cuddling in his bed nude.

Something Peter said last night flits through my brain.

What if it doesn't give us any options other than what it wants?

Could he be right? Could Neverland have more control over us, of me, than I had known? The only reason I even consider the possibility is because of how I've changed. Of course, I don't think I've changed all *that* much, only where Peter's concerned. That has to mean that it's Peter who's changed me, not Neverland who molded me into what it wanted. Who I am in Neverland is who I've always been my entire life. It didn't alter me. It didn't make me into Peter Pan's perfect adversary.

Which means it can't do that when we return.

Still, the doubt lingers.

"Did you mean what you said last night?" Peter asks, pulling me from my thoughts.

"Hm?"

"About not wanting to be enemies in Neverland."

"I meant it," I answer quietly, staring up at the ceiling. "I think I much rather prefer this."

I can hear him swallow. "Even if…even if I can't…"

"Did you know I came here a hundred years ago?" I tilt my head down so I can look at him now. There's a crease between his brows as he shakes his head. "I didn't think so."

"Why?"

Sighing, I peer up at the ceiling again. I can't tell him this while looking into those damn forest eyes. "It was shortly after you cut off my hand." I feel his body go rigid beside mine. "I guess I wanted to see this world one last time before I died."

"*Died?!*" He jolts up and stares down at me, distraught.

"Calm down, Peter." I reach up to smooth the crease between his brows with my thumb. "I didn't die, did I?"

"But why would you…"

I sigh again and drop my hand, looking back to the ceiling despite him still sitting up and staring down at me. "Because I *wanted* to die. I was angry. Distressed. Ashamed. I lost my hand. To an insolent little brat at that."

When I peer at him again with a grin, he doesn't appear amused.

"The point is…I couldn't do it. I was a coward. You once said to die would be an awfully big adventure, but…I wasn't ready for that one."

"I said a lot of stupid shit back then."

Laughing, I grab his arm and pull him back down to me. "At least we agree on that." I bury my nose in his hair to inhale his earthy scent, then shut my eyes before saying what I need to say next. "I don't think I've ever loved anyone. I'm not even sure I can. Maybe neither of us can. Whatever the case, this is just another adventure too. I refuse to be a coward this time."

Peter's silent for a long while as he bites on his bottom lip, his fingertips lightly tracing some of the tattoos on my chest and abdomen.

"What's going on in that head of yours, Peter?"

He says nothing for another moment, then he reaches over me, grabs my hook, and pulls it closer to him. "I really *was* playing games, you know," he says quietly, thoughtfully as his thumb grazes over the smooth metal. "When I did this. But...I thought it was all pretend. I thought I imagined it all because I had no one else in Neverland. I always thought I was alone." He sniffs. "I thought it was all make-believe."

I gently remove my hook from his hand and place it beneath his chin so that I can lift his face until he's looking at me. There are deep pools in his green eyes. "I'm real, Little Star."

"I know that now."

"You were only a child. I don't hate you for it anymore."

Moving my hook, I gingerly brush the hair off his forehead before running it down the side of his face. His eyes flutter closed, and he shivers. I can't stop my smirk, nor the way my cock now stands at half mast.

"How could I?" I whisper, raising my head until our lips are a breath apart. "When you seem to like it so much?"

He opens his eyes, and they aren't as wet as before. Instead, they're full of unbridled, wanton lust. His face looks so pretty, full of longing, with my hook caressing down his cheek. His cock is already hard against my thigh.

Wrapping my hand around his throat, I close the distance between us, kissing him hard, my tongue clashing and tangling with his. Then I lick his lips before biting down on his bottom one, not as hard as last night as there's already a small bruise there, but it's enough to make him whimper and my dick twitch.

My cock is such a needy fucker. At least that hasn't changed.

I brush my lips against Peter's softly, then say, "I think you should move that gorgeous mouth of yours a bit south, Little Star."

His eyes go as wide as they can in his aroused state, his eyelids still heavy with desire. I snag the sheet with my hook and throw it off us. My hand moves to the top of his head, and I push him down until he's situated between my legs. He grips the base of my cock, licks the pre-cum from my head, and then his mouth is all around me. The soft warmth has me throwing my head back against the pillow.

"Fuck," I groan, tangling my fingers in his hair. "I love your fucking mouth."

Despite my hold on him, he has complete rein of his own movements. And they're perfect. *He*'s perfect. His hand moves around the base of my shaft, and his cheeks cave in as he sucks the rest of me eagerly.

Since he seems to have this under control, I reach for his other hand, bringing it to my face. I suck two fingers into my mouth. Peter moans around my cock. I swear my resulting thrust is involuntary as I try to chase that feeling. But Peter takes it so well.

After I make sure his fingers are nice and wet, I pop them out of my mouth. "Get yourself ready for me."

He does. He reaches behind him, and judging by the next vibration that rumbles through his throat, he uses both fingers. Good. I threw that damn bottle of lube across the room last night, and neither one of us is getting up to get it.

As he fucks himself on his fingers, he starts rutting into the mattress, and I imagine his erection rubbing against the sheets.

"You're so fucking needy for it," I say, unable to stop watching him.

My dick vibrates again with his moaning and whimpering, and if I'm not careful, I'll come down his throat before I get to fuck him.

And I'm not having that.

My hand goes back to his hair, and I yank him off my cock, repressing a groan at the loss of his mouth.

"Get up here."

He crawls up my body, straddling me, and immediately crashes his lips against mine. I think the control I allowed him to have went to his head because he delves his tongue into my mouth in a dominating kind of way, making me taste myself. Like he knows exactly what he's doing, and he loves every second of it.

I can't say I mind all that much either.

Again, I tug his hair to pull him back. I place my hook beneath his chin until he opens his eyes to look at me. "Are you going to fuck yourself on my cock, Little Star?" My voice is rough and deep even to my ears, deep and swimming with desire.

He nods, the movement sluggish.

"Such a good boy," I say as I move my hook down his neck to his chest, pressing the smooth, rounded part of it against him until he starts to raise himself. With my hand, I grip his hip. "Take your pleasure. Take whatever you want from me. It's yours."

Those are words I've never spoken a day in my life, and I don't plan on taking them back.

He stares at me, something swirling in his eyes. Then he places one hand on my chest and reaches behind with the other to take my length and guide it to his entrance. He lowers himself on it, slowly at first as he pants, moaning when my crown breaches the ring of tight muscle.

He pauses, his eyes screwed shut.

I decide not to punish him for it when he says with a strained voice, "You're too big. It hurts."

My length is still drenched with his saliva—I know that was a conscious effort on his part—and he's still dripping with mine from his fingers. But I can tell it's a little more than uncomfortable for him.

"Peter." I brush my hook against his cheek comfortingly until he opens his eyes. "You can take me, Little Star. You were made for me as much as you were for Neverland. Let me prove it to you."

His chest hitches, his eyes swim with emotion. He begins to move again, lowering himself more and more and more, slowly, until my cock is fully sheathed inside him. His moan is so fucking loud.

Then I realize that it's both of our moans blending together in the space around us.

I can't help but stare at him as he moves on my cock, doing exactly as I said and fucking himself on it. He's practically glowing. It's the most beautiful sight I've ever seen. I've been alive for hundreds of years, seen multiple worlds, traveled the seas under all sorts of skies, but this…this right here is what I want to remember the most vividly. This is the moment I never want to forget.

The longer I stare up at him, the more convinced I am that he actually *is* glowing. It could be an illusion, the sunlight casting a halo around his form like the silver lining of a cloud. Or it could be Neverland's star that I'm seeing, the magic that fuels it.

If he is the sun, then I think I'm the moon. Used to the darkness, but living for those moments where his light shines on me.

A sheen of sweat glistens on the smooth, sun-kissed skin of his heaving chest. His head rolls back on his shoulders, and an erotic moan escapes from his perfect, delicious lips. "Fuck, Hook. *Fuck*. You feel so fucking good."

"I told you you were made for me."

As I grip his left hip tighter, his hands on my chest move down to my abdomen, his nails digging into my flesh. I wince but finish with a satisfied groan.

"That's it, Peter. Take it. Take it all. I'm yours."

He starts moving faster, and I grab his length in my fist. Pre-cum drips onto my abdomen.

"Mark me, Little Star."

He drives himself twice more on my cock before he's coating my abdomen and I'm filling his insides. I barely get a glimpse of his mark before he collapses on top of me. Our chests heave in tandem with only sweat and cum between our skin.

And judging by the sting, there may be a bit of blood too.

Peter glances over at the clock on his nightstand, drops his forehead to my chest, and grumbles, "I'm late for work."

I chuckle, watching his hair bounce from the movement. "Don't go."

"I have to." He sits up, grabbing one of our towels from the foot of the bed.

He moves off me, and my spent cock slips from his hole. I hate the way the empty air hits it, already missing being inside him. As he cleans himself off, I stare down at my torso. Tiny beads of blood dot the angry red marks he left.

"You made me bleed."

Peter looks down and shrugs. "I think you owe me more blood than that."

I smirk as my eyes go to the scar across his chest. "I'm not complaining. Well, except for the fact that you're leaving."

He moves to sit on the edge of the bed, his back to me. "I'm quitting today."

Sitting upright, I stare at a trickle of sweat as it cascades down the curve of his spine. "What?"

"We're going back to Neverland." He peers over his shoulder at me. "Tonight."

26

PAN

"Are you sure?" Hook asks.

As much as I'd love to stay in this bed and let Hook fuck me six ways from Sunday, the anxiety of returning to Neverland is too great. Of facing my shadow again. Of facing the truth of my existence. Of facing Hook's feelings for me in that place. I have to rip it off like a Band-Aid.

And then decide if I'm even going to stay.

Fuck. How did everything get so messy?

Standing off the bed, I twist around and look down at the state of Hook's chest and stomach.

Yeah, messy indeed.

Suppressing a grin, I nod. "Yeah, I'm sure. But right now, I need a shower." I backstep toward the bedroom door, no longer holding back my grin. "Would you care to join me?"

Hook's eyes darken. "That's not even a question."

When he swings his legs over the side of the bed and

stands on his feet, he groans. I can tell it's due to all of our extracurricular activities in the past few hours, possibly the sting from my scratches on his torso, but…I can't help myself.

"You need help, old man?"

His eyes snap to mine, darkening further as his expression turns into a scowl. "What the fuck did you just say?"

Adrenaline pumps through my system as though it was shot directly into my veins. I realize now that it's my favorite drug. I get a similar feeling when I'm flying, the higher the better, but there's something about the rush that Hook gives me. It's even more potent. The way he looks at me, the way he stands there, naked and confident and lethal. Covered in my cum and his blood.

When he takes a step forward, I bolt, turning and running through the open door into the hallway. I don't get far. Then again, I didn't expect to.

Hook's arm snakes around my waist, pulling my back flush against his chest. I struggle halfheartedly because I'm not ready for the adrenaline to go away, the high to vanish.

But when he pushes me against the wall, I give up, realizing how heavily I'm breathing. Hook's left arm stays around me, the point of his hook pressed into my side, and his right hand comes up to wrap around my throat. He turns my face to the side, then bites down on my neck, wrenching a strangled cry out of me.

"Another game, Little Star?" his rough voice whispers in my ear, making the hairs on the back of my neck stand. "Do you like it when I chase you?"

I whimper, only able to nod.

He presses his body harder against mine. I feel his soft cock twitch against my arse. "Careful, Peter. I may just fuck you again, right now against this wall. I'd fuck you so hard you wouldn't be able to sit down for a week."

My own dick attempts to rally at his words. "Just because I called you old?"

"No. Because you'd love it."

And then the heat of him is gone.

So is the support he offered me. When that's gone too, I realize how weak my knees are. Before I'm able to collapse from my own shaky weight, Hook's there to catch me, his deep, wicked chuckle in my ear.

"Come on, Little Star. Time to clean up."

He helps me to the shower where we wash each other off. Even as I use a soapy washcloth to clean his chest of blood, sweat, and cum, he doesn't flinch or make a noise. He simply stares at me while I work.

When his hook comes up and gently brushes the wet hair off my forehead, I sigh and finally meet his gaze. "You're distracting me."

"You've been distracting me since I got here."

Yeah, I'm never getting out of this apartment if he keeps this shit up.

After that, I hurry to finish cleaning myself so that I can escape the shower, trying to avoid looking at Hook the rest of the time. Of course, I fail more often than not, but I still manage to finish before him. I'm out of the shower, dried off, and dressed in a fresh pair of jeans, a long-sleeved army green shirt, and Converse by the time Hook is exiting the bathroom in nothing but a towel.

Holy fuck.

Beads of shimmering water roll down the tattooed valleys and ridges of his abdomen, and I follow their path with my eyes until they get to the edge of the towel wrapped around his waist. When my gaze snaps back to his, his eyes are less ice-blue and more flame-blue. My face, my entire body, burns when I realize I've been caught. He stares at me with a wicked smirk. And still, all I want to do is run my fingers through the wavy, wet hair that frames his face and drips more water onto his shoulders that threaten to continue the vicious cycle.

Keep it in your pants, Peter.

I was just in the shower with him. How can he have this effect on me every time I see him, even if it's been mere minutes?

I don't think I'll ever get used to how fucking beautiful he is.

He was always just a pirate to me. A make-believe pirate, part of my imagination, someone to play the role of the villain in my story.

Now? He's the most ravishing pirate I've ever laid my eyes on.

"Meet me tonight?" I ask as we stand in the hallway, a few feet apart.

"You're not coming back here?"

I glance around, peer over my shoulder into the bedroom, then to my right into the living room. With a sigh, I shake my head. "No. It's better if I just leave this place behind."

Is that because it'll make it easier if I choose to come back or because I'm already prepared to leave this life behind and return to Neverland? Either way, I realize now that it won't be an easy choice no matter what I decide to do. I think coming back here before tonight would only make that choice harder.

"But feel free to stay as long as you like," I say as I move through the hallway into the living room. I can hear Hook's steps following me. "I'll be at the school for a little bit, and then I want to say goodbye to Wendy. So let's say around dusk? Meet me on the beach by the Coastline Cafe."

Before I reach the front door—saying nothing of the bag of takeout food that's still there, old and forgotten—Hook grabs my arm, spins me around, and his lips collide with mine. At first, it's deep and brutal and intense, just like him. But then it turns softer, his hand cradling the back of my head.

By the time he releases me, I'm breathing heavily and seeing stars.

"What was that for?"

He rests his forehead against mine, his chest heaving as much as mine is. "Because I think I'm more enamored by you than you are of me."

I don't know when he started acting so vulnerable around me, but I think he's wrong.

He smiles, then takes a step back. Without warning, the smile falls and a frown creases his face. "Are you sure I shouldn't go with you? You know, in case...your shadow..."

"No." I shake my head with conviction. "I refuse to be afraid of it. I'll see you tonight."

Then I'm out the door before he can stop me again.

TRUTHFULLY, I'M STILL fucking terrified of my shadow. The only reason I'm not locked in my bedroom, cowering and curled up beneath my sheets, is because of Hook. Because he took care of me, because he distracted me and helped me forget, even if only for the night. What happened last night shook me more than I care to admit. Hook saw it.

But I won't let him see that I'm still afraid.

I'm the only one who can save Neverland, who can stop my shadow. I don't have the luxury of tucking my tail between my legs and running away.

Besides not wanting Hook to know how scared I am, I didn't want him coming with me to the school because I want to say goodbye to Simon. And, well...last time I had a conversation with Simon with Hook around, Simon nearly became the captain's next catch. He was that close, wouldn't have even needed bait on the hook.

Now that I think about it, Simon may not even care that I'm leaving.

But he's still my friend, so I have to try.

Leaving the main office, I head to the music hall. I didn't quit like I told Hook I was going to. Just in case I do decide to come back, I don't want to come back jobless. Instead, I let them know that I had a family emergency that I need to leave town for.

Technically, it's not much of a lie.

Neverland is my home, and the mermaids and the fairies and the other native creatures were all born from Neverland just as I was. They're my family. And I *am* leaving town. They don't need to know that it's a little further than that and that I'm actually leaving the *planet*.

Opening the door to the music hall, I see a few students milling about. There's not a class going on right now, so I ask one of them if they've seen Simon. The young woman points to one of the practice rooms.

I take a seat in an empty chair to wait, my legs bouncing anxiously.

When the door to the practice room opens, a student exits with their clarinet in hand. Next comes Simon. He only gets a few steps before his gaze locks on mine. His body immediately stiffens, and I don't blame him for it. His eyes move around the room. I'd call it paranoia, but again…I don't blame him.

I stand, and we slowly approach each other.

"It's just me," I assure him. "I'm really, really fucking sorry about the other day."

He nods, lips pursed. "You were late, so I had to take a couple of your practice spots."

"I'm sorry." I can tell he's still upset about the concert, so I get right to the point. "You're probably going to have to take a few more. I'm leaving tonight. Family emergency back in London. I'm not sure when I'll be back."

His face falls. "Shit. I'm sorry, Peter." He shifts on his feet for a moment, clearly awkward and uncomfortable. His mouth opens once, closes, then opens again. "Look...you don't, like...need help, do you? You're not in some kind of toxic relationship, right?"

I almost laugh, but I stop myself.

Toxic? Probably.

Okay, undoubtedly.

Everything I could imagine ever wanting? Absolutely.

"I'm fine, Simon. I swear."

He still looks uncertain, but he eventually nods and lets it go.

"If I don't see you again," I say, offering my hand, "I just wanna say good luck at USC."

Simon shakes my hand and finally smiles. He gives me a quick, skittish kind of hug that makes me chuckle. "Thanks, Peter. Good luck to you too."

Before heading over to Wendy's, I stop by my favorite Mediterranean restaurant for lunch. It's the same place Hook got that takeout food from last night. I have no idea how he knew, but when I saw the bag this morning, I felt so incredibly light, like my feet were going to leave the ground. The hum of my magic was stronger, louder than it's been in fourteen years.

At least I'm pretty sure now that I'll be able to fly when it's time.

I show up to Wendy's in the early afternoon and knock on her front door.

She opens it with a blanket around her shoulders like a shawl, her hair a little wild, wearing extremely wrinkled pajamas. More wrinkled than usual.

Laughing, I enter the house when she opens the door wider for me. "Afternoon nap?"

She closes the door, nodding while she yawns.

"Oh, to be a writer."

Wendy spins around with the blanket stretched wide like wings, showing off her mismatched pajamas—a blue and pink striped T-shirt and white pants with little...*Christmas trees* on them. It's April. She has no makeup on and is wearing fluffy gray socks.

"Glamorous, isn't it?"

Laughing again, I head into the kitchen. "I'll make you some coffee."

When I get back to the living room with two mugs full of steaming coffee with cream and sugar, Wendy is curled on the couch, her blanket enveloping her, making her look like a burrito. She must be exhausted after working her arse off to meet her deadline. Her hand peeks out to grab her coffee, and I sit down beside her.

Like a Band-Aid, I remind myself.

"Hook and I are going back to Neverland tonight."

My words interrupt her tentative sip, and hot coffee spills down her chin. She winces and curses as she wipes it off with her blanket.

Shit. Maybe I should've led with that before giving her the coffee.

"Sorry," I mumble.

She looks at me, a deep crease between her brows and a frown on her lips. "You're going back *tonight*?"

I nod. "I don't think it can wait. My shadow attacked me last night." Before she can get worked up, I add quickly, "I'm fine. Hook was there. He saved me."

Her eyes practically bug out of her head. "Wow. Captain Hook saving Peter Pan's life. I don't think I'll ever get used to that."

"I don't think I ever will either," I confess.

We drink our coffee, then decide to make one last trip to Coastline where we drink *more* coffee. We sit inside for half an hour and talk about Jeremiah and the upcoming wedding. When we finish our drinks, we head out to the beach.

My stomach twists knowing I'll be leaving this world from right here in a few hours, but then it settles a little when I remember that I'm leaving with Hook.

I won't be alone.

We stroll along the beach, both of us holding our shoes in our hands as we walk barefoot through the sand toward our spot. We talk and talk and talk, more than we have in a long time. It's so nice. I'm going to miss this.

But then she brings up Hook and wants to talk about *us*, and I blush for the entire very short conversation before I quickly change the subject.

I don't tell her that I'm simultaneously scared of loving Hook and not being capable of loving him.

We climb onto the rocks and sit in our spot, looking out at the ocean and watching as the waves roll in, the surf foaming below against the bottom of the crag. The sun is still pretty high in the sky. It's warm, kissing our skin as we reminisce about our days in Neverland together. Including memories of Tinker Bell. I'm thankful for them, that I have those memories back and that I'll always have them. It's still difficult to talk about her, but it's a little easier than it was. Happy memories help.

"I think that's what I miss most about Neverland." Wendy's face glows beneath the sun as she stares out into the glittering ocean. "The fairies. They were so beautiful. Even though Tinker Bell kept trying to get me killed."

Since she's able to laugh about it, I join her.

"Tink was a menace," I admit, still grinning.

"But you loved her." Wendy turns her face to stare at me as though she knows my secret. And I think she might.

My heart patters in my chest at that word. That one word. But it's so much more than a word, isn't it? If I didn't love Tinker Bell, then how could her death have affected me so strongly to make me leave Neverland? My *home*, a place that's more than just a part of me. How could I have felt her loss even when I didn't remember her?

"I think I did," I finally whisper. "And if I did, then I love you too."

She smiles, and I swear it's knowing.

The afternoon turns into evening, and we agree to hang out the last couple of hours back at her place before I have to meet Hook. I have to take her back anyway since we brought my moped. She let slip that she wanted one more ride on it—she's never tried to drive it herself—and then turned a rosy shade of pink. I knew Wendy secretly liked Lily.

We get back to her house, have a couple cups of mint sage tea, and talk even more.

After having so much fun hanging out with Wendy most of the day, I fail to realize how much time has passed. The color of the light coming in through the windows has changed from a daytime white to a glowing, waning sunset orange.

"I should probably get going," I finally tell her, looking at her with a cross between a smile and a frown.

She frowns too and asks the question I know she's been dreading. "Will you come back?"

Sighing, I shake my head. "I don't know. If I survive," I add, attempting a grin to lighten the mood my words bring, "I'll for sure be here for your wedding. I wouldn't miss that for the world. *Any* world."

A small smile crosses her face briefly.

"Come here." I open my arms, and she launches from one end of the couch to the other to hug me. I hold her tight as she buries her face in the crook of my neck. I kiss the top of her head.

"I'm going to miss you, Peter Pan," she whispers.

"I'm going to miss you too, Wendy Darling."

I give her instructions for my things in case I don't ever return. She almost refuses to hear it, but when I tell her to sell everything in my apartment and use the money for her honeymoon, she perks up a little.

Of course, she does so jokingly.

At least...I think she does.

After I give her one last hug, I leave. I ordered an Uber since I decided to leave Lily at Wendy's house. I know she'll take care of the moped in case I return. She can sell it if I don't.

As I'm on my way to meet Hook, the sun slowly sets and paints the sky in pinks and golds. My stomach flutters. I realize it may be butterflies.

I know I want to come back here one day, even if it's only to visit Wendy and see her get married.

But maybe I could be happy in Neverland.

27

HOOK

Eddies of gray smoke from my cigarette, thick and acrid and swirling, rise into the air against the backdrop of the beach at sunset. It's my last one. Once back in Neverland, it's back to the pipe.

The waves of the ocean crash against the shore, and I close my eyes for a brief moment to enjoy the sound of the surf. It reminds me of Neverland and how ready I am to get back.

Opening my eyes, I flick the ash of my cigarette onto the sand. My hair is tied at the nape of my neck so the beach breeze doesn't blow it around my face. On my way here, I stopped by my motel room to change into clean clothes. Jeans, gray T-shirt, leather jacket. I rather like this jacket. Maybe I'll wear it in Neverland sometimes.

I also have another jacket draped over my left arm, one I found in Peter's closet. It's a black parka, and the images I conjured of Peter wearing it when I found it *definitely* had no effect on me whatsoever.

Okay, fine.

I made myself come in his bed.

I take a deep drag of smoke at the memory of having to do the work myself and not having the feel of him to get me off. Fuck, it pissed me off.

But now I'm here, standing on the beach waiting for him. I calm down a little at the thought. I may have had to go most of the day without him by my side—something I've become annoyingly attached to over the weekend—but at least I know he'll be here.

Well, I *hope* he'll be here.

He could've easily told me to meet him here at dusk to give himself the day to leave town and get a decent head start. With the things he was saying last night, I'd be lying if the thought hadn't occurred to me. Gutted me. But I'm here, trusting him. Trusting that he'll show up to take us both to Neverland.

He was scared last night. More than scared. He was so terrified I feared his heart might give out on him. This morning, he hid it better, but I could tell he was still afraid. I wouldn't blame him if he decided to run. I could handle Peter running from his shadow.

But, fuck…I couldn't handle him running from *me*.

I really have been on edge all day.

If he shows up, if he takes us back to Neverland, all this tension wound inside me may actually loosen. Because right now, as the last rays of the sun are slowly sinking beyond the horizon, the heavens darkening with its descent, I feel like I can't breathe.

Dusk. Peter said dusk.

He's still not here.

The line of gold between the blue of the ocean and the blue of the sky shrinks with each blink of my eyes. My heart is like a galloping horse inside my chest.

I take the last hit of my cigarette and stomp it out beneath my foot.

The two blues of the horizon meet, bleeding together, the last sign of the sun gone as dusk turns to night.

"Sorry!"

Peter's voice. Hurried steps in the sand behind me.

My eyes close. My shoulders slump. I can finally breathe.

"Here, try this."

I open my eyes and look at Peter who's standing beside me now. He's holding out a drink in his hand and breathing heavily. He rushed across the beach to reach me. My heart relaxes along with the rest of my body.

"Are you okay?" he asks, brows pulled together.

Clearing my throat, I take the drink from him to avoid answering his question. It's cold, ice clinking together as condensation drips down the plastic cup. I take a sip from the straw. The initial flavor is a momentary shock to my tongue, causing me to grimace, but then I enjoy the taste.

"What is it?"

"A mint iced coffee with pistachio milk," he answers as if those words strung together is the most normal thing ever. He bounces on the balls of his feet. "It's from the cafe. I wanted one last one before we left."

He's twitchy, like he's already had a few *last ones*, but I don't mention it.

"It's not bad." I hand it back to him, and he takes a drink. I stare at his lips as he sucks from the straw. Only when I'm able to force my gaze away do I hold up the jacket that's still hanging over my arm. "I brought this for you. You may need it since Neverland is currently experiencing an ice age."

He looks from the jacket to me and smiles. "You know, I don't think I'd get cold in Neverland, what with my magic and everything."

"Oh." I drop my arm.

"But," he starts quickly, "who knows. Maybe I will need it. There's a chance my magic may need to recharge once we're there."

I don't know if he's just trying to make me feel like I'm not totally useless, but I appreciate it either way. He takes the jacket from me. After finishing off his drink, he jogs over to the nearest trash bin, throws it away, then rejoins me. He throws the black parka over his shoulders and slips his arms through the sleeves.

"So you ready?" he asks as he zips up the jacket.

At least, I think that's what he said.

I was right. He looks fucking breathtaking in black.

Green has always suited him, sure, but my black heart has a thing for black. And the way it contrasts with his hair and eyes, making the strands appear a little redder and his irises a little greener, has me about ready to rip the jacket off of him instead.

Or maybe fuck him while he wears it.

Peter clears his throat, and I'm jerked back to reality.

"Careful, Captain," he drawls with a grin. "You're looking at me like I was looking at you this morning."

An involuntary grunt escapes my throat, and I have to reach down to rearrange my erection straining against the zipper of my jeans. "Fuck. You cannot call me that right now."

A mischievous glint sparkles in his eyes. "Oh, there's a nifty little trick. *Captain.*"

I glare at him, lean forward, and growl inches from his face, "You better be careful before you get sand in places you really don't want it."

Peter laughs. The sound helps calm me.

Me. Not my needy cock that wants to be inside his smiling mouth.

My hand goes to the nape of his neck. I grip hard and smash my lips against his, swallowing the last of his laugh. It turns into a moan in my mouth, and I swallow that too. Relentlessly. I don't let him go until he whines from the lack of oxygen.

We break apart, panting.

"Are you ready *now*, Captain?"

That glimmer in his eyes only grows more luminous when I scowl at him. "You're really trying to test me, aren't you, Peter Pan? If you haven't figured it out by now, I don't have much restraint. Especially when it comes to you."

He smiles sincerely, and after a moment, the sexual tension abates. A little.

Peter holds his hand out. "Let's go home."

Something in my heart skips, but it's not from the idea of finally returning to Neverland.

It's going home with Peter Pan.

Taking his hand, all I can do is nod because I can't find my words.

He squeezes my hand, smiles at me as he stands beside me, and says, "I hope I can still do this. Think happy thoughts."

I return his smile. "You're the only happy thought I need."

Peter's chest hitches. There's a wetness that's pooled within his eyes, but behind that, they shine brighter than I've ever seen. He moves back in front of me to wrap his arms around me. It's a tight hug, and I'm briefly stupefied. Then I return his embrace. He kisses me on the jaw, then looks at me with those bright, brilliant, scintillating eyes.

He really is my Little Star. I *know* he can do this.

Clearing his throat, he steps back into place. He takes a deep breath. "Ready?"

I repeat his earlier words. "Let's go home."

We smile at each other.

"Don't let go," he says.

"Never."

Peter stares up at the darkening sky, the deep blue turning blacker. We stand there in silence. I don't rush him. I know he's having to work up the courage or the will or the magic. Either way, I wait there with him until he's ready.

Stars begin to wink into existence, and the moon shines radiantly over the water. The golden ripples that the sun had cast over the ocean earlier have been replaced by silver.

Several minutes later, Peter speaks again. "I'm sorry if this doesn't work."

"It'll work. I have faith in you."

"I don't even have the star to guide the way."

"You don't need it. You *are* the star. You know the way."

A few minutes later, we're lifted into the air by Peter Pan's magic.

And we're going home.

THE TRIP TO NEVERLAND is the same as when I left. A tunnel of stars. A moment of breathlessness. Instead of a burst of yellow at the end of the tunnel, it's dreary and gray. Snow falls on our backs as soon as we've entered the atmosphere over the island. The cold bites into my bones.

"Fuck."

I glance over at Peter at the sound of his voice. Anguish is etched all over his face as he looks down at the state of his home. How cold and dark it is. How the shadow has claimed over half the island, thrown it into absolute blackness.

When I see his eyes glass over, I say, "We're going to save it, Peter."

He simply nods, then dives us down, down, down.

The dive makes me sick. My stomach is in my feet.

As soon as we're leveled out, everything settles where it's meant to be.

Peter flies us toward the opposite edge of the island from where the shadow has taken over. We approach the treeline along the beach not too far from where the Jolly Roger is docked.

Goddamn, I missed my ship.

We land in the snow. It's a soft landing, our feet crunching into the white powder blanketing the once sandy beach. I have to admit that I missed the cold and the overcast skies. I'm not quite ready to see the heat and the blinding sun return, but considering the difference means whether Neverland lives or dies, I'll grin and bear it.

Peter lets go of my hand and walks away from me toward the shore where the snow meets ice. He stares out at the frozen cove, and by the slump of his shoulders, I can tell he's brooding.

I don't want him to brood.

So I stalk off in the opposite direction, making sure my crunching through the snow is loud enough to attract his attention.

"Hook?"

I don't stop. I keep marching toward the tree line. I'm halfway there when I hear him following after me.

"Hook! Where are you going?"

I'm at the first tree, then I'm crossing into the thick of the frozen forest. It's even darker here. Snow drifts down from where it's been caught in the leaves of the canopy. My steps turn louder as twigs snap beneath the snow.

Then I stop behind a tree.

"Hook?"

Only when I hear him on the other side do I round the trunk, put my palm flat against his chest, and push him against the tree. I lean into him, lifting my hook to place it beneath his chin.

"So what did we decide, Peter Pan? Back to enemies?"

His eyes are wide, glossing over again. I recognize the look in them. Fear. And something deeper than disappointment, like maybe I just stabbed my hook into his heart and twisted. His bottom lip trembles.

Shit.

I can practically hear the thoughts racing through his head, loud and clear.

"Shh," I sooth, moving my hook to brush the hair off his forehead. "It's me, Little Star. It's still me."

He takes a shuddering breath, his body relaxing between me and the tree. "I can't be your enemy right now, Hook. I need you. I need you to help me save Neverland."

"We'll save it," I assure him, hating that he's too afraid or too distraught to play the game. I brush my lips against his. "I'm sorry I scared you."

"I just thought—"

"I know what you thought." I hold his gaze, stare so deep into his eyes I fear I may fall into them. "But Neverland will *never* have that kind of hold over me. It will never be able to dictate how I feel about you. If it does, then I'd no longer be me."

He sniffs, then nods.

I kiss him softly. His lips creep into a grin against mine.

"For the record, I'm not scared of you, Captain Hook."

I pull back, arching a brow. "Oh, really? Are you sure that's wise?"

He smiles, but then it falters, then drops completely. He swallows, our gazes never breaking. "I *am* scared though. I lied when I said I wasn't afraid of my shadow. I'm afraid of going back to that place. To the dark and the cold. Being trapped there forever. Alone."

"And here I thought Peter Pan wasn't afraid of anything."

"I'm all grown up now. I was a stupid child back then, not brave."

"You don't have to be fearless, Little Star," I whisper as I gently skim my hook down the side of his face, a breath between our lips. "But I promise you that you *are* brave. You can be both brave and afraid. Because one cannot exist without the other."

Peter's eyelids flutter closed, and he sucks his bottom lip between his teeth, his body reacting to how close we are.

I don't want him to be afraid. I want to help him, even if all I can do is offer a momentary distraction.

My hook grazes the side of his neck as my hand goes to the erection that's starting to strain against his jeans. He instinctively bucks against my palm as I stroke him through the fabric.

"We should probably take care of my shadow first," he says in between moans.

"I'd rather take care of you first."

He opens his mouth, but his protest dies on my lips.

28

PAN

"I'd rather take care of you first."

Well, I can't argue with that.

Okay, I could, and I may have tried. But then Hook kissed me and is currently stealing all the air from my lungs, the thief he is.

Not that I'm complaining.

I know what he's doing, trying to distract me. Because I'm absolutely fucking gutted after seeing Neverland in the state it's in. It's so cold and dark, and I know my shadow wants to turn it into a place like he sent me last night.

Last night.

It feels like it was forever ago.

It feels like ages since Hook saved me, comforted me, claimed me. It's as though I can't remember a time that existed before I belonged to him and he belonged to me. It may not have been that long, but when you live as long as I have, as long as *we* have, time doesn't exactly work in a standard manner. A long time can pass in the blink of an eye, and a very short time can feel as though it stretches on and on and on.

I think that's how we got here as quickly as we did.

And I never want this time with Hook to end.

If I stay, it doesn't have to.

If Hook and I save Neverland, we could have this forever. This heat, this feeling of his lips on mine, this uncontrollable desire to let Hook fill that missing piece of me so I can feel whole. This doesn't have to end.

Neverland is a world without end.

Hook's hand tugs on my hair, and his husky voice is in my ear. "Stop fucking thinking."

"S-sorry."

"Stay with me, Little Star," he says as his hand leaves my hair and goes back to my jeans, unzipping them and taking my length into his large, warm palm.

I moan against his lips as he strokes me, too gently. I need more.

"Please, Hook." My warm breath blooms between our mouths as I plead with him. "Be my distraction. I don't want to think about anything but you. I don't want to feel anything but you. Please. *Fuck...*"

My begging spurred him on as he steadily stroked harder, faster, while I spoke. My head falls back against the tree trunk, my mouth open in a silent cry.

Then his hand is gone, and he's pulling my jeans and boxer briefs down to my ankles. I lift one of my feet so I can step out of them. Once he's back up, pressing me against the tree, I shiver. But it's not because of the cold. The cold bites into my skin, but it doesn't bother me. Not like it probably bothers him.

It's the look he's giving me. Like he's about to rip me apart, devour me, ruin me.

"Wrap your legs around my waist," he commands.

I bite my lip. Grin. "Aye, *Captain.*"

His eyes darken even more. He growls.

I don't get the chance to obey him by myself because before I can, he's lifting me in the air and my legs are wrapping instinctively around his waist. My hands grab his biceps for leverage. I don't know when he unzipped his own jeans, but his erection is already pressing against my entrance.

"I'm warning you now," he snarls. "I'm not going to hold back."

"Good. I don't fucking want you to."

With a groan, he reaches between us, first smearing my pre-cum on his thumb, making me whimper desperately as I watch him. He lifts me a little more and adds it to his own, rubbing it all together as he coats the head of his dick with our mingling pre-cum. Then he spits into his hand and adds that.

We're gonna have to get this fucker some oil.

When he doesn't enter me right away, I look up, startled to see him staring straight into my face. His blue eyes appear even icier against the frozen backdrop.

He grins, showing off his canines. "You look so fucking hot in black."

The head of his cock breaches the ring of muscle, and we moan together while he thrusts gently until he's fully sheathed.

The initial sensation is pain, but it's soon followed by pleasure. I don't think I'll ever get used to his size.

Keeping one hand on his bicep, I bring the other up to his hair, untying the knot keeping it held back at the nape of his neck.

"And I love your fucking hair," I breathe as I run my fingers through it.

He kisses me again, fervently. His beard burns my face, but I relish the heat. The sparks between us seem to melt the cold away, and we become trapped in our own little bubble of heat and passion and longing.

Having to come up for air, I throw my head back against the tree, panting.

"You're still mine, aren't you, Little Star?" His lips brush my throat as he continues to fuck me. "Even though we're back in Neverland?"

It's less a question than it is a challenge, a reminder.

"Yes. Yes, I'm yours, Hook."

"Then look at me."

I do, and his lips crash against mine for a fast, rough kiss.

"You don't fucking belong to Neverland. You belong to me."

All I can do is nod and hum in agreement.

As he continues pounding into me, I feel confident enough in his hold on me to release his other bicep and grip my dick in my hand.

"Oh, fuck," I moan against his lips, then kiss him. "Hook." Kiss. "Please."

"Please what, Peter?"

I don't even get the chance to beg for release before he drives into me so deep that everything but the two of us fades away. I come into my hand as I cry out. Hook sneaks his tongue into my open mouth, kissing me as deeply as he's fucking me. My hand tightens in his hair, and he groans, grunting as he spills inside me.

Panting, he rests his forehead against mine. "Fuck," he says, voice raspy. "I love hearing you beg."

"I know." I smile lazily at him. "That's why I do it. Well, and because I like it too."

He smiles back, kisses me, then pulls out. I drop my legs from around him, a little unsteady on my feet at first like a newborn fawn. I lean over to wipe my hand in the snow, then pull my jeans back up.

Once we're both tucked back into our clothes, Hook pins me against the tree again. This time, he's gentle. He places his hook under my chin affectionately, his hand roaming the side of my body as he kisses me tenderly. It's gentle and warm, and I melt into it, allowing him to distract me for one last moment.

But eventually, it has to end.

We pull apart, Hook takes my hand, and we walk out of the forest back onto the snow-covered beach. The ice over the frozen cove in front of us stretches all the way out to sea through the narrow space between land. A ways off on our right sits the Jolly Roger. It's not rocking like I'm used to, anchored in place by the ice. The ship itself seems to be covered in a layer of frost, icicles hanging off its bow and its mast.

I look at Hook and catch him staring longingly at his ship. Grinning, I ask, "Am I going to have to compete with your ship if I stay?"

Realizing my mistake the second the words leave my mouth, I shut my eyes and grimace.

"*If?*"

Peeking one eye open, I see him scowling at me, his nostrils flaring. He rips his hand out of mine. I frown up at him, giving him my best puppy dog eyes.

It doesn't work.

"What the fuck is that supposed to mean, Peter?"

My face falls, and I sigh. I didn't mean to let him know this was something I had been contemplating. I didn't want to hurt him. I especially didn't want to talk about this before facing my shadow. I *need* him on my side. Something tells me

I won't win if he's not. I never thought I would need Captain Hook in this way—or in the other ways that I do—but I do. I really fucking do.

I hesitate, then say, "It just means that I hadn't decided if I was going to stay if we managed to get rid of the shadow. I wanted to wait and see..."

"See what?"

"If we're still the same," I answer honestly. I place my hands in the pockets of my parka, square my shoulders, take a deep breath. "If you still want me here. If I still want you. If Neverland respects my wishes and lets me be who I want to be."

He takes a step toward me, nearly closing the distance between us. "And who's that?"

The man who loves you.

I don't say that. I can't say that. Because what if Neverland doesn't allow it?

Instead, I say, "Someone with the freedom to *choose* who he wants to be."

Hook nods slowly, and I can tell he's working on accepting that this cryptic answer is all he's going to get right now. But I think he knows what it really means.

"Then...I hope Neverland gives that to you."

He doesn't say it, but I still hear the words he doesn't speak. He doesn't want me to leave.

Taking another deep breath, I step back, needing that distance between us before I let myself drown in him all over again.

"First thing's first though," I say. "We'll need a plan. I think I should go scout the island, see how far and deep my shadow runs. I should be safe in the air. My shadow may have all its magic here, but I've always been able to fly circles around it."

It's the truth. Another truth...I really fucking missed flying.

Honestly, I wasn't sure I was going to be able to. The fear and uncertainty had been there all day. But the longer I stood on that beach, holding onto Hook's hand, the louder the humming inside me grew, the stronger my magic felt. Then once I was in the air, I never wanted to come back down.

But the sight of Neverland was enough to make me.

However, since returning, I've felt a boost to my magic as well. I was worried that I would feel other things too—like Neverland's control over me. But I haven't.

If anything, I feel more like myself, more free.

"I should get to my ship," Hook says. "Let my crew know that I'm back, let them know what's going on."

I nod, but I hate the idea of us separating. Dread settles deep in my gut, and there's a pang in my chest.

Neverland is not the same.

It's dangerous.

Anything could happen.

"I'll fly you to your ship," I offer, relieved when he agrees.

"Just...give me a moment."

He stares pensively out at the Jolly Roger, and I wonder how he feels about being back here—aside from the obvious that he missed his ship. Snow flutters around us in little flurries as we stand there side by side.

Nearly two minutes pass before I break through the hush. "What are you thinking about?"

"The last fourteen years," he answers languidly, his eyes still on his ship. "I thought I was happy, but...I don't think I was." He says it like it's a revelation he never expected. "I think I was...*bored*." Turning his head just enough to look at me, he smiles. "Don't get me wrong. I'm bloody glad you left. I'm glad you grew up. *This* Peter Pan...well, turns out I don't want to kill *this* Peter Pan."

I can't help but grin and roll my eyes. "Glad to hear it."

He chuckles and looks back at the Jolly Roger. "But it's not only the shadow that made this place dreary and dull. It was your absence. The absence of what made this world fascinating, of what made this world what it is, what made it *Neverland.*"

My gaze remains fixed on him as he sighs, still deep in thought. I get the urge to reach over and smooth the crease between his brows.

"Or maybe I'm just thinking too hard." He shrugs, looking back at me with a grin. "Maybe I only missed the thrill of having someone to fight with."

My own grin turns into a smirk. "I'll fight with you all you like, Captain Hook."

He takes my hand, pulls me to him, and kisses me.

Relentlessly.

Once again, he steals my breath.

The pirate. The scoundrel. The thief.

My pirate. *My* scoundrel. *My* thief.

I tangle my hand in his wavy hair that's damp from the snow, knowing that I would let him steal anything from me if it meant he's mine.

The humming of my magic is so damn deafening that I wonder if he can hear it too.

When he breaks the kiss, we're both breathless.

"Take me to my ship, Peter Pan," he says, voice husky against my lips. "And then take your flight."

29

HOOK

Peter drops me off at my ship on the stern deck. It's the highest deck at the back of the ship above my captain's quarters that overlooks the quarterdeck and the main deck. None of my crew are up here, but a few of them on the lower decks see us land.

Staring at Peter for a moment, I don't want to let him leave, but I know he needs to understand what we're dealing with if we're going to fight this thing.

"I'll be back," he says, a small, sad smile on his face as my fingers slip from his.

"Be careful."

He flies away, and I watch him go.

It's such a surreal sight, so bizarre knowing that the boy I used to hate has been replaced by this beautiful man who makes my heart ache when he flies away from me. He's not wearing clothes made from the forest, instead flying in jeans and his black jacket. I can't explain why it's so tantalizing, the way he dips and dives in the air as the wind whips through his auburn hair.

"Captain, you've returned!"

I close my eyes, sigh, and gather myself before turning to face Smee. "Aye. Gather the men on the main deck."

"Aye, Captain."

As a red-faced Smee runs off, I turn back to where I last saw Peter. He's now just a dot above the canopy of the Neverland forest.

MANY OF MY CREW give me strange looks as I step up to the rail of the quarterdeck and peer down at them all on the lower one. I know that my clothes are odd to them, but I don't want to waste time changing. Not to mention I foolishly took my best frock coat with me to that other world and left it there.

All is not lost. I think I like this leather jacket better.

I spot Starkey among the men below, and I have to bite back a grimace. He was the only one of my men that I ever regularly engaged in any kind of sexual activities with, but that never meant we had any semblance of a romantic relationship. He's my first mate; I'm his captain. What we did together was purely carnal, physical. There were never any feelings attached.

At least not on my end.

The thought puts a sour taste in my mouth.

I like my first mate. I may be a ruthless bastard and the list of people in the universe I like may be brief, but I've never had the proclivity to be cruel to those people.

Well, not intentionally and not unless they deserved it.

Okay, so I can actually be pretty heartless.

But centuries is a long time to be on a ship with someone who's been your occasional casual lay. And your friend. Ending that part of our relationship isn't exactly going to have me walking on air.

"I found Peter Pan and brought him back to Neverland," I tell my crew when I realize they've been staring at me expectantly.

"Is he going to help us?" one of the men asks.

"He's going to do whatever he can." My voice carries over the ship in the frigid air. "I'm going to help him get rid of this shadow. I don't know what the plan is yet, but I want you men to be ready in case we need you. Understood?"

They answer in unison. "Aye, aye, Captain!"

I head down the stairs from the quarterdeck to the main deck. Starkey is already moving through the crew, wearing his usual royal blue tunic, making his way toward me. I shouldn't be surprised.

"My cabin, Starkey."

He follows me to the steps leading below deck. We take them down, and I open the door to my quarters.

Something inside of me clicks into place the moment I step inside, like a missing puzzle piece of my heart. This is my home. And nothing has changed. Not that I would've expected it to since I was only gone a few weeks, but it felt so much longer.

I take in the room, my glass cabinets of knickknacks and treasures, my favorite antique floor globe depicting the world I just returned from, my desk covered in maps and doubloons. My bed tucked in the corner. I stare at the latter as an image conjures itself in my mind. Peter Pan and I both on top of it, bodies slick with sweat, my aching, throbbing cock buried deep inside him as he moans my name.

"Captain?" Starkey asks in his deep timbre.

"Shut the door."

I tear my gaze away from the bed, but the visual lingers. I want that. I want Peter Pan in my bed. I want to share my home with him.

Fuck, I hope he chooses to stay.

I feel a presence at my back, Starkey's warm breath on the back of my neck. Once upon a time, his breath would have done something to me. But now, I ignore it and step away in the same second that his hand touches my shoulder.

"Care for a drink?" I ask as I walk over to my small rum bar.

I'm definitely going to need a drink for this.

"Are you sure you want a drink?" Starkey follows me over to the bar and watches as I pour rum into two glasses. "I thought maybe..."

"You thought what?"

I'm grateful to hear my usual authoritative and assertive captain voice come out of my mouth. I had truly feared that my time in the other world, my time with Peter, had softened me. And as a captain of a ship, I can't afford for that to be the case. Even if I do have to give Starkey news he won't want to hear, even if it hurts him, even if I do consider him a friend as much as a member of my crew. As his captain, I can't compromise my status.

"I thought you may be tense, Captain," he says, speaking with a sultry tone. Neither the tone nor what he calls me does anything for me anymore. "I thought you may need me. Maybe on my knees?"

Handing him the glass of rum, I say simply, "I don't."

"Oh." He doesn't look hurt, only surprised. He drops the tone. "Even after dealing with Peter Pan?"

"Actually—"

The words I was planning on saying were going to come out easier than I expected, but I don't get the chance to speak before the large window looking out of the stern of the ship opens and Peter Pan flies inside. He does a flip in the air—I'm impressed that he can still do that even as a grown-up—and lands directly next to me on the other side of the bar from Starkey.

Both Starkey and I stare at him with wide eyes and slack jaws.

He throws an arm casually around my shoulders, and my body instantly heats.

"Starkey, right?" Peter smirks at my first mate.

It's familiar. Dazzling. Cocky, with all his boyish charm.

Peter Pan is back in his element.

"It's been a while," he continues with a nod even while Starkey remains shellshocked. "I'm not sure how to tell you this, mate, but Captain Hook will no longer be requiring your...*services*."

Fuck. He must have been listening at the window before flying inside.

I stare at him for several seconds. This is clearly his Peter Pan schtick. Beneath it? He's jealous. I can tell by the barely perceptible tension in his jaw, the way his arm drapes possessively over my shoulders.

It warms my heart. And makes my cock twitch.

I'm not surprised at the latter, but...my heart...is the thing even still black?

Starkey's eyes ping-pong between us. A grin slowly creeps onto his face as he places his drink on the bar, still full. "Seriously? You two?"

"Is there a problem, Mr. Starkey?" I snap, forcefully, and maybe a little aggressive.

"No." He shakes his head and speaks adamantly. "Of

course not, Captain. Just surprised is all. You're my Captain and my closest friend. I'll always respect you."

I'm positive Peter can feel my shoulders relax beneath the weight of his arm. The last thing I wanted to deal with was a jealous first mate.

"Ready your men, Starkey."

"Aye, Captain."

The moment my first mate is gone and the door is closed, Peter's arm drops from around my shoulders. My heart gives a stutter as he takes one step away from me, like it wants to follow him.

"You didn't tell me about Starkey." His tone is indecipherable, his back to me.

"Because it wasn't important."

He picks up Starkey's glass of rum and swallows the contents in one gulp. After placing it back on the bar, he turns to face me, his hands in the pockets of his jacket. His act has ended, and now he stands there, apprehensive. I sense his insecurity, and it guts me. I feel ashamed for causing it and angry that it's there at all.

"How long?" he asks, his voice small.

My nostrils flare with rage—not at him, but because he feels the need to even ask.

I close the space between us and grab him by the jaw. "It was *not* important," I repeat. "It was a matter of convenience. Can you imagine going untouched for hundreds of years?"

Instead of my words comforting him, they appear to have the opposite effect.

He frowns, his gaze flicking between my eyes and my chin. "And you can end something that lasted that long just like that? Like it meant nothing?"

"Peter." His name comes out soft, pained, pleading. I

move my hand from his jaw to the side of his face, gently brushing my thumb across his cheek. "Compared to what I feel for you, it *was* nothing. Some twisted part of me may like that you get jealous over me, but I give you my word. You are the *only* one I want to be with. If you'd like, I'll take you up on deck right now and claim you in front of my crew to prove it to you."

The muscles of his face work in an attempt to suppress a grin, but it doesn't work. He rolls his eyes. "You're crazy."

"For you."

That hint of a grin lingers briefly before vanishing completely, replaced by another frown. "How do I know you won't tire of me too after a few hundred years?"

"I can assure you that you'll tire of me far before I will of you. And I'm willing to bet that for me, that would take an eternity. Probably not even then." I lean my forehead against his, brushing my thumb against his cheek again. "As for how long it takes you, I'm willing to take the risk."

I kiss him, and for one terrible second, I'm afraid he won't kiss me back, afraid that I'm not worth the same risk. Afraid that he still might not decide to stay.

But then he does kiss me. His soft lips move against mine, warm and pliant. I slip my tongue into his mouth, and the moment it makes contact with his, all the blood rushes south. I pull back as though his tongue burned mine.

We have work to do, and as much as I'm sure we'd both love to distract ourselves again, we have a shadow to defeat.

While the heat abates and our breathing evens out, we stare at each other. There's no doubt in my mind that I want Peter Pan to be mine for all eternity. I want to ask him to stay, to stay in Neverland with me. But I don't.

Would I even want to stay if he leaves again?

That's a bridge I'm not ready to cross.

"So what's the plan, Little Star?" I ask, still close to him, unable to pull myself out of his orbit.

It appears he's having the same problem, his eyes glued to my lips. He licks his own, then rakes his teeth over his bottom lip.

"Um..."

I clear my throat, and his gaze snaps up to meet mine.

"I think I have a plan," he finally says. "But..."

"But what?"

"I don't know if I can do it," he admits. He sighs as he turns to the bar and helps himself to another drink. "It's going to take a lot of magic. Magic I'm not sure I have anymore."

Watching as he pours rum into the glass and throws it back, my eyes get stuck on his throat as he swallows. He's so beautiful, and I don't think that it's just because he's *made* of magic. But he's both. Both beautiful and full of magic.

He *is* magic.

I'm not worried.

"Believe in yourself, Peter." I pick up the bottle of rum and pour us each one more drink. "Because I believe in you. I always will."

There's a ghost of a smile on his face as he picks up his glass.

I hold mine and clink it against his. "To defeating this godforsaken shadow."

We drink.

I run the back of my hand over my mouth, then say, "Now tell me what to do."

My crew and I are scattered about in the snow-covered woods near the very edge of the shadow in the center of the island. From my spot behind a tree, I watch as Peter approaches the dividing line. A sword hangs in its scabbard at his waist, one of mine.

I hold my hand in the air, signaling my men to stay put for now.

My heart is pounding away like a storm in my chest, the tempest growing more insistent with every beat, more violent with every breath.

Other than that, everything is quiet, as though a dreadful hush has fallen over the island like a blanket. Snow continues to drift down steadily, swirling in little flurries in the air. My black hair, my black jacket, all of me is covered in icy flakes. I should be freezing, but the blood is pumping through my veins so fast, so erratic, that it keeps me warm. I think I even feel a bead of sweat roll down my back.

Peter is too damn close to the shadow. This is how my men and others have disappeared, vanished within the dark cloud living on the island with us. He raises a hand, palm toward the shadow, and I swear my heart stops.

But he doesn't get sucked into the black, doesn't fade.

In fact, he...*glows*.

The shadow extends like a wall in front of him, stretching across all of Neverland. In stark contrast to the blackest of black, Peter Pan is glowing like the sun.

But not quite as bright. His light flickers, dims, shines more brilliant. It's inconsistent, struggling to stay steady, to grow as bright as it needs to be. I hold my breath and start a silent chant.

I believe in you, Peter Pan.

It takes a strong burst of will to tear my gaze away from him so that I can scope things out.

Looking around, I see the faces of my men peeking out from behind other trees. I peer up, into the gray skies that I can see through the breaks in the green and white canopy. There's no sign of our nemesis, none other than his wall of black.

Returning my eyes to Peter, I'm nearly blinded by a flash of light that shoots out of him, like lightning. It's gone just as quick. He stands there, seeming unaware that it happened at all, his eyes closed, his lips moving.

I believe in you, Peter Pan, I repeat silently again.

As he continues to work, I'm feeling hopeful. Unfortunately, that hope vanishes in an instant.

The wall of shadow right above Peter appears to flutter like the sail of a ship, then morphs, stretches. Something attempts to come through. A form pushes against the veil as though it's made of fabric, then it breaks out in a wisp of cloud and flies through the air.

It's the form of a man, but he's shaded in, a silhouette.

The *shadow*.

It lands right behind him, but his eyes are still fucking *closed*.

"PETER!"

I don't hesitate. I bolt out from behind the tree and hurl myself forward like a cannonball, tearing through the snow to get to Peter.

But I'm too late.

The shadow has a sword in his hand, a blade that's as dark as *he* is, but I'm sure if he wills it to cut, it will. And when he swings it through the air and brings it down just as Peter turns around, my heart stops for the second time in the span of a minute.

Peter's reaching for his sword, but he's not fast enough. His other arm comes up, the only means to block the shadow's blade.

He screams.

And goes down.

I stop in my tracks as shock floods my system, my body paralyzed with it.

I yell his name again, and the shadow turns. I think it's facing me now, but it's difficult to tell because it doesn't have a face.

And then it does.

Peter's face.

My men come barreling out from the trees now amidst a cacophony of howls and war cries, brandishing their swords, ready to attack. They probably hesitated when I failed to give them a signal, but I had been too damn scared for Peter.

That fear turns my insides to ice, crystals forming in my veins when I see the snow beneath him turn red.

The shadow's attention has shifted to the rest of my crew, so I force my feet to move, feeling as though my brain is on manual as I give the instructions to one foot at a time. Halfway to Peter, it becomes a little easier. The easier it is, the faster I move. Until I'm barreling in his direction, collapsing beside him.

The snow has soaked up the blood to make it look like there's more than there actually is. When I inspect him, I find a long, nasty gash straight down his forearm and a smaller one on his forehead. It's dripping blood down the side of his face.

"Peter?" I press, scared to touch him.

He groans, but he doesn't move.

Fuck.

The noise of my men suddenly turns from battle cries and rallies to that of bloodcurdling shrieks. It has my head snapping up, finding a shocking, ghastly scene.

Out from the shadows extend tendrils of smoke, extensions of itself. They snake across the ground and around the trees, growing like vines. They latch onto the legs of my men, pulling them out from under them. The men scream as they're dragged through the snow toward the tenebrous wall.

All I can do is watch in absolute horror as every last one of my men disappears through the barrier into the blackness. The last thing I see of any of them is the blue of Starkey's tunic.

Pan's likeness stands in the middle of a cluster of trees, staring at me with dark gray eyes. His sword at his side. Challenging me.

I don't want to leave Peter, but I don't have much of a choice. If I don't do *something*, the shadow will take us both.

After checking to make sure Peter is still breathing, I slowly stand to my feet, my eyes now zeroed in on his shadow. I take my sword from its scabbard, swing it in the air. I'm fueled by rage as I run at him.

I'm mad at the shadow for taking over Neverland.

I'm angry that he took my crew.

I'm furious that he hurt Peter.

I bring my blade down, and it clashes with his above his head as he blocks it.

The shadow's imitation of Peter Pan is different here. Darker. Less solid. It really is like night and day.

And then something hits me.

Smirking, I lean my face forward an inch. "You can't destroy Peter Pan. You would destroy yourself along with him."

"Perhaps." His voice is nothing like Peter's now. It's deeper, rougher, with a bit of an echo. "But I can still destroy you."

A white hot pain shoots through me. I gasp. At first, the pain is everywhere without a source. My whole body is simply on fire, and then it's radiating through my stomach. When I look down, I see a second shadow blade piercing my abdomen.

The shadow cheated.

It fucking cheated.

I open my mouth, cough, try again. My voice doesn't sound like mine. Raspy, already dead. But I barely manage a strained, "Bad form."

I don't know what I was expecting death to feel like, but I don't think it was this.

I black out. The last thing I remember seeing is the shadow's sword protruding from my stomach before I'm lying on the cold snow. Blood from the wound is seeping, pouring into the frost. My vision swims with red.

I see Peter, several meters away. He's barely stirring. I try to speak his name, but no sound comes out.

As I lay there dying, I'm fraught with guilt.

Guilt for the things I've done.

Guilt for letting the shadow get so strong.

Guilt for not trying to stop it sooner.

Guilt for my lost men.

Most of all, guilt for letting Peter Pan down.

Neverland will die.

But not before me.

30

PAN

When I wake, all I know is pain. It beats like a living thing inside me, all around me. In my brain, in my bones. It feels like I got hit by a fucking freight train.

It's quiet. Why is it so quiet?

Except for a ringing in my ears, I hear nothing. The ringing grows louder and louder, drowning out the usual humming as I try to move. Everything is dark because I haven't opened my eyes. The ground is soft beneath me.

Snow.

Then it all comes rushing back.

The shadow. The sword. Hook screaming my name.

My eyes fly open. My vision is blurred like I'm looking at everything from underwater. There's a contrasting of black and white. Shadow and snow.

And red.

The snow beneath me is red. I raise my arm, and an

intense pain lances through the entire limb. I scream as I blink back tears. The sleeve of my jacket is torn, and the gash from my shadow's sword extends the length of my left forearm. It's deep. So deep that I swear I can see bone somewhere beneath all the blood.

As my scream fades into the darkness, I realize again how quiet it is. It makes me too aware of my own heartbeat.

Thump. Thump. Thump.

When I finally have the strength, I manage to sit up. I get even more dizzy than before, but then my vision slowly comes into focus. I take in the Cimmerian wall of darkness, then the snow-covered forest. I see no one around. No shadow. No Hook. No pirates.

Except…there's a lump in the snow some distance away. And…more red.

I squint my eyes. My head pounds.

A leather jacket.

Hook.

No.

I'm not sure how long it takes me to make it to two feet, but it feels like too long. And when I do, I don't get far. I manage a couple of steps before dropping back into the snow. I stumble my way forward between steps and crawls, desperate to reach Hook.

There's blood. So much blood.

His eyes are closed, and his face is as white as a ghost's.

I place my hand on his chest, hold my breath as I wait for the rise and fall.

It doesn't come.

I shake my head. "No, no, no, no."

I stare down into Hook's face, not breathing, trembling all over. My pain has become an afterthought. All I care about is Hook. All I want is for him to open his eyes.

"He said I couldn't destroy you."

The voice is right behind me, deep, grating, taunting. I don't turn around.

"Looks like he was wrong."

Tears track down my cheeks. My jeans are covered in bloody snow. I can't stop fucking shaking, and it has nothing to do with the cold. Everything inside me is being ripped to shreds as I stare down at Hook's lifeless body. I can't look away. Even as an agony so excruciating and visceral, worse than any physical pain I could ever endure, is tearing through me, slicing open my body and soul, taking everything I have.

I have nothing.

I'm a black hole.

All I want now is to curl up beside Hook, in that crook of his arm where I fit so perfectly. Close my eyes. Let it go.

I want to die with him.

"You both should've stayed in that world," my shadow says somewhere behind me. "He could've lived out his life with you."

Even if I thought my shadow was right, Hook would've died one day, but I wouldn't have. At least, I'm pretty sure I wouldn't have. I had magic there. I think I had my immortality too. I don't know when I would've stopped aging, but I'm pretty sure I would've had to watch Hook die and then live for the rest of eternity with everyone else I cared about dying around me, destined to be forever alone.

Of course, if I live through this, that will be my fate either way.

As though he can't get enough of hurting me, my shadow says, "As I'm sure you've already guessed, I killed Tinker Bell too."

I swallow thickly. I'm not surprised, but his words still cut me.

"You planned all of this," I say, my voice choked with misery. "You wanted me out of Neverland so you could unleash your darkness."

He doesn't confirm, but I know I'm right.

My shadow has taken too much from me. I won't let him take anything else. I won't let him take Neverland. Not without a fight.

Tears drip from my chin onto Hook's jacket. All I can do now is try to keep my promise to him.

Leaning over, I place a kiss on Hook's pale forehead. Against his icy skin, in a raspy whisper meant only for him, I say, "You are my happy thought, James Hook. Now and forever."

It takes everything in me to stand, to put any kind of distance between him and me. But I do it. I rise on shaky legs, tears still spilling over my cheeks as I slowly round on my shadow. He stands there like a reaper, an inauspicious black shape against pure white snow.

Rage like I've never felt before starts a fire somewhere within me. Instead of melting away the anguish and the hopelessness, it all begins to swirl together in a vortex of flames.

"If one of us dies, we both die." I'm reminding my shadow as much as I'm reminding myself. Because I *really* want to fucking kill him. "If we both die, Neverland dies with us."

"I'm aware. But I don't have to kill you to let my darkness consume you." He has two swords in his hands, one of them dripping with Hook's blood. The droplets of crimson soak into the snow below. "I'll just send you back into the darkness. I'm sure you remember that place. That's where you'll live out the rest of eternity."

Turns out, I'd rather die and take Neverland with me.

"And what of this darkness?" I ask. "Won't you just be damning yourself to the same fate?"

"*This* darkness is *mine*, not the prison that Neverland made for me. I'll thrive here."

"I don't fucking think so."

I draw my own sword from its scabbard. It doesn't matter that he has two and I only have one. I don't plan on fighting him.

Over the past few hours—though it feels like much longer than that—I've come to realize something. Or *feel* something may be more accurate. The magic inside of me growing more intense. Louder. Hotter. More powerful.

I used to believe that the only thing that fueled my magic was Neverland itself. That it simply existed in an unalterable, constant state.

Now I know better.

I stand here, consumed with an overwhelming amount of emotion, more than I have ever felt in my life.

Fury.

Sorrow.

Determination.

Love.

The humming inside of me is resounding, thrumming, roaring. Louder than ever before, vibrating my bones. It's a torrent, a whirlwind, an avalanche, a waterfall.

A fucking cataclysm.

And somewhere inside of me, it turns into the most powerful magic I've ever possessed, ever wielded. It scares me, and yet…it doesn't. I feel more assured, stronger, unwavering.

Light erupts all around me. *From* me. Through every vein, every bone, every sinew, every pore. Through my arm and through the sword. The blade directs the light. It bursts forth as I aim the sword at my shadow, the light brighter, more luminescent than anything I've ever seen. I fear it may blind me.

The light strikes its target. When it hits my shadow, the brilliant beam passes through him and refracts into a billion tiny rays that shoot out of him in all directions until he looks like the sun itself.

Then he's gone, burned by my light.

Beams of light explode out from where he stood. They pour out of me too, shooting off in every direction, piercing the shadowy veil, rocketing into the dark sky like fireworks.

The world is a burst of light.

I shut my eyes. I count my heartbeats.

One…two…three…four…

The blaze is so bright that it shines through my eyelids.

…seven…eight…nine…

I hear footsteps. The fluttering of wings.

My eyes open.

I'm no longer alone.

All around me in the forest are pirates, American Indians, fairies, as though they've magically materialized, freed from their shadowy cage. They're all staring at me with looks of wonderment and confusion. I have no energy to answer their questions, to explain things. I don't have the desire.

I can't even focus on them or this victory because the center of my world is behind me.

Even in death, his gravity pulls me.

I turn and trudge through the snow, my feet dragging, dropping the sword on the ground on my way. I collapse beside Hook, fresh tears in my eyes.

His own eyes are closed, his skin an ashy white. The blood has stopped pouring from his wound and dried on his hand that rests where his gray shirt is stained a dark crimson. His hook is half buried in snow. The warm sun shines down on him through a break in the canopy of trees above us.

The sun.

My shadow is gone, confined once more to the darkness, the darkness that can no longer devour and feed on Neverland now that my star is back.

We saved Neverland.

We did it.

But it doesn't feel like a victory.

Hook is supposed to be here. He's supposed to see my star in the sky. See the shadow gone. Feel the warmth on his face. Watch the snow melt. He's supposed to do all of that with *me*, not be lying here dead.

I sob. The noise is so loud, like it had been trapped in my chest for centuries.

All around me in my periphery, I see the pirates removing their hats and holding them to their chests, bowing their heads for their fallen captain.

I can't watch.

I throw my body over Hook's and bury my face in the crook of his neck. He still smells the same, like leather and amber. His hair is still soft, but his body is so cold.

Am I always doomed to lose the people I love in Neverland?

Love.

Fuck. This fucking hurts.

Once again, I'm falling apart, being shredded from the inside out. This anguish, this heavy, agonizing sorrow, makes me wish I was dead with him. Or that I could take his place. Instead, I'm alive, my insides being twisted, my stomach churning, my chest aching. I'm breaking like glass, shattering into a million shards. I'm imploding, my heart and soul spilling out onto the snow, melting with it in the sun.

When I speak, I'm surprised that I can at all. My voice breaks like everything else in me is breaking. "I love you, James Hook."

Neverland owes me, goddamnit. *It fucking owes me.* I saved it from being razed by the darkness that *it* created. It *can't* take Hook from me.

But Neverland owes Hook even more. Hook hated me, loathed me to the very pits of hell when he came to find me. He resisted the urge to kill me. He never gave up. He fought against our hundreds-year-old feud for this. He's dead because all he wanted was to save Neverland, save his home, save *our* home.

Lifting my face, I raise it to the sky and bellow, "You owe him!"

My voice carries, reverberating through the forest, ricocheting off the trees.

There's no answer.

I lower my head again, then lay my body down beside his. I'll stay here with him until someone drags me away. I don't even feel the pain in my arm or in my head anymore. All I feel is a much more excruciating kind of pain.

"I love you, James Hook," I say again.

I close my eyes, tears spilling over the edge onto my cheeks. And then I say it again.

"I love you."

And again.

"I love you."

Now that I know, I may never stop.

"I love you, James Hook."

Something flickers behind my eyelids. A flash. A spark.

My eyes snap open. Nothing has changed in front of me. Hook hasn't moved. He's still dead. But *something* has changed. I think it's inside of him and inside of me. Just a spark, a spark of something. A spark of life? If there still exists such a thing inside of Hook, then maybe I can reach it. Maybe I can ignite it with my magic.

I close my eyes again.

"I love you. I love you. I love you, James Hook."

This may not work. I sob at the thought but try again, my voice turning more desperate.

"I love you. I love you. I love you, James Hook."

Nothing.

I won't stop trying. I'll keep chanting until my voice gives out. Even then, I'll say the prayer silently.

"I love you. I love you. I love you, James Hook."

Something burns inside me. I embrace it. Send that burning, that spark, straight to Hook.

"I love you! I love you! I love you, James Hook!"

A resounding gasp fills the forest. My own follows when I open my eyes and see that Hook's are open as well. I watch, eyes wide and mouth agape, as he stares up into the sky and inhales one breath and then another. The sight of his chest moving as oxygen travels in and out of his lungs has me forgetting to breathe myself. The sight of the color returning to his skin has me struck speechless. His forget-me-not-blue eyes have me never wanting to look away.

Then they find me, his eyes.

There's movement around us in the melting snow, happy whispers, but it's all just background noise.

"You're alive," I say with awe, my hand coming up to caress his cheek.

"I am," he says, like he has to confirm it for us both. Then his face breaks out into the most dazzling, heartstopping smile I've ever seen. "And I love you too, Peter Pan."

I lean down and kiss him. I kiss him like it's the first and last time.

A violent racket erupts around us. I think it might be fireworks. It doesn't make me stop. Even when I realize it's the clamor of clapping and hollering and cheering of those surrounding us in the forest, I still don't stop. I simply smile against Hook's lips, tangle my fingers in his hair, hold him close.

Because I'm afraid to let him go ever again.

He has to be the one to break the kiss because if it were up to me, I never would.

He sits up with my help, and the world around us comes into focus once more.

The American Indians give us one last look, respectful nods, then disappear into the forest. The pirates are hugging each other or rolling around in the melting snow like they're not fully grown men who have murdered and pillaged several seas within their very long lifetimes. Fairies are flying about like disturbed butterflies, sprinkling their fairy dust over everyone and everything.

"You did it," Hook says, still smiling.

"We did it." He opens his mouth to argue, but I beat him to it. "I never would've been able to do it without you."

And I know it's true. It was my love for him, and his love for me, that gave me the magic I needed to send my shadow back to where it belongs. I never would have had the power to do it otherwise.

To ignite Neverland's star.

To *be* Neverland's star.

My gaze goes down to his blood-soaked shirt that sticks to his body. There's a hole in the fabric, and I gently graze my fingertips over the unbroken, unblemished skin beneath it.

When I look back up at Hook, there are big fat tears in my eyes that threaten to fall. Fairy dust drifts down on us like snow even as the actual snow around us melts. Hook's hair shines with the iridescent glitter and makes him look more beautiful than ever.

"Don't you dare ever try to leave me again, James Hook."

He pulls my face to his, brushes his lips against mine. "Never, Little Star."

Then he kisses me.

And I know I'll stay in Neverland for as long as he's mine.

I hope it's forever.

EPILOGUE

HOOK

I don't know what the fuck I'm doing at a goddamn wedding. What the bloody hell was Wendy Darling thinking inviting me to her *special day*? I mean, I get that I'm with Peter, and Peter is and always will be her best friend. But after everything I did?

Then again, I guess I shouldn't be surprised. Wendy Darling will always be a better person than me.

It's September, and the wedding is taking place outside at a fancy park in the countryside in the outskirts of London. I'm sitting in one of the front rows of white chairs, rolling a doubloon across my knuckles while my hook carelessly digs into my thigh. None of it helps ease my anxiety. If Peter were with me, I probably wouldn't be so anxious, but seeing as how he's Wendy's man of honor, he has other responsibilities than babysitting a pirate at a very formal wedding.

Even after my time in this world all those months ago, I'm still not quite used to being around so many people.

It's a few minutes before the ceremony starts, so they're all still milling about, congregating. Round paper lanterns hang on wires above the attendants. A white wedding arch stands at the end of the aisle, covered in peach roses and white wisteria.

I'm wearing a suit. A fucking suit.

Peter's lucky I love him.

To distract myself from the tie that's hanging around my neck like a noose, I let my gaze wander. I spot two men staring at me—one with dark hair and glasses and a younger one with bright red-orange hair and freckles. Their heads are together, their gazes flickering back and forth to me, whispering to each other.

It takes me a moment, but I eventually recognize them.

I quickly avert my gaze. I didn't come here for a reunion with John and Michael Darling.

A group of three women are on the opposite side of the aisle from the two men, so I stare at them instead. Two of them are wearing pink dresses, the third wearing green. It's been so long since I've seen a woman in a fancy dress. Admittedly, they're all beautiful. And while I know I still find women attractive, it doesn't matter. It doesn't matter that my attraction isn't limited to gender. I already know who I'm going to spend the rest of eternity with.

As though my thoughts were the cue, the music begins. I quickly tuck my doubloon into my pocket.

The groomsmen appear and walk down the aisle, followed by the groom, Jeremiah Nibs. There's not much fanfare for their entrance, but I do recognize a few of the faces besides the groom's. They're some of Peter Pan's Lost Boys. I was never great with their names, but Peter's talked about them over the last few months. I recognize the twins from Peter's Instagram post, and I think the other two might be Curly and Tootles.

I really hope they don't go by those names here.

I also hope they didn't invite Slightly to this thing.

All those random thoughts vanish the moment Peter appears at the end of the aisle with the rest of the bridal party behind him. Those women blur into the background as they walk down the aisle toward the arch because all I have is eyes for Peter.

His gaze finds mine, and I swear my heart stops beating.

It wouldn't be the first time.

He looks fucking mouthwatering in a suit. His smile is dazzling. I can't believe I'm so fucking lucky he's mine.

The wedding party is all lined up on their respective sides. Peter stands beside Wendy's three bridesmaids, and for the first time, I realize that he's wearing a peach tie that matches the women's dresses. His pants and suit jacket are black, and I can't wait to rip it all off him.

The music changes. While everyone shifts in their chairs to get a look at the bride, my eyes don't leave Peter.

It's never easy to take my eyes off him.

He's trying to keep his own eyes on his best friend as she strolls down the aisle, but it appears he can't help but be drawn to me too. His face flushes when he realizes I've been staring at him without pause. A beautiful blush creeps into his cheeks, and I grin devilishly. In a subtle gesture, he blows me a kiss.

My heart stutters.

Wendy is very near the end of the aisle when I finally tear my gaze away from Peter to look at her. I have to admit she looks stunning, her white dress hugging her soft curves and flowing down around her legs. Her hair is up in a plaited bun.

Her father gives her a kiss on the cheek, then hands her off to her about-to-be husband.

The officiant steps up behind them and begins to speak.

I barely listen to a word. During the entire ceremony, my eyes remain glued on Peter, and when he sneaks peeks at me, I cherish every smile that graces his beautiful lips.

"I CAN'T BELIEVE you invited Captain Hook to your wedding."

I clear my throat as I step up beside Wendy's brothers in the receiving line in what they call the Acacia Room—the largest room inside the venue where the reception is taking place. It's a vast space with high ceilings and filled with white tables, more paper lanterns, and lots of rose gold decorations. It's the end of the line, and I'm the last one. I took my time because I knew Peter was going to be busy.

Except, now that I'm here, I don't see him.

John Darling spins around, and his eyes instantly widen when they land on me. I see fear in them, and it gives me a sick kind of satisfaction.

I'm trying to be better. I truly am. Sometimes I just can't help myself.

"Behave, John," Wendy hisses behind him.

I grin. "Nice to see you again...*Redhanded Jack*."

His eyes grow even bigger. Michael, who's standing beside him, snorts.

The Darling brothers and the Lost Boys all stare at me as though I've grown two heads and they have mixed feelings about it. There's some fear, some amusement, some bewilderment.

It occurs to me that if any of them still harbor ill feelings toward me, they may decide to do something about it. Before,

I always had my crew to back me up when I fought them, but they're not here now. And these are no longer children. I don't even have a sword. All I have is my hook—I could at least probably do some damage before I'm taken down.

This may be a wedding, but once upon a time, none of us would've cared about that.

For several seconds, there's a tense silence that hangs over us as Wendy glares as though daring us to do something at her wedding. I don't know about them, but I don't think I'm willing to take the risk.

Fortunately, I'm saved from any necessity to defend myself when Peter shows up, bounding across the floor with a grace that I'm still amazed by. He has eyes for no one but me as he approaches. Without a word, he puts both hands on the sides of my neck and kisses me in front of everyone.

It steals my breath away just like every other time I kiss him.

Pulling back, he smiles. "Sorry for disappearing. I'm here."

I say nothing. He's taken my words as well as my breath.

As he laces his fingers through mine, he turns to everyone else with his classic charming smile. "Everyone have a nice reunion?"

Now they're staring at *both* of us as though we've fused into one and grown a whole bunch of extra heads.

Michael Darling breaks the silence with a loud laugh. "This is *wild*."

The tension eases a little after that. I congratulate Wendy on her nuptials before I end up sitting at a table with Peter, the Darling brothers, and the twins. Turns out, the dark cloud over us may have dissipated a little *too* much. Michael Darling starts cracking jokes at my expense, and the twins think it's such a good idea that they eagerly play along.

"How does Captain Hook run his ship?" Michael asks.

"How?" the twins ask simultaneously.

"Single-handedly."

They all burst into laughter, and my jaw clenches. I glance at Peter who's sitting beside me, and his mouth is in a thin line. His chest heaves with the restraint it takes to suppress his own laughter.

"Who has two thumbs and loves Peter Pan?"

"Not Captain Hook."

"Hey, that joke doesn't work anymore."

My face heats. I slam my hook down onto the table. A few curious gazes drift our way, so I lean forward and speak through my teeth in a low, strained voice. "And here I thought all you little urchins *grew up*."

Their faces fall, but it looks anything but genuine.

Michael frowns the most dramatically like I just stole his candy. Then he clears his throat. He points down at my hook, then scratches the side of his nose to cover up the gesture. "You know, he does have a *point*."

The table erupts in howls and cackles.

Even Peter can't help but laugh with them this time.

By now, my face is practically on fire, as though there are flames beneath my very uncomfortable dress shirt. I'm breathing through my nose like a raging bull because my jaw is clenched so tight.

Okay, so I clearly still have anger issues. But it's good to know that Peter Pan didn't change *everything* about me.

When I'm on my ship, I'm still the best bloody pirate captain that ever lived. When I'm forced to deal with insolence and harassment from those who may as well still be *children*, images in my mind's eye show my hook buried deep in their chests.

It's only when it comes to Peter that anything's changed.

But…he's still chuckling, and I'm still seeing red.

I round on him. "If they don't fucking stop, I'm going to gut each and every—"

Peter's lips are on mine.

I forget whatever it is I was saying, why I was saying anything at all.

My anger vanishes, melting in the passionate heat with which Peter kisses me. I'm pretty sure there's some cheering going around the table, but it all blurs in the background. His tongue briefly slips into my mouth and massages mine. The wicked crusade of his tongue sends all my blood rushing south.

I may still be a despicable beast, but Peter Pan has a firm hold on the leash that he's wrapped around my heart, body, and soul.

When we pull apart, there's a devious smirk on his lips.

I growl at him, but I effectively feel tamed.

At some point during Peter defusing the bomb inside me, the song playing through the speakers changed. It's softer, slower. Wendy and her new husband walk out onto the dance floor, and everyone watches as they begin to sway to the music.

I, on the other hand, am distracted by the way Peter intertwines his fingers with mine. He watches his friend with rapt admiration and genuine happiness while I watch *him*.

When the song changes again, others join the bride and groom on the dance floor.

"Dance with me," Peter suddenly says.

I freeze, my gaze on our enlaced fingers, and I'm filled with trepidation.

Dance? When was the last time I danced? Have I ever danced? In my hundreds of years of living, I can't remember ever having moved my feet to any kind of musical rhythm.

Just what the Lost Boys need. More ammunition for more jokes.

But when my eyes slide up to meet Peter's, I know I'll give him whatever he wants.

Sighing, I silently curse. "I've never danced before."

He smiles and brushes his lips against mine. "So let me lead."

When I arch a perturbed brow at the ridiculousness of the idea, he simply chuckles, stands, and pulls me up by my hand. I go without a fight, if not a bit reluctantly.

Peter pulls me out onto the dance floor. He and Wendy exchange radiant smiles as he stands in front of me and others move around us. When he places his hand on my lower back, I still, my eyes burning into his.

After Peter saved Neverland and I saw the forest without its frost for the first time in fourteen years, my earlier thoughts were confirmed. Peter's eyes really are the same color as the Neverland forest.

And it turns out, I don't hate Neverland's sun as much as I once used to.

"Put your hook on my shoulder," he says.

I'm surprised he doesn't accidentally slip up and say hand. He's never done anything like that. I don't think he lets himself forget.

With a faint smirk, I do what he says. "You just like my hook anywhere."

He takes a step forward, making me take a step back. "I like any part of you anywhere."

Fuck. I don't know how long I'm going to last in this place with him saying things like *that*.

Peter moves, leading our bodies to the music drifting throughout the large room. With him leading, it's surprisingly not as difficult or scary as I imagined it would be. The only thing that has me uneasy now is the way my cock is enjoying this closeness a little *too* much and is threatening to prove it.

"You should be careful, Little Star," I growl close to his ear as we dance. "I may decide to fuck you right here on the dance floor in front of everyone."

His warm breath fans my cheek in short, erratic waves. "You look so goddamn erotic in a suit that I might just let you."

I don't realize that we've stopped moving until I pull back to stare into his face. There's a veil of lust-induced euphoria over his brilliant green eyes as he bites and sucks on his bottom lip. Just like when we're in Neverland, time stands still for us while it continues moving everywhere else.

He blinks lazily, staring at me through his lashes, a silent plea.

Then, one whispered word.

"*Captain.*"

He knows damn well what that does to me. What it's done to me every single time he's used the word in the past few months. So I know exactly what it is he wants, what he's begging for.

And of course when he begs, I give him what he wants.

Before the mast in my pants becomes too noticeable, I lead Peter off the dance floor, holding onto his hand as though I'm scared to let go.

Sometimes I am. Sometimes I'm afraid he'll simply fly away from me one day.

The moment we've exited the Acacia Room, my hand is all over him, my lips on his, my eyes peeking open long enough to check the rooms that we pass. This venue is huge, so there's bound to be an acceptable place to claim this man of mine.

I smile against Peter's lips as we slip into an empty room,

the golden glow of the dying day pouring in through the windows.

As I help him lose his clothes, I can't get that one word out of my head.

Mine.

Neverland might have made him, but sometimes I think it made him just for me.

EPILOGUE

PAN

I wake to the cool touch of metal against my heated skin. Something sharp skates across my chest and down my abdomen.

Groggily, I blink my eyes open.

Everything is black.

That's when I register the feel of soft cloth covering my eyes and tied behind my head.

When I begin to squirm, a low, husky whisper in my ear stops me.

"You're my prisoner of war, Peter Pan."

The voice, the words, the hook exploring my body, all of it draws a whimper from me.

The bed we're on rocks gently beneath us, the Jolly Roger no longer anchored in ice. It sways on the sea waves, docked on the island of Neverland.

I remember when the ice first melted, the ship lurching for the first time in years. We were standing out on the deck, staring off into the thin, breaking sheet of ice over the water. Hook stood behind me, his arms around my waist, his chin on my shoulder as he admitted to me how much he missed the feel of being on his ship at sea. After that, we left on a month-long journey.

Sailing on a pirate ship was fun.

All the sex was even better.

Occasionally, we'd do something like this. Turns out, we both enjoy games.

My entire body shivers when Hook, lying beside me, leans over and brushes his lips across my chest, stopping to take one of my nipples into his mouth before biting it. I arch beneath him as his hair hangs down and brushes softly against my skin. His hook makes little circles above my pelvis.

He kisses the length of the scar on my chest, and I don't think it's because he's sorry. I think it's because he loves that he marked me.

I honestly don't mind. I'll bear whatever markings he wants to give me.

His lips travel back up my chest, over my collarbone, up my throat. Sucking my bottom lip into his mouth, he bites, making me moan. By now, the sheet over my lower half is an Egyptian cotton tent.

"As my prisoner," Hook says as his hand snakes around my throat, "I get to do whatever I want with you. Are you going to be a good boy and let me? Or are we going to have to do this the hard way?"

I'm not sure how much *harder* it could get.

My mind is so muddled with sleep and lust and Hook's touch, but I try to think about his question.

I love being his good boy, receiving his praise. But there's another part of me that does want the hard way, that wants the fight, that wants him to be rough, that wants to beg. I've long since accepted that having all of that with Hook turns me on more than anything. Only with Hook. I don't think it would be the same with anyone else. And even without it, I'm sure he would figure out other ways to affect me like this.

I think my body makes the decision before my brain does.

My hand comes up and grasps Hook's wrist. I dig my nails in. He hisses and lets go.

I still can't see anything because of the blindfold as I struggle to move without his hook slicing into my side. As I slide to the edge of the bed, his hand grips my arm, pulls me back toward him. He flips me over so I'm lying on my stomach. I writhe beneath him as his body blankets my back, weighing me down, pressing me into the mattress.

We're both naked, his erection hard against my backside. His hand wraps around my throat from behind, and it doesn't take long before I'm putty in his hold.

"I think you're just begging to be punished," he growls in my ear, thrusting against me.

I whimper and nod desperately, pitifully. I absolutely crave his punishments. I'm ravenous for his touch. This man, this ruthless, ravishing man, does things to my mind, body, and soul that no one else ever has. Ever will.

All I want, forever and ever, is to be his.

"Show me how bad you want it, Little Star."

I'm already rutting into the mattress with how bad I want it, chasing whatever friction I can get.

When Hook realizes, he spreads my legs with his knee and lets go of my throat. Sitting up between my legs, he pulls my hips into the air, putting too much space between my dick and the bed.

So, naturally, I reach down to take matters into my own hand.

He catches me around my wrist. With his hook, he snatches up my other one and holds them together behind my back. My face presses into his pillow.

I practically sob without anything to grind against.

The sharp point of his hook roams down my back along my spine, causing my whole body to arch and tremble with insatiable need.

"Prisoners of war don't get to come unless given permission." His hand tightens around my wrists. I wince, loving the way it hurts. "Is that understood?"

I bite down on my bottom lip, then swallow. My voice comes out thick and raspy. "Please."

"Please what?"

"You know what."

The words come out shaky, the plea full of so much desperate longing. Judging from the way Hook's cock twitches against my arse, he loves it as much as I do. I love it because of the way it affects him just as much as it affects me. I love his control.

He grips my wrists tighter. "Say it, Peter."

"Please fuck me." I roll back as much as I can, grinding my arse against his dick. With another whimper, I say the next words like a prayer. "Please, Captain."

Now I've done it.

I think I've unleashed a monster.

He thrusts hard against the crack of my arse and growls, "*Fuck.*"

I feel his hook come down over my wrists, pinning them in place as the sharp point presses lightly into my back. Then his hand is gone. I hear a bottle open, and I squirm for about ten seconds in anticipation before I feel him against my hole. His fingers are slick with oil. He presses one against the rim and pushes inside me.

Unintelligible noises escape from somewhere deep within me as I tremble and writhe on the bed.

He adds a second finger. A third.

"Fuck," I moan, moving back and forth, panting, fucking myself on his fingers. "Fuck, that feels so good. Please, don't stop, Captain."

He pulls all his fingers out.

"No," I cry, letting out another sob. "Why?"

I start squirming again, trying to free my hands. He digs the tip of his hook into my back, and I wince again when it feels as though he may have broken skin.

Like I said, let him mark me. It only spurs me on.

"You're only allowed to come with my cock buried inside you."

"Then please fuck me," I beg, trying not to move anymore but failing. My body continues to seek out any kind of touch, any friction, that it can possibly get. "Please. I need you inside me, Hook. I promise I'll be good."

Then the soft, velvety head of his erection presses against my hole.

"I know, Little Star," Hook says breathlessly as he begins to push his cock inside me. "You're always so fucking good for me."

With one slow, steady thrust, he fills me. My resulting moan is *so* loud.

Once he's in to the hilt—stretching me, completing me—he stops and stills just like that for several heartbeats. Allowing me to adjust, allowing us both to bask in this feeling of being whole, fitting perfectly together, like puzzle pieces. Celestial bodies drawn together.

He lets go of my wrists, wraps an arm around me, and pulls me up until my back is flush against his chest. When he gives a tentative thrust, the new angle makes him hit that spot inside me with impeccable accuracy and the perfect kind of friction. I'm seeing stars when he pulls the blindfold off my head and tosses it away—we both enjoy these games, but he still makes sure I watch the most important parts. He grabs my chin to tilt my head to the side so our eyes meet.

I have to blink a few times before my vision adjusts to the dim, early morning light of his captain's quarters. When it does, I'm greeted by a sight that still manages to release butterflies that flutter all around in my stomach. His dark, wavy hair drapes around his pale face as he looks at me with even paler eyes that will never stop being capable of piercing my very soul, destroying it completely if that's what he wanted.

"I love you, Peter Pan," he says as he stares intensely back at me.

"I love you too, James Hook."

And then he's fucking me and kissing me. I moan into his mouth as his beard scrapes against my face.

His hand leaves my chin, and his palm travels down my neck, over my clavicle, my chest, my abdomen, leaving a scorching trail in its wake. Then his hand is around my length, tightening, his thrusts behind me causing me to rut into his fist.

"Oh, fuck fuck fuck."

All the sensations are almost too much, too overwhelming. The pleasure is so intense it's almost painful. I revel in it, drink it up, let it intoxicate me.

And then I realize…

"I don't want to come yet," I practically mourn. "I never want this to end."

Hook kisses below my ear, then whispers between pants, "We have forever, Little Star."

I unravel, shooting my release all over Hook's hand and the bedsheets. Letting my head loll back onto his shoulder and my eyes roll into the back of my head, I fall limp in his grasp, totally blissed out. There's an idyllic glow in the edges of my vision. Euphoria fills my veins, my bones.

Hook pumps inside me a few more times, following me over that brink into paradise.

We collapse in a heap of sweat, cum, and tangled limbs. Hook eases out of me but then wraps his arms around me to make up for the loss. I'm not sure how long we lie there, curled up, panting until we catch our breath, stealing slow, soft kisses.

This is why I stayed in Neverland.

It was a little bit because it's my home. A little bit because I love the magic that permeates this place, that's imbued into my blood. A little bit because I love the games that I can play here.

But most of all…it's because I'm so head over heels in love with James Hook.

"I should get going," I say quietly when I realize how much brighter it's gotten inside the cabin from the morning sun—my star.

"Aye, can't be late for the games," Hook says, mouth curled into a grin.

"You love it as much as I do. Admit it."

"I don't deny it."

I kiss him, then climb off the bed and dress in a pair of old, faded, ripped jeans. I think they're the same ones I wore the day I returned to Neverland for the first time after fourteen years.

"You know we can still be ourselves, right, Peter?"

Tying my sword and scabbard to my side, I turn back to look at Hook lying on the bed in all his naked glory.

Fuck, he's drop-dead gorgeous. It should be a sin to look as good as him.

But there's something in his eyes there I don't like. Fear, uncertainty. It's faint but there.

I crawl on top of the bed in my jeans and lean over him, running my fingers lightly through his hair. "I love you, *James Hook. You.* The man. The pirate. Everything you are." I take his hook in my hand, raise it to my lips, and kiss it. "If you never wanted to play one more pirate game with me, it wouldn't change how I feel about you. Ever. I love fighting with you, but I love making love with you more."

He gives me an easy smile, moving his hook to lift my chin. "Get out of here while you can, Peter Pan. Gather your Lost Boys. We duel at noon."

"You mean you'll be getting your pirate arses kicked at noon."

He scowls, a playful glint in his eyes. "Proud and insolent youth."

I smile so big it hurts my face. "Dark and sinister man."

Our last kiss is deep, slow.

Then I'm flying out his window.

IT'S BEEN NEARLY A year since Wendy's wedding. At least, I think it has. It's difficult to keep track in Neverland where time doesn't work the same as it does in her world.

I went back about a month ago, met her baby daughter Jane. I can't believe Wendy's a mother. Though, admittedly, it suits her.

While I was in that world, I may have picked up another Lost Boy, an orphan. It's honestly insane to me how many there are, how many children exist in that world who have no family or a horrible family.

I'd bring them *all* to Neverland if I could.

The last one I found was trying to steal several bags of beef jerky and some Zingers from the convenience store nearest Wendy's house. He looked to be about thirteen, and his left eye was black and blue and swollen. I cornered him outside, asked him what happened, and told him if he didn't tell the truth, I'd haul his arse back inside and turn him over for stealing.

Of course, I wouldn't have.

But when he told me his foster father hit him, I didn't skip a beat. I asked him if he wanted to come with me to a better place where he would never have to see that man again. He hesitated only briefly—stranger danger and all that. He's a smart kid. But I'm glad he accepted. Before we left, I went back into that store and bought them all out of beef jerky and Zingers.

When we showed up back in Neverland, that's what the other boys decided to call the new recruit.

Zinger.

All the other boys are younger, so Zinger slipped right into the role of their leader.

When I fly into the treehouse, he already has them all geared up and ready for battle like good soldiers, swords dangling from their sides and warpaint on their faces.

They remind me of my original Lost Boys, and it makes me a little nostalgic. Zinger reminded me of Nibs the first time I saw him, and there are two young brothers, ages nine and ten, who are similar to the twins when they were their age. There's a boy with tight blond curls, just like Curly, and the other two aren't all that different from Tootles and Slightly.

I swore to myself I'm not going to fuck up with these kids like I did them though. All of these boys know what this place is, and I won't let them forget it, won't let them forget where they came from. I want this place to heal them. Because each one of them has their own trauma, and that's why they're here.

Neverland can help them.

If any of them ever want to go back, they know the choice is theirs.

But for now, they're all ready to play the game.

"Ready to fight some pirates, Lost Boys?"

"Ready, Peter!" they answer in unison.

"They stole our treasure! Let's go get it back, boys!"

The *treasure* is a small chest with a handful of doubloons and some jeweled necklaces. And technically, it belongs to Captain Hook, but he was willing—*barely*—to part with the small amount for these purposes.

Hey, he's still a pirate. And I love him.

I fly out of the treehouse, the Lost Boys trailing after. We make our way through the Neverland forest as I fly above the canopy of trees, keeping an eye on the boys below through the breaks in foliage. A perfect breeze tousles my hair as I flip and spiral in the air. The pure joy that comes with flying has only grown since returning. Sometimes I never want to come down. Few things land me on my feet.

For old time's sake, I crow.

They crow back.

I smile.

Neverland is exactly how it's meant to be. Fairies fly around freely, and the air is practically suffused with glittering dust. Their fairy songs carry on the breeze. Sometimes I play the flute I brought back with me from the other world, harmonizing with their melodies. It often makes me think of Tinker Bell. Fuck, do I miss her. Neverland isn't quite the same without her, but the memory of her no longer makes me want to run away. It makes me want to stay and never forget her ever again.

We pass by the lagoon. Mermaids lounge on Marooners' Rock, basking in the warm sun high in the sky. Tail fins splash in the water around the rock.

The Jolly Roger looms in the distance.

And fuck me if my heart doesn't do a little dance.

I fly ahead to make sure the plank of wood that I had set up is still in place, offering a direct bridge up into one of the gunports in the side of the ship. When the boys reach it, I silently motion for them to climb up. Lifting a finger to my lips, I indicate for them to remain quiet until I give the signal.

Once they're all in the ship, I fly up, gliding in circles, staring down onto the deck where pirates saunter around, working various jobs.

When I don't see Hook, I frown.

But the game must go on.

I crow, loud, louder than I ever have.

The doors and hatches to below deck are thrown open. The Lost Boys come pouring out. The clanging of metal against metal rings out as blades clash below.

I circle above the ship one last time before diving down, withdrawing my sword from its scabbard on the way. My heart begins to pump adrenaline through my body, and I love every dose of it.

I look for Hook again, but when I still don't see him, I aim for one of his crew.

Before I reach the deck, something comes crashing down on my back. A net. It bears down on me, surprisingly heavy, and the weight shoves me straight down to the dirty floor of the deck. I struggle against the material, my sword stuck in the rope. I try to cut it, but I don't have enough room to work, my limbs contorted like a pretzel.

Then Zinger's there to help untangle me, throwing the net off me.

"Thanks," I say with a nod.

He nods back, then runs off to fight pirates.

Me? I only have one pirate on my mind.

And he's still not here.

Where the fuck is he?

I see Starkey in my periphery. He's a blue blur in his usual tunic as he rushes at me. Starkey and I have no real quarrel, even after I claimed Hook as mine.

But of course we're going to fight because that's the game.

When he's close, his sword comes swinging around. I lift mine just in time to stop it.

Then there are more. Pirates surround me, their swords inches from my bare chest, my bare back. My skin glistens with sweat under the noon sun. Adrenaline has my heart racing, my lungs heaving. I turn in a circle, but there's a fence of sharp blades all around me.

"NO!"

Hook's voice draws my attention to where he's arrived from below deck, sword in hand, wearing a black and red frock coat, black hair framing his beautiful face. The thrill of the games mixes with my feelings for this man—an unslakable desire and the most passionate love.

His crew backs away from me as he approaches.

He smiles at me, sinful and sensuous. "Peter Pan is *mine*."

I raise my sword, the point inches from his chest. I smile back. "And you're mine, Captain Hook."

Our blades clash.

Then the game really begins.

ACKNOWLEDGMENTS

THE PROCESS OF WRITING a book may typically be a solo endeavor when there's only one author, but the journey to publishing is anything but. It's so much of a team effort that this debut romance novel wouldn't be what it is today without so many people.

Thank you to my very supportive family and friends, the ones who know I wrote this book and what kind of book it is, the ones who support everything about me. Your unconditional love means the world to me, and I hate to think where I would be without it.

To all my beta readers for your thorough and careful handling of this story. Your valuable feedback played such a huge role in the final version of this book that I'm sure I would cringe if I ever tried reading through the first draft.

To my absolutely amazing street team, your support and kindness have made my heart happy in oh so many ways. You were the first ones to welcome me as a romance author, and I am forever grateful.

Lastly, but certainly not least, thank you to everyone who took the time to read this story of Captain Hook and Peter Pan. I hope you loved them as much as I do.

MORE BY RIVER HALE

FAR FROM SERIES

Far From Neverland

Far From Camelot

More coming soon!

THE ECHOES DUET

Memory Lane (#1)

Echoes of the Past (#2)

Echoes: A Novella (#2.5)

When Lightning Strikes
(A Darkish Sapphic Romance)

ABOUT THE AUTHOR

River hale is a pseudonym, created because her mother once told her that she'll read everything she ever writes. She's a writer with a tea addiction and a love for everything dark, twisted, haunted, and beautiful. She's written and published more appropriate books that her mother is allowed to read under her real name, but she'll always have a special place in her heart for dark romance.

River's Newsletter:
https://riverhale.com/newsletter

Join River's Reader Group:
https://www.facebook.com/groups/riverhaleshellions

instagram.com/riverhaleauthor
tiktok.com/@riverhaleauthor
facebook.com/riverhaleauthor

Printed in Dunstable, United Kingdom

77691481R00188